Paris

Life will t[illegible] many Chang[illegible] strength from grandma Calden and those who love you. Always remember to love yourself, and to never accept that your dream is an impossibility.

Yvonne Weems

UNREQUITED LOVE

BY

YVONNE A.WEEMS

Hope you enjoy my book!

Unrequited Love

A Second Time Media & Communications Book/published by arrangement with the author.

Printing History
First printing: January 2010

Cover design and production by Miller Design Studio

For bulk order information address:
Second Time Media & Communications LLC,
P.O. Box 401367
Redford, MI 48240-1367
313-263-2711

ISBN: 978-0-9840660-7-0

www.secondtimemedia.com

Printed in the United States of America

SECOND TIME MEDIA COMMUNICATIONS™

DEDICATION

I would like to thank God for allowing me to follow my dream, and for allowing me to be a part of a family that provided undying love, support and encouragement.

To my son Ronnie Clopton Jr.: Thank you for reminding me at a critical time, not to allow adversity to stand in my way. Without your encouragement, I may have once again allowed time to distance me from my dream.

To my sister Renee Weems Gardner: You have been my biggest supporter. You have uplifted me for as long as I can remember. You were always the first to see any and all of my creations.

There are so many who have helped me with my book in one way or another. I just want to let you all know that I appreciate what you did for me:

Betty Chapel, Barbara Carter, Myron Wilson, Deborah Davenport, Tamika Hart, Mary L. Weems, Kenneth & Tina Smith, Charnelle McCree, Michelle Williams, Courtney Carr, Tamica Lane, LaTonya Morgan, Jackie Knight and Silvia Gordon.

Thank you so much Erica N. Jones, for getting this book off the ground for me. I appreciate your diligence and professionalism.

Yvonne A. Weems

Unrequited Love

Prologue

Jerome Ware was on the football team at Redford High School. Shavon was so much in love with Jerome but no matter what Shavon did, Jerome just wasn't interested. Shavon tried everything to attract his attention. When she got it, it was only momentarily. Then one day Shavon thought she had Jerome right where she wanted him.

"Going to the party tonight?" she asked.

"If all goes well, I will."

Shavon looked into his eyes and gave him the biggest smile she could muster. She knew that his lack of words could only mean that he was hinting for her to go along with him.

"I'm going too," she replied. "Maybe we can--"

Cynthia interrupted, "Hey Jerome, you ready?"

Jerome looked back at Shavon.

"See you at the party."

Shavon was crushed. She tried to keep her smile as she waved him off. On the inside she felt as though it was the end of her world. She knew there had to be someone in Jerome's life but she thought she could handle that; until she saw her. Cynthia was tall, slim, light complexion with hazel colored eyes, and long sandy-colored hair. Shavon imagined Cynthia might be cute, but she didn't expect her to look like one of Europe's most prominent Black models. She found herself feeling jealous. She tried to compose herself as she thought of a way to get back at Jerome. Of course! She would do it at the party tonight…

***

It's good to see you too, Jerome," Shavon said timidly hoping he would read between the lines. She looked around the room for familiar faces spotting her closest friend and waving.

"Where's your friend?"

"Friend? Oh, you mean Cynthia." He signaled for Cynthia to come over. Shavon stood completely still. The last thing she wanted was to meet Cynthia, but she didn't dare show her jealousy. Cynthia approached them.

"Shavon, this is Cynthia; my fiancé."

Shavon stared at Cynthia's finger and tried to camouflage her pain.

"What a pretty ring, Cynthia."

"Thank you. After we graduate, we're getting married. But I'm sure Jerome already told you about that."

Shavon evinced a fictitious smile. Cynthia rubbed it in royally. Shavon had to get away from Jerome.

"Excuse me," Shavon said with another forced smile. "And congratulations, you two!" Shavon turned away. "You two deserve each other," she whispered.

After that night, Shavon decided Jerome wasn't good enough for her anyway.

CHAPTER 1

As Shavon stood in the mirror, she made sure everything would be perfect for tonight. October 17, 1983 marked her and Tracy's anniversary. She and Tracy had been going steady for two years now since Shavon was in the tenth grade at Redford High.

Shavon was a cheerleader at Redford and participated in many school activities. It wasn't until a graduation party that Shavon found out Tracy was on the football team at Redford. Initially, Shavon wondered why she had never noticed Tracy before. He was about 6' 3", very lean, (especially for a football player) with slightly waved black hair and a golden brown complexion. He was extremely handsome. Shavon knew exactly why she had overlooked him… because of her love for Jerome Ware.

While Shavon put on her makeup, she picked up a photograph of her and Tracy, which had been taken at his prom last June. She thoughtfully admired it. "You lucky devil," she said out loud. She felt very fortunate to have Tracy.

She briefly thought of the adversity she had gone through with him and other women. She knew they'd had their share of problems but had overcome them. All of that was in the past now.

Shavon's daydream was interrupted by the telephone.

"Hello!" She spoke in a high-spirited voice thinking it was Tracy.

"Hi," Myah said. "So, what are you doing tonight?"

"You know today's our anniversary. Tracy and I are going out to celebrate."

"Oh, yeah. Where are you going?"

"I don't know yet. You know how Tracy is. He's always full of surprises. I know we'll probably go to dinner. He'll be here around six."

"Guess what happened, Shavon?"

"What!"

"Ronny and I broke up again last night. One of his lady friends called me again. I just let him know that I didn't appreciate that and I'm not going to put up with it. He fed me that same old line he did about two months ago. He claims he doesn't know who this girl is either. I get so tired of him sometimes. I know he'll be back in a week or two. What do you think I should do?"

"If I were you, I would think about it long and hard because nobody has the answer but you, Myah."

"Why are you so good at evading my questions, Shavon?"

"Myah, I just want you to do what's right for you. What I think shouldn't matter."

"But you're my best friend, Shavon," Myah whined.

"I know, Myah, but being there for you as a friend is fine, but telling you how to solve your problems is another thing. I'm not a counselor. I'm here for you and I want you to be there for me too but I know the answers to my problems shouldn't come from you. And I know later on down the road you'll say, I should have known better than to listen to Shavon. She didn't know what she was talking about."

"Okay, okay. I read you loud and clear. Uh-oh, the boss just came in, gotta go."

Shavon looked in her closet and decided she would wear the burgundy and black dress Tracy bought her for her 17th birthday. She remembered how well Tracy liked her in that dress. 'It flatters you in all the right places,' he had told her.

She knew wearing that dress would put a smile on his face. The spandex dress was half burgundy and half black in the front. The back was solid black. It was sleeveless and fitted which showed off her slender and perfectly proportioned figure. Shavon found the dress to be one of her favorites too. She knew when she wore the dress, she wore it well.

***

"Hey, Tracy, what do you say we go play a little basketball?"

"Not today, Darryl. Shavon and I have a date. Today's our second anniversary and if I'm a minute late, she will have a natural born fit." Darryl looked at Tracy and laughed.

"You don't have to hide your feelings from me, man. I know you wouldn't miss it for the world."

"I wouldn't lie about that," Tracy conceded. "I think everybody knows how close we are."

"Yeah, and I have to tell you, Tracy, you really surprised a lot of people – including myself."

"Hey, man, I just couldn't stay away from her. She carried herself with more finesse than any girl I've ever met. She's smart, pretty and extremely mature. Every time she smiled, those dimples and slanted eyes were about the prettiest features I'd ever seen. What can I say; she's the best. She never played those hard to get games or any other games for that matter. She was really candid with me and I was just mesmerized by her. No other woman had ever been that way with me. And you know me. I was the one who called all the shots. Whatever I wanted, I got. Shavon made it a little more difficult. I remember when I first began to realize she really cared for me. I called myself putting my foot down. I told her I was the man in our relationship and what I said was final."

"No you didn't, man."

"Yes, I did."

"What did she say?"

"Well, up until then all the other girls went along with that, but not Shavon. She slowly walked up to me and said, 'this world does not evolve around you, and if you don't want me to have a voice in this relationship, then we may as well stop it right now. I got along fine before I met you, and there won't be any tears when you're gone.'"

"That was certainly straight to the point," Darryl laughed.

"Yes it was, and I've loved her ever since," Tracy laughed then continued. "And man, just like me, she has goals. She'll be the perfect wife but it will be a long time from now, my friend. I've got to do something for myself first, like getting my career established. I've got some good news for her too."

"Yeah? Like what?"

"I got a promotion today."

Darryl threw out his hand for a play, "Hey, man, congratulations! I'm really happy for you. That's good news all right."

"Well, I look at it this way, Darryl. I'll continue writing for the magazine, and maybe later I can expand my short stories into novels. Maybe even do a little song writing. Who knows? Darryl, I don't know if I've ever told you but Shavon likes designing clothes. I've seen some of her designs and she's really good. After she graduates this year, she plans on going to college to study fashion designing." Tracy looked at his watch. "Well, Darryl, I'll check you out later. I gotta pick up some flowers before the florist closes."

"Okay, man. Tell Shavon I said hello. You two have a good time."

***

Tracy got home just in time to smell his mother's down home cooking. Mrs. Gaines was preparing her favorite: southern fried chicken, squash, a small fruit salad and homemade buttered rolls.

Mrs. Gaines had loved cooking since her childhood. She was raised in Tennessee where her mother cooked fresh meals everyday, which she traditionally carried on to her family. She often wondered why her children were so thin considering all the healthy meals she religiously prepared.

Maria moved to Detroit when she was twenty-three years of age. Two years later she met and married Darnell Gaines. Tracy was the first born of three children. Neicy, Tracy's sister, was 17 and his younger brother, Delaney, was 14.

Six years had passed now since Mr. Gaines had suffered a fatal heart attack. After his death, Mrs. Gaines raised her children alone. The demise of Tracy's father put much pressure on him. He felt that he had to take care of his family. Maria wanted Tracy to live his life as he would if his father were still alive. She welcomed the day Tracy came to her and confided that he couldn't be like his father. With tears streaming down her face, she hugged Tracy. She told him he would be more of a man being himself, and that she loved him for who he was as she had done his father. Her words were a great relief for Tracy, and instantly opened the door to a better friendship with his mother. Tracy leaned over and kissed his mother on the cheek.

"Hi, Mom."

Unlike her children, Maria spoke with a southern accent.

"I didn't think you'd be here for dinna, bein today's Fridee and all."

"I won't. Shavon and I are going out for our anniversary. I'll be with her for the rest of the evening."

'*What you know bout a anniversary*,' she thought. She looked at her son with half a smile. She knew how much he loved Shavon, but she couldn't help wanting to see her son with Sherry Witton. Sherry had been Tracy's childhood girlfriend. Sherry's father owned a construction company and Maria knew that if Tracy married Sherry, he would have a future with her father's company. But she also found Sherry to be very attractive, intelligent and compassionate. Maria knew that Sherry would love and take good care of her son. Oblivious to the fact that Sherry and Tracy hadn't seen each other in three years, she still hoped one day they would be married.

***

Shavon opened the door and Tracy grinned. "God, you look good in that dress. I wonder what handsome fellah bought it for you. Whoever he is, he sure knew what he was doing."

Shavon threw her arms around Tracy giving him a tight hug. Tracy pulled one hand from behind and handed her a dozen red roses. Shavon laughed inviting him in and gave him a dozen red roses. Shavon and Tracy combined the roses, exchanged cards and they were off.

"Where are we going, Tracy?" she asked.

"First, we're going to get some dinner."

"I know that silly, but where?"

"That's a surprise! Hold tight, woman, you'll see."

Shavon looked at Tracy with a smile on her face and love in her eyes.

"Did I tell you that you're the most handsome, generous, considerate, and loving man I've ever met and that I love you with all my heart?"

"Well," Tracy responded, "Did I tell you that you are the most beautiful, the most intelligent and benevolent woman I've ever met and that you couldn't possibly love me as much as I do you?"

Shavon moved a little closer to Tracy and kissed him softly on his neck while breathing deeply.

"Please, Shavon, not while I'm driving. You know how I get when you do that."

"Okay," she agreed with light laughter. "Besides, the night is young," she said.

Tracy looked away from the road and gave her a devilish smile. "I know," he said with pleasure as he reached for her hand.

She looked around thinking that she had never been in such beautiful surroundings in all her life. She spotted a sign which said, "Welcome to Beverly Hills." She looked at Tracy as he pulled into the parking lot. Tracy got out and opened her door.

"Tracy, it's beautiful out here."

She saw Lombardy Poplar trees nearly 12 feet high as she observed the stunning beauty of the landscape. The walk leading to the entrance was bordered in red and white geraniums. In the center of the grass were letters created from multi-colored flowers that read: *The Crystal Palace*. It was the most beautifully designed restaurant she had ever seen. She could tell from the large lighted picture window that it was huge inside. She could see the crystal chandeliers and the well-dressed waiters. She had never been to such an extravagant restaurant.

Once they were inside, it was even more beautiful. There was a waterfall display with red floodlights with trees and plants set up to look like the Garden of Eden, she thought. To the right were vast fish aquariums with fish, Shavon nor Tracy had ever laid eyes on. To Shavon's surprise, there was familiar music as they entered.

"May I help you, sir?" the attendant asked.

"Yes," Tracy responded. "A reservation for Gaines, please."

Shavon sat down still nearly dazed as she looked around. There were candles lit and wine glasses on every table. She looked to the stage as the live band was about to play.

"Tracy, this is beautiful beyond words. I couldn't even imagine a place like this. You really outdid yourself this time," Tracy blushed.

"Yeah, but I think my lady deserves the best, don't you?"

"Nothing could ever be better than what I already have," she said. They met each other half way for a kiss.

Shavon was consummately pleased with what Tracy had done to assure her that she was indeed special. They both enjoyed dinner. Shavon's highlight of the evening was when the vocalist came to the table and sang a love song that Tracy had requested prior to their arrival. Shavon had a picture taken and requested prints be sent to their homes. This would be a night they would never forget.

They capped off the beautiful evening with a long walk.

"Guess what, babe? I've got some good news. I got a promotion today."

Shavon was so exuberant she nearly knocked him off his feet when she hugged him.

"Congratulations, Tracy! I knew you would and I know there will be many more."

Tracy softly touched her cheek pulling her to him and kissed her passionately.

"Tracy."

"Yeah," he responded recognizing the seriousness in her tone.

"When you get rich and famous, you won't forget me, will you?"

"Never! Forgetting you would be forgetting myself."

Tracy and Shavon returned to the city at 8:30 p.m. He took her to the Detroit West Club in Detroit. They danced until they could dance no more.

"Where are we going now?" Shavon asked half high from her third glass of Canei wine.

"Well, are you ready to go home?"

"No! Not if you have anything else up your sleeve," Tracy looked at Shavon and laughed.

"You may as well finish what you started earlier," he said.

She looked out the window of the moving car, "Well, I'll think about it."

Tracy pulled over and parked the car. He began kissing Shavon on the neck as he moved his hands from her waist to her hips. Shavon slipped her arms around him pulling him close and pushing her breast against him. Tracy's hands began to roam as she aroused him. His hands were moving up her thighs now as she responded stroking his back sensually and kissing his neck as she knew he enjoyed. Before Tracy realized what was happening, he had loosened Shavon's bra strap, half way undressed her and was lying on top of her. Shavon had already begun unbuttoning his shirt.

He whispered to her, "So Shavon, now that you've had a little time to think about it, what do you wanna do?"

She slowly got up and put her clothes back together.

"Can you take me home?" she asked innocently.

They looked at each other and laughed loudly. They both knew that would never happen. Tracy took Shavon in his arms once again.

"Shavon, I love you."

"I love you too, Tracy."

Tracy's friend, Mark had given him the keys to his apartment since he was staying overnight with his girlfriend. Everything had worked out beautifully for them.

When Shavon awoke, it was one o'clock in the morning.

"Wake up, Tracy!" She shook him. "It's one o'clock in the morning. If we leave now I'll beat mama home. She said she'd be in late tonight. She'll probably be in by one thirty. I think she already suspects we sleep together but I don't want her to know for sure."

When Tracy pulled into the driveway, he kissed Shavon three times, reluctant to let her go before she went inside. She looked out the window and watched the back lights of Tracy's new silver Riviera go up the street.

She made it home ten minutes before her mother. Just as she got under the covers, her mother's car pulled up. Shavon heard her coming up the stairs. Dana peeked in her daughter's room to make sure she was home before going to bed. Shavon was so happy she smiled in her sleep all night long. Nothing could penetrate her happiness.

CHAPTER 2

Shavon picked up the crystal swan. "I don't know, Myah. Maybe I should get Mama something more personal this Christmas."

"More personal? I thought all of her gifts from you were personal."

"You know what I mean Myah, something ideal. Something I know she'll get some use out of." Shavon hesitated before she continued. "But I do like this swan and I think she'll probably like it too."

Myah studied Shavon's face. "Mark my words, Shavon. If you get her some more clothes, she'll never wear them. She hardly goes out and I would hate to see you spend your money and watch it set in your mother's closet."

"Maybe I'll just look around some more."

"It's only three o'clock, Shavon. Northland doesn't close for six more hours." Myah looked in the window of a jewelry store as they walked pass.

"I asked Ronny to get me a ring for Christmas but I know that's out of the question. He went part time last month and he's behind on his child support payments. His ex has called him three times since then. She knows his hours have been cut but she couldn't care less. I think she uses most of that money for herself anyway."

"Poor Ronny," Shavon said. "It's bad when a girl tricks a guy the way she did."

Myah interjected, "Oh he regrets it. But even though things are much harder on him now, he loves his baby girl. He can't have a lot of things he really wants but he's learning to make sacrifices."

Myah ran into a nearby store. "Oooh! Look at this, Shavon; this is beautiful! Maybe I can get Ronny to help me get this coat for Christmas instead of a friendship ring. What do you think?"

"If he's as fashion conscious as you say he is, he'll love this." Shavon examined the lining and inner stitching of the wool coat then held it up to Myah. "It's very well made--I'll tell you that. Look at this detail. It's definitely quality. Try it on, Myah. I bet it will look good on you."

As Myah tried on the coat, she remembered it had been a while since she had seen any of Shavon's designs.

"Speaking of sharp…Have you created any new designs lately?"

"Yes, as a matter of fact, I have. I have an idea for a winter, business suit line using mostly wool fabric but I'm not finished yet. I'll show them to you later."

From across the room, Myah spotted a pearl white party dress with fringes along the hemline. Shavon followed as Myah went toward the mannequin.

"This is so sharp. This dress is made of Lycra and Nylon and was definitely made to fit." She removed it from the rack. "I'm trying this bad baby on."

Myah began to talk to herself while she tried on the dress. "Heavenly Father, do your best, please don't let me bust this dress." Myah came out of the dressing room glowing. "This dress was made for me. I look so sexy!"

Shavon took one look and asked her if she could breathe.

"Shavon, this dress is made to fit." She turned around.

"Myah, you'd better buy that dress. I'm not trying to be funny but it looks like you've got a rear end."

"I didn't hear you, Shavon, but I could have sworn you made a comment out of jealously. But I'm sure I was mistaken."

Shavon laughed, "Girl, you know you need some help back there."

Myah lowered the dress to her shoulder blades. Shavon could see that Myah was pleased and she too thought Myah looked nice in the dress. Myah looked up and down at herself in the mirror.

"I guess it does look like I can't breathe, doesn't it?"

"That never stopped you before, Myah."

"That's right and it won't this time either." She glanced at Shavon. "You've got a lot of nerve. Remember those stone washed jeans you used to wear when you and Tracy first started dating?"

Shavon laughed as Myah continued, "Correct me if I'm wrong but those jeans were so tight you couldn't have passed gas if you wanted to."

Shavon burst out in laughter. She knew she couldn't argue that point. Myah stepped back into the dressing room and changed her clothes.

"Oh, did I tell you, Myah?"

"Tell me what?"

"Grandma's coming up in two weeks for the Christmas holiday."

"Is she flying?"

"No. You know Grandma loves long rides. She'll probably come on the bus."

"Well, I don't remember the last time my grandmother stayed for more than three hours when she came to visit us. She and Mama really don't get along."

"Why not?" Shavon asked.

"I don't know, maybe because Mama never got married. Mama didn't want to marry Gerald's and my father but he did ask. She said she loved him but not enough to marry and spend the rest of her life with him. He wanted her to be what he thought she should be and you know Mama. She wasn't going for that. So here I am. He supports us and sends us Christmas and birthday presents, but he doesn't visit a whole heck of a lot. What about your father, Shavon? You haven't mentioned him in a few weeks."

Myah stepped out of the dressing room and put the dress back on the rack and they headed out of the store.

"Well," Shavon began in a half saddened voice. "I spent the day with him Wednesday after school."

"And?" Myah urged.

"Well," she started in an excited voice that slowly descended. "After dinner, we just sat around and talked."

"So, what's wrong with that? Did you expect him to fly you to Paris for dessert?"

"Well, I didn't expect his girlfriend to be there."

Myah looked at Shavon with sympathetic eyes and they both began to laugh.

"You're still hoping your parents will get back together, aren't you?"

"Well, they've only been divorced for a little over three years. Thing is, when Daddy comes over, I can tell that he and Mama enjoy each other's company."

"Well. Shavon--look!"

"Look at what?"

"That guy over there! I haven't seen a man like that since I don't know when--that's what! Oooh look, Shavon. He's coming this way." Myah smiled, blushed, twitched and switched as she walked. She raised her head for the look of sophistication she knew men liked so well. As he approached them, Myah smiled batting her eyelids. "This is it, Shavon. Watch me dazzle him," she whispered.

"Hi," he said in a sexy baritone voice. "How are you beautiful ladies doing today?"

Shavon had a brief thought of how typical he sounded. Probably with a lot of practice, she assumed.

"Let me introduce myself. I'm Larry--and you?" He looked at Myah.

"Myah, but all of my friends call me--"

"And what's your name?" He directed his attention to Shavon.

"Shavon."

Myah stood back and looked from his face to Shavon's. She couldn't believe it.

"Shavon. That's a pretty name, for a very pretty lady I might add."

"Thank you." Shavon blushed.

"So, how would I get in touch with you, Shavon?"

Myah stood there mouth open now. She couldn't take anymore. She walked on. When Shavon caught up with Myah, Myah had a strange look on her face.

"I don't believe it."

"Believe what?" Shavon asked.

"I don't believe after all that sign language I evinced, he looked right at you. Did he see me or what? And you weren't even interested. I just don't believe it. God's gift and he didn't even look at me!"

Shavon looked at Myah with a smile and they both began to laugh. Shavon knew that Myah wasn't totally serious, or so she thought anyway.

Shavon found herself wandering back into the gift shop where she had seen the swan. "I really do like this swan. I wanted to get something bigger but I know she'll love this. Tracy's going to help me out with the money for my parents' gifts if I need it."

"Well, who's gonna give you the money for his gift?" Myah asked.

"Daddy is. We've already looked at a leather jacket. I made some money by making outfits for a couple of Mama's friends"

"Some of us have it made," Myah said with admiration.

"For now," Shavon assured her. "I'll be pulling my own weight next year, you'll see."

Shavon spotted a cologne booth. "Look, Myah. Let's sample some new fragrances."

Myah didn't respond. Shavon noticed Myah's eyes were focused in Marshall Fields. Myah sniffed into the air, "I smell smoke."

Shavon sniffed and raised her brows, "I don't smell anything, Myah."

"Well, you're about to cause I'm about to start a fire." Myah marched quickly toward the store as Shavon followed.

"What is it, Myah?"

Myah stared at a woman a few feet from her.

Shavon whispered, "Who is that, Myah?"

"Ronny's ex, Cassandra. She is his little girl's mother. All she does is squeeze more and more money from him and now I know what she's doing with it? Look at the way she's dressed, trying to look like she's got something."

"Myah, that's no reason to start trouble." Shavon grabbed Myah's arm. "Let go."

Myah pulled her arm away from Shavon's grasp.

"I ain't gon' do nothing!"

"Do I look stupid or something? I know you, Myah."

Myah continued to stare at the woman ignoring Shavon's pleas. Shavon threw her hands up, "I don't want any part of this. I'm leaving."

Myah walked towards Cassandra who was engrossed in perusing through the clothes racks. Cassandra didn't see Myah but she sure felt her. Myah bumped her hard enough to make her stumble. Cassandra grabbed at the clothes rack to keep from falling but she went down with the rack. Myah snickered and ducked behind another rack. She enjoyed seeing the look of embarrassment on Cassandra's face.

Myah laughed out loud as she left the store. Shavon looked back as they walked away. She saw Cassandra brushing off her clothes as she talked to the sales person and a customer who was pointing at them.

"What happened?" Shavon asked.

"I knocked her right off her feet."

"Did she see you?"

"No, she was too busy falling to see me. She didn't know what hit her."

"I don't know about that, Myah. I saw a customer pointing at us. I'm not sure if she saw us but if I were you, I would watch my back."

"Trust me Shavon, I'm not worried about it."

Shavon laughed as she looked at Myah who was now humming Jingle Bells. Her face revealed no remorse or concern for what she had done. Shavon just shook her head. Myah looked up as if she had no idea what the look was for.

"What?"

"Myah, one of these days you're going to make a mistake and grow up."

Myah laughed, "Not likely, Shavon."

The girls walked through the crowded mall for hours and didn't buy a thing. They saw many things they liked but they always thought it best to think it over before they bought something.

By the time they got home they were exhausted. Shavon bathed, ate dinner, and after talking with Tracy, she went straight to bed.

CHAPTER 3

Tracy stopped at a red light and looked over at Shavon, "And what are you in such deep thought about?"

Shavon looked up as if she had been shaken by someone, "Oh, nothing really."

"If it were nothing, you would be paying more attention to me," Tracy said. "Maybe you just don't want any company today--with your mind preoccupied and all."

"Don't be silly, Tracy. You know I always enjoy your company. Just because you're the last person I saw last night, and the first person I saw this morning..." She giggled.

"Very funny," he said blushing. "Do you think you can walk from here?" He laughed loudly.

"Very funny," she said. She pinched him on the earlobe and lowered her head. "Well, I just don't know what to get Mama for Christmas. Myah says I shouldn't get her any clothes, because the last dress I bought her is still in the closet with the tags on it. I saw something at the mall last week I thought she might like."

"Is that what's so heavy on your mind?"

"Yes!" She answered defensively.

"What's wrong now?" he asked.

"You act like it's so trivial."

"Well," he said slowly.

"Tracy! It is important."

"I know it is, Shavon, but you acted as if it were a matter of life or death!" She pouted teasingly as she always did. Tracy put his arm around her shoulder. "Come here you big baby. You're my big baby," he said with a smile.

Shavon returned his smile as she rubbed his thigh. Tracy kissed her quickly and looked back toward the road.

"I saw the most beautiful crystal swan in one of the gift shops at the mall and I've been thinking about it ever since. I wish you could have seen it. It's diamond cut and it's so beautiful."

"So, what's stopping you from buying it? Is it the money?"

"No. It's not--"

"Shavon, your family knows you're not working and they don't expect much from you."

"But, Tracy, I wanna get them something they would absolutely love. I'm trying to decide between the swan or that camera for Mama. She could really get some use out of that camera at the art shows but I can't stop thinking about the swan."

"Hey, let's go see it."

"Are you serious, Tracy?"

"Sure, let's go."

Tracy examined the swan as Shavon watched with excitement.

"Well, what do you think?"

"You were right. It is beautiful. It would look good on your mother's entertainment center."

"If it were only a little larger," she said.

Tracy walked over to the cashier. "Excuse me, Ms. Does this swan come in a larger size?"

"Yes, it does, sir. It's in the catalog. There's just so much here to display, we could never display all we have. Let me show you. The 8 inch size comes with a base."

Shavon walked up and put her arm on Tracy's shoulder. "Oooh, Tracy. That one is really beautiful."

"I know," he said looking at the cashier. "We'll take it."

Shavon's mouth hung open in surprise for a moment.

"Are you crazy? Look at the price of that thing, Tracy!"

"Don't you think Mom is worth it?" he asked.

"Well--yea-yeah, I do, but she'll be just as happy with the smaller one."

"Why not go all out, Shavon?"

"Because--well--Tracy--," she began without knowing what she was going to say.

Tracy looked back at the cashier and pulled out his checkbook. Finally, Shavon composed herself. "You really don't have to do this, you know."

"I know but I'm crazy about your mother and I'll do anything for you--you know that." Shavon blushed.

"Okay, but it's from you too, Tracy!"

On the way home, Shavon and Tracy talked of her mother's love for art. Shavon knew her mother would like the swan because of her intrinsic interest in art itself. Dana Robertson loved art and studied from childhood to develop her natural talent. She attended Michigan State where she obtained her degree in teaching. She knew she needed something to fall back on if her paintings weren't enough.

After Dana divorced Casey, she tried to support Shavon and herself with the profits from her paintings. When she realized it couldn't pay all of the bills, she worked as an art instructor. Casey had insisted Dana and Shavon keep the house but Dana had been raised with such independence, that she initially refused. She reminded him of how hard he had worked to get the house and how much she wanted to accomplish her own security. In the end Casey convinced her that keeping the house would be best for her and Shavon.

Dana and Casey both went through many sleepless nights without one another and often dreamt of each other. Casey's outlook on his marriage changed after the divorce was final. He then realized that he should have had more respect and appreciation for what he had at home. Over the past 14 years,

Dana had taken all she could and decided she could no longer endure the agony he induced. One more affair would have literally taken her off the edge. They parted as friends for Shavon's sake.

***

Shavon looked around the station but no sign of her grandmother Jesse. She hoped that Jesse hadn't changed her mind. She looked forward to seeing her. She looked just beyond the passenger entrance and to the left, where she spotted a lady sitting on her suitcase in the corner.

Jesse looked up as someone approached her but she never got a chance to see who it was. Shavon gave Jesse a big squeeze, knocking her off her suitcase. Jesse sat there for a moment trying to get over the shock and pull herself together. While Shavon picked up the glasses Jesse wore, she smiled with excitement.

"Hi, Grandma." She realized Jesse was still sitting down. "Oh! Let me help you up, Grandma. I'm just so happy to see you."

"Me too, Shavon," Jesse said looking at Shavon closely. You're still beautiful I see. Child, you look more like me every day."

Shavon's giggle was followed by a smile.

"Where's your mama?"

"She's in the car. She couldn't find a parking space, so I came in to get you while she's waiting out front," Shavon smiled at her grandmother as they walked toward the door. It was always a pleasure seeing her grandmother.

"You enjoy your ride, Grandma?"

"Yep sure did. Sort of relaxes your mind, you know."

Dana leaped from behind the wheel of her Continental and grabbed her mother throwing her arms around her tightly. Dana didn't notice the falling bags her mother carried on her right arm.

"Oh dear, not you too!" Jesse exclaimed. "I've been down once already," she said with enthusiasm. "I just hope when I leave I'll be in one piece." They all laughed and hugged.

Jesse mentioned how beautiful the city was, as she had remembered. She always wished her daughter would come back to Indiana, as she had mentioned a few times. But she knew Dana had done well and she was proud. Dana had a beautiful home in a nice neighborhood, a fine daughter and everything she ever wanted.

"So, Mama, how are you?"

"Just fine--couldn't be better."

"How's Daddy?"

"He's okay, I guess. He's doing better. Janelle's staying with him while I'm here."

"Is his mind still coming and going?" Shavon asked.

"I'm afraid so, child, but the arthritis isn't so bad right now. He's not complaining about it anyway. He said to tell everybody hello."

Jesse looked at Shavon's jet-black hair which was longer than it was on her last visit. "When are you going to see your grandpa? He asks about you all the time, when he's in his right mind." Jesse laughed lightly. "He always says, 'I'd sure like to see my little Shavon.'"

"It's kinda hard right now, Grandma, but as soon as I get out of school, I'm coming to stay with you two for a couple of weeks."

Dana looked at her daughter, "If she weren't so in love, she would probably stay the summer like she used to."

Shavon blushed and looked out the window.

"You still with that same young fella, Shavon?"

"Un huh."

"Well, that's good. When I was your age, I couldn't get a man to stay with me that long. The only time they stuck with me was when I didn't want them."

Shavon and Dana laughed.

"He's a really handsome boy too," Jesse added. "If you two get married, you'll have some beautiful children."

"We'll get married one day, Grandma but no time soon. We need to get our careers established first before we even think about getting married and starting a family. I have too many things to do. Tracy is just getting started and he doesn't want kids either--not for a while anyway. He's getting closer and closer to a management position. Mama, did I tell you about his promotion?" Shavon asked turning towards her mom.

"Yes, you did. And I think he is going to go far."

"Me too," Shavon said proudly. Jesse cut in.

"No, child, you don't need any babies now. Make something of yourself first then have the husband and the children. You're lucky. Most of these boys today can make 'em and that's about it. I'm hip to that. Janelle keeps me informed. Mmm hum."

Shavon giggled at her grandmother's use of slang.

"Well you don't have to worry about me and Tracy, Grandma."

Shavon looked in the mirror and caught her mother's expression. Dana glanced in her rear view mirror at Shavon and back at the road. Shavon felt a little uneasy when her eyes met her mother's but she put it out of her mind.

As they pulled into the driveway, Jesse admired the house. "Oh! The house looks different. What did you do?"

"I had the trim painted," Dana answered. "And Shavon put out a few garden decorations. Mama, you remember Johnny Fields, don't you?"

Jesse frowned as she tried to remember.

"You know, the landscaper."

"Oh, yeah. I remember him."

"Well, he put the fountain in for me. He and his brother take care of the lawn."

"You sure enhanced the property, Dana." When Jesse went inside, she looked around. "I see you redecorated inside too!"

"No Ma'am. I just changed it around a little." She pointed to the corner where the television was setting. "The sofa used to be here. The table was here." Moving around the room, Dana showed Jesse what changes she had made.

"I see you've painted some new portraits. I didn't know you still did that."

"Yeah, just a few sunsets. I've had a little spare time. We'll talk later, Mama."

Dana put her arm around her mother's shoulder and gave her a big hug. "Let's get you settled and get some dinner on."

"All right by me," Jesse agreed.

Shavon walked into the kitchen and announced that she was going over to Tracy's to prepare dinner, and later to the movies.

"Why don't you invite him to dinner over here, Shavon?" her mother asked.

"I'm cooking for him tonight," Shavon replied.
Dana laughed, "Poor thing; don't kill him, Shavon."

Shavon put her hands on her hips with a shocked look on her face, "I didn't kill Daddy. As a matter of fact, he loves my cooking."

Jesse sat on the side and watched with hysterical tears.

"Well, he was supposed to tell you that, Shavon," her mother said.

They all laughed.

"Well, remember some of those times you came home dead tired and I had already cooked dinner for us? You didn't complain then," Shavon pouted.

"I know," Dana responded with loud laughter. "But I..." She leaned over and grabbed her stomach and they all laughed hysterically.

"That's okay, that's okay. I just hope you don't come in tired and hungry again, Mama," Shavon said as she laughed.

After Dana and Jesse wiped the tears from their eyes, Dana admitted how well Shavon cooked and that she just needed a good laugh.

***

The dinner with Tracy went well. His mother had taken the others to visit old friends of hers leaving Shavon and Tracy with complete privacy. Shavon prepared spaghetti and meatballs with garlic bread. Tracy loved Shavon's cooking and knew that she would make a good wife one day. Things got intimate and comfortable and they resigned the thought of the movie and stayed home and enjoyed each other's company.

When Tracy took Shavon home, he went in for an hour and talked and laughed with Dana and Jesse. Shavon's mother adored Tracy. She told her mother again that she felt he had a lot going for himself and he was really good for Shavon. He had given her the utmost encouragement and support as far as her future was concerned. She knew he would go somewhere in life and Shavon needed the assertiveness he projected.

CHAPTER 4

The week went by quickly. Christmas Eve was joyous for everyone. Dana gave a small Christmas Eve party inviting only close friends. Shavon invited Tracy, Myah and Ronny to be her guests for the evening. Everyone seemed to have had a great time, even after Myah and Ronny had an argument.

Everybody had a good laugh when Myah started singing *"What Do The Lonely Do At Christmas.*" In the middle of the song, she turned to Ronny and promised him that he would be lonely next Christmas if he messed up one more time. Ronny wasn't pleased. He told her she should just say he'll be without her.

Myah stared him down a moment before she spoke. "You know, you should donate your brain to science." Shavon closed her eyes as she braced herself for what her witty friend would say next. "I think scientists would be very interested in knowing how you lived for 20 years without using it."

Shavon sensed that if she waited another second, things wouldn't go well. She signaled to Tracy to help her break the monotony. They turned on the stereo and started to dance. By night's end, Ronny and Myah had made up and everyone was happy and having fun. At 10 p.m. they turned off the stereo, TV and all the lights and lit up the Christmas tree. They sang Christmas carols until two in the morning.

"Merry Christmas!" Myah yelled into the phone.

"Merry Christmas to you," Shavon returned. "How are things going at your place, Myah?"

"Things are just fine. I'm going over to Ronny's sister's house later. We already opened our gifts. Mama bought me that coat we saw at the mall, that black and blue wool one. Do you believe that? You told her didn't you, Shavon?"

"Well, she asked me what you wanted and you know you would have had a baby if I hadn't told her."

"You're right. Thanks a million. Is Tracy there yet?"

"Yes. He's in the living room and he came in empty handed," Shavon said slightly disappointed.

"He did what!" Myah yelled in Shavon's ear.

Shavon continued to whisper, "He came in with the gift for daddy from us and a gift for Grandma but that's all."

"Maybe it's too small to see."

"Don't say that, Myah. You might get my mind roaming in the wrong direction."

"Well, it could be."

"Maybe--" Shavon's mother interrupted telling Shavon to go back and entertain Jesse and Tracy.

"I'll call you later, Myah." She turned to her mother. "Where are you going?"

"I'm going to the store for a few last minute things. I'll be right back."

"Tracy and I will go for you." Dana turned quickly.

"No. You just entertain and I'll be right back." Dana quickly walked out and closed the door.

Shavon walked back into the living room, grabbed her camera, and took some pictures of Tracy and her grandmother. Minutes later Dana walked in. Shavon noticed her mother wasn't carrying a bag but she dismissed the thought.

"Let's open the gifts, it's eleven thirty!" Jesse yelled. Everyone agreed and moved around the Christmas tree. Dana called out the names.

"Let's see, from Tracy to Jesse."

Jesse reached up and took her gift with a look of embarrassment look on her face she replied, "That was really nice of you. I'm sorry I didn't get--"

"Oh, that's okay. You'll make up for it next Christmas," he said as they all laughed. Dana continued until all the gifts were gone. Shavon and Tracy were right. Dana was in awe of her crystal swan. Shavon sat quietly feeling left out for a moment. She gave Tracy a crooked smile. He took her hand and led her to the window. She looked out of the window then back at him. He pulled some keys out of his back pocket.

"It's all yours."

Shavon brushed the tears from her eyes as she stared speechless out of the window. He grabbed her and gave her a hug. He knew it was too soon for her to speak. It was just too much to take in. He just held her while she stood there as if dazed and stared at her car.

"Oh, Tracy." She turned to look at her mother and grandmother who stood behind her grinning.

"You see why I love him so much."

"I sure do child, I sure do," Jesse said.

"What are you standing there for, Shavon? Go try it out!" her mother yelled.

Shavon took Tracy's hand and walked out the door. They stood outside nearly a half hour looking at the car. Shavon fell in love with her royal blue Camaro. Tracy assured her that it wasn't new, it didn't cost a lot and that he had the consent of both her parents.

"I thought you would catch on when your mother said she was going to the store and went to move the car."

"I knew something was funny when she came in empty handed but I never thought this would be the reason."

Shavon wrapped her arms around Tracy. She knew her mother and grandmother were in the window but she couldn't control herself. She smothered Tracy with hugs and kisses.

CHAPTER 5

It had been two weeks since Myah had seen Ronny. He had taken a trip to Wyoming to visit his mother and Myah couldn't wait to see him. Her heart jumped when she heard the doorbell. She ran to the door and smiled when she saw her baby. Myah closed the door behind Ronny and squeezed him.

"I sure missed you."

"I missed you too. I couldn't wait to see my baby again," he said.

Myah smiled, "I've got plans for you, Baby. Did you bring the whipped cream?"

Ronny smiled, "Maybe I did. Maybe I didn't."

"Well, I'll just have to frisk you and find out."
Ronny raised his arms as Myah frisked him.

"Bingo," she said. She pulled the can out with a confused look and asked, "What is this?"

"It's whipped cream, Baby."

"You know I like Cool Whip. How dare you come in here with a bargain brand!"

"Aw, Baby!"

"Don't you 'aw baby' me. If you'll skimp on this, you'll skimp on me."

"Aw, Baby. Don't say that."

"Bargain brand! I don't believe you. You remind me of my father. He must have tried them all. But, I'll tell you one thing, he didn't try that cheap whipped cream. What did you save? A dime?"

Ronny laughed and put his arms around her waist. "That's not fair, Myah." He didn't mind so much. He could tolerate a lot from Myah. He knew how irrational she could be at times.

"You spoiled the mood!" she yelled.

Ronny leaned against the wall and listened as she went on and on about the whipped cream.

"Well, I'll just come back some other time with the right stuff."

Ronny took two steps and Myah turned around.

"What? I know you don't think you're going to leave me like this, do you?"

Ronny laughed, "I knew you would see it my way."

"I know you know better not darken my doorstep with some bargain brand next time," she pouted settling back into his arms.

"Yeah, yeah, yeah," he agreed. "Now let's get busy."

She nearly snatched him out of his shoes and pushed him in the basement.

"What's down here?" he asked.

"You'll see."

Ronny took one look in the corner and bucked his eyes. He knew he was in trouble.

***

Shavon opened the letter and held her breath momentarily as she read it, hoping it would be good news:

Dear Ms. Robertson,
Thank you for your inquiry and interest in our company. We too, feel that we have a very reputable company and we are very selective of our prospective designers. Due to your lack of experience, we cannot consider your employment with our company at this time. However, we have listed a few companies who may consider your work, despite your lack of experience.

Shavon disappointedly looked at the letter and threw it in a pile with the rest. *Another disappointment*, she thought. She sat in her room planning her next step. In her muse, she began to doodle with her colored pencils. Before she knew it, she had created what she thought to be one of her most beautiful designs. The design was of a long flowing satin, lavender gown. The sleeves laid on the edge of the shoulder blades with the front dipping slightly revealing cleavage. The gown slightly flared from the waist and had pearl-like buttons down the back.

As Shavon sketched the gown, she imagined herself wearing it. *Hey, I'll wear it to the prom*, she thought. She began to add accessories which made the dress more alive. Suddenly her excitement declined. She began to think about the letter she had just received and put her design in the closet.

***

Tracy had done well for himself with *Classic Magazine*. He had gone from mailroom clerk to a contributing writer of a monthly column within a year and a half.

Tracy stood in the window near his desk thinking of how he had come to be with this company. He had entered an amateur writer's contest. He had heard about it through a co-worker at *Classic Magazine*. No one even knew he could write. His story was chosen over 500 entries. Marcus Tate, the president, was so impressed with Tracy's writing ability that he had him write a few more pieces and moved him into the position of writer. Though Tracy was nervous, after the first few months he got better. He was a new writer with new ideas. Just what the company needed.

Tracy was waiting for a call from Shavon. He glanced at his watch. It was now 12 noon. He had expected her call an hour ago. He smiled as he looked at the photograph they had taken on their anniversary. He suddenly felt dizzy. He stumbled to his chair as he took deep breaths. “Hey, what’s going on in here?” said a voice coming through the door.

Tracy opened his eyes. “Oh,” he said groggily as he tried to pull himself together. “Just a dizzy spell, that’s all. What’s up, Jim?”

“I have some good news, Tracy. I wasn’t supposed to tell you but I can’t hold it another minute.” Tracy looked at him with raised brows.

“Yeah, spill it.”

Jim Stephens was Tracy’s Editor. Jim was a handsome man who was 47 years old with blond hair and blue eyes. Despite his age, he had the face of a younger man. He had found Tracy to be a very intelligent, wise and creative individual. He never treated Tracy as if he were superior to him or like he was any less important than the older employees as others had done.

When Jim’s wife died in a car accident, almost everyone had given up on him but Tracy was there. Jim tried to kill himself and Tracy helped him work through his grief. Tracy told him how he needed him as a friend and how the company needed him. He also told him how he himself had felt when his father had died. Tracy explained how alone, burdened and useless he had felt and how he had overcome his own grief. Though Jim was devastated by his wife’s death, Tracy’s patience and concern touched him deeply, making him realize that his wife’s memory and the love they shared was enough for him to live for.

“Our readership has nearly doubled in the past year and we think most of it is due to your stories. You’re a very good writer, Tracy,” he said as he lit a cigarette. “We still get letters of praise for some of the stuff you’ve written long ago.”

Tracy sat up straight looking puzzled as Jim lit a cigarette and continued.

"I thought fifty percent of the readers bought the magazine because of the gossip columnist, Melissa Stax. Well not anymore, pal. She's good but I think you're a few points ahead of her. It doesn't take much to dig out some gossip on the stars but what you write is your own creation. That takes brains and imagination. Getting to the point though, the company is expanding and we need a smart young fella to oversee the Children's Literature Department in the new headquarters. Some of us are staying here, like me. I've been here for so long, I don't want to leave."

He took a puff from his cigarette and continued," But anyway, the boss has been watching you for a while now, Tracy. He knows you've got the brains and good organizational skills. And he says with some training, you can supervise the department. He says you're a natural and you know a good story when you see one. When you wrote that story about that young kid growing up and facing responsibility, I think it touched all the mothers who read it. It sure brought tears to my eyes." Jim sniffled and wiped his eyes to humor Tracy.

"Rob said it was ingenious. He says you seem to be versatile and he wants to help you expand your capacity. I don't have to tell you that good employees help the company grow."

Tracy smiled as he listened. Before now, Tracy had not known what an asset he was to the company. And now his future had promise. Jim continued smoking his cigarette, taking shorter puffs as the excitement grew.

"The boss was delegating more responsibility to you for the last several months for a reason, pal."

Tracy stood and went to the window. He watched as the snow fell. On the other side of the street he observed two children making a snowman, a snowplow in motion, and three little boys carrying shovels, *to make money*, he thought. Tracy turned to Jim as he tried to contain himself.

Jim went on. "The boss thought he would condition you first. So there you are, pal. What do you think?"

"I don't know. I need some time to grasp it all. I--I mean everything is just flying right before me and I don't know what to think."

"Well, Tracy, you've got twelve months to think about it." Jim turned to leave the office. He stopped at the door. "Oh, I hope you like New York." Tracy's mind was blown. New York?!

He thought to himself, 'A new place, new people; away from my family. What would I do? I've never been on my own.' He thought about his mother. '*New York! Why can't you work here?'* she would say. And Shavon would just scream.

Then he remembered she had not called. He looked at his watch. It was now 12:30 p.m. Tracy became worried. It was not like Shavon to neglect to call when they had a lunch date. He called her house but there was no answer. He wondered where she could be. He went to lunch alone.

After work Tracy dashed over to Shavon's house. Dana sat and talked with him for about 15 minutes before he realized Shavon wasn't there.

"Where's Shavon? She said they had a half-day of school and we were supposed to meet for lunch but she didn't show up. I got worried, so I came straight from work."

Dana gave him a puzzled look. She too was surprised at Shavon. Shavon would never forget about a date with Tracy. Tracy stayed for half an hour longer before leaving.

Dana sat watching the 6:00 p.m. news when Shavon came in.

"Good afternoon, Shavon. How was your day?"

"Hi, Mama," Shavon's face revealed a fictitious smile. "My day was okay. How was yours?" she asked without emotion.

"Long as usual," Dana replied. Shavon headed toward the stairs. "Tracy came by. He wants you to call him. He said you two had a lunch date and you didn't call."

"I forgot," Shavon said in a low whisper. She began to climb the stairs again.

"Shavon, are you hungry?"

"No. I stopped and got something to eat on the way home."

Shavon went straight to her room. Dana knew something was wrong with her. She had never seen her so withdrawn but she wouldn't pry. She would wait for Shavon to come to her.

The following morning Dana received a call from Jesse saying that her father had gotten worse and he was in the hospital. Dana thought it was best to take some time off and go to her father.

"Will you be all right here alone, Shavon?" Dana asked noticing that Shavon looked a little better today.

"I'll be fine, Mama, don't worry about me. Give Grandpa my love. I'll be praying."

Dana left that morning.

***

"I'm glad you could make it this time."

Shavon looked away.

"Shavon, what's with you? You've been so distant. Are you mad at me or something?" Before she could answer, he continued. "I didn't say anything to you after the first day because I thought maybe you were having a bad day but, Shavon, this has been going on all week."

He looked across the table at her. He didn't know what to think. *Was it another man? No. Of course not!* Tracy refused to believe such a crazy thought. She would never love anybody else.

"Shavon, is this because of that innocent little kiss Stephanie gave me? I told you before she was only congratulating me on my story. You should know there was nothing to it. Please, talk to me."

Shavon turned toward him and shook her head no.

"Tracy, I forgot all about her and that kiss. It's just that I'm really worried about Grandpa. He was already ill and now he's worse." Shavon looked at him earnestly.

He reached across the table and held her wrist. "I know you're worried about your grandfather but this started before he got sick."

"Tracy!" She nearly yelled. "I told you I didn't feel well the day I missed lunch."

"Why couldn't you call me, Shavon? I know your mother gave you my message. Shavon, I waited until ten o'clock and you never called me, why not? What did I do? I just don't understand, Shavon."

Shavon looked at Tracy and saw the hurt in his eyes. She knew she should tell him what was on her mind but she couldn't bring herself to say it. She was afraid of what he might think.

"Shavon, I love you, you know that. Whatever it is, I just wish--I wish you would talk to me about it."

She rose from her seat and put on her sweater.

"Shavon, you hardly ate anything. I know you'll be starved by dinner. How about dinner tonight? Anywhere you want to go."

"No. I think I should be home in case Mama calls."

"Well, I can come over to your place."

"Not tonight, Tracy. I've got a lot of homework to do."

"Okay, Shavon, I won't pressure you." He stood and kissed her on the cheek. She managed a smile as they walked out of the restaurant.

After school, Shavon went home and straight to bed. She wanted to call Tracy. She picked up the phone and put it back down. She awoke to the ringing of the phone.

"Hello?"

"Hi, Shavon. How are you?" Myah asked.

"I'm fine. Just a little hungry that's all. I skipped dinner but I'll get something in a minute."

"Did you talk to Tracy?"

"No."

"Where's your mother?"

"She'll be back next Thursday. Grandpa's much better now, but she wants to stay to help Grandma out."

"Well, get some sleep, Shavon, you're gonna need it."

Myah was right, she should get some rest. Shavon had cried herself to sleep most of the week but tears didn't help. Her confrontation with Tracy was inevitable.

In the week that followed, Shavon was still reticent. Tracy had tried to shake her mood but couldn't. Tracy was frustrated beyond belief. Every time he attempted to penetrate her attitude he hit a brick wall. Tracy became impatient and went to Myah.

"What's wrong with Shavon?"

"What do you mean?" She insisted on playing the innocent act.

"Why is it that you're the only one she can talk to?"

"Look, Tracy, if you have a question about Shavon, ask Shavon."

Tracy became angry. "She won't talk to me, damnit! You know what it is and you're going to tell me, Myah!"

"Get the hell out of here," she demanded. "Who do you think you are coming in here trying to tell me what I'm gonna do. I don't owe you anything so get out!" She opened the door.

"For Christ sake, Myah, you're her best friend. I know she talks to you." He calmed his tone. "Myah, I need to know what it is. Is it something someone said?"

Myah looked at Tracy as he stood in the doorway. She felt sorry for him but it wasn't her place to tell him, she had promised. She looked away.

"Look, Tracy," she said in a low voice, I'm sorry but I can't help you. I gave Shavon my word."

Tracy walked toward her. "If there's something wrong with her, I should know about it, Myah!"

He looked at her and saw that she was looking behind him at the open doorway. He turned and saw Shavon standing there. The last thing she wanted to see was her best friend arguing on her behalf with the man she loved, because she couldn't stand up for herself. She turned from the doorway and began running toward her car. Tracy ran close behind and grabbed her by the arm. She tried to pull away from him.

"Don't fight me, Shavon," he said in an understanding tone. They sat in her car for about an hour. Tracy held her while she cried.

"I'm sorry, Tracy. I'm sorry. I didn't mean to."

"You didn't mean to what?" Shavon fell silent.

They sat for another 15 minutes before Shavon finally broke the silence.

"Tracy, I'm pregnant."

Tracy's heart dropped. "Pregnant? How can you be?"

"I don't know! I just am."

"Are you sure?"

"Yes."

"What did you do, take one of those *do it yourself* tests?"

"No, I went to see Dr. Kline."

"But, Shavon you were taking birth control pills."

"I know but Dr. Kline says that it's rare but it can happen."

"Well, why didn't it happen before now?"

"He couldn't answer that, Tracy."

"Shavon, do you think that maybe you forgot--"

"Why are you blaming me, Tracy? It's not my fault the pills didn't work." Her tears were streaming but Tracy inadvertently ignored them.

"How far are you?"

"Two months."

"What about your period?"

"I did a little spotting last month but I thought it was just an irregular period. I felt some abdominal pains and went to see the doctor." Tracy looked out of the car window.

"Shavon, I don't want a baby," Tracy said blankly.

Shavon pulled some Kleenex from her purse.

"I don't either." They both stared out of the window in silence for a minute.

"What are we gonna do with a baby, Tracy?" Shavon asked with a lump in her throat.

"I don't know." He looked over at her. He had never seen her like this, so sad. He wiped her face where her mascara had smeared and leaned close and kissed her.

"We'll think about it first then we'll decide what to do," he said. They embraced.

Shavon slept better for the next few days. She was still unhappy about the baby but the worst part was telling Tracy and that was over. She thought he would hate her and say she had planned it so that he would marry her but he didn't. Shavon knew Tracy was hurt and disappointed but he loved her and they would work it out together.

She thought about things long and hard for the next few days. What her grandmother had said during her visit rang in her ears now. "No! You don't need any babies now. Make something of yourself first." Over and over, it haunted her. *Mama, Grandma and Daddy are going to be so disappointed in me,* she thought. *But the fact still stands, I'm pregnant.*

She began to come to the realization of being a mother. She still didn't want or need a baby but the baby was on the way. She began to think about the baby when she ate her meals. She imagined she would have a boy as smart and handsome as his father. And maybe later in life, a little girl, she thought with a smile.

She dreaded having to tell her mother but it had to be done. With Tracy at her side, she felt stronger about facing everybody. *I know Mama's gonna ask about marriage but I don't think Tracy's gonna agree with that and frankly, I don't either*, she thought. *Well, I won't worry about that now. I'll wait and talk to Tracy first*. Her thoughts were broken by a call from Tracy.

"Hi, Shavon. How do you feel?"

"I feel fine."

"How was school?"

"It was okay. I passed that English test with a B+."

"Good! I'm glad to hear it and I'm not at all surprised." She could tell he was smiling. Shavon had always gotten good grades but over the past two weeks, her grades had begun to drop. Her mind was so preoccupied that she couldn't think straight or study but now, things were better.

"I quit the cheerleading squad today. I'm going to miss it, but it can't be helped."

"No, it can't," he agreed, "not for a while. You don't want to do anything to hurt yourself."

"Well, how are you?"

"I'm fine. It's not me I'm worried about." For a moment there was silence.

"Have you had enough time to think about things, Tracy?"

"Yes, have you?"

"I think so. I'm already two months. We'd better talk soon. I thought by now I should be showing but I can barely tell when I'm undressed."

"Maybe it's a small baby," he said.

"That's what I thought too."

"Well, I'll be off at four thirty so we'll get something to eat and talk about things then."

"Tracy, Aunt Florence is going to be here a little later so if we can go over to Mark's place."

"Okay, I'll give Mark a call and I'll see you later."

***

Myah and Shavon sat on the living room floor playing checkers.

"So, Myah, what did you say happened to your ankle?"

"I didn't."

Shavon laughed.

"Alright. What did you try this time?" Myah smiled and turned away.

"I fell."

"Sure you did. And I bet Ronny fell too." Myah laughed.

"You think you know me so well, don't you?"

"Better than your own mother. Come on, Myah, tell me what you used."

"No, that's not your business."

"That's beside the point, Myah. Come on. You can tell me," Shavon teased.

"Okay but you have to promise me it won't end up in print with Tracy's name by it."

Shavon giggled and put her pinky out for a pinky swear.

"A trampoline," Myah whispered.

"A what? How can you-- I've heard it all now."

"Shavon, it gets worse. Do you know he came to my house with some bargain brand whipped cream?"

Shavon screamed, "Ohmigod! Girl, you need to quit. Whipped cream? And what difference does the brand make?"

"It makes a lot of difference to me. There's nothing like Cool Whip."

"Girl, sometimes I just don't know about you. A trampoline, a sprained ankle, bargain brand whipped cream. I told you about that kinky stuff."

"Kinky? I'm not kinky. I'm just fun and adventurous. You're too traditional and boring," Myah told her.

Myah noticed Shavon had looked at the clock several times. "Expecting Tracy?"

"Yeah, how did you know?"

Myah placed her head on her hand. "You've only looked at the clock a thousand times, Shavon."

They laughed. Myah looked up at Shavon who was now standing.

"It's good to see you laugh again, Shavon."

"Shhh," Shavon motioned. "Aunt Florence is in the kitchen. She'll be keeping me company while Mama's gone." Shavon smiled. "Since I told Tracy, I feel a lot better about things."

"Did you tell your mother?"

"No. I thought Tracy and I would tell her together."

"So, what did Tracy say?"

"He's okay with it but we haven't really talked about it yet. We're going to settle things today."

"What do you think he's gonna say, Shavon?" Shavon looked toward the floor.

"Probably the same thing I'm going to say."

"What's that?"

"What else? I can't give up my own baby. I think he'll agree to that. I know I'm still in school but there are plenty of pregnant girls who finish and graduate on time. I'm only two months and I'll be in my (she counted on her fingers) seventh month in June. It'll work out fine as far as school is concerned. I know the baby will put us back a little. It will affect my education and it might affect Tracy financially but I think we can handle it. I'm going to assure him that I don't want to rush into marriage right now. He's probably thinking about that too."

Myah looked at Shavon in a sympathetic fashion. She didn't dare say what she was thinking. She briefly thought about what she had gone through with Ronny. When he had found out she was pregnant, he immediately set up an appointment for a termination of pregnancy. She didn't think she could handle things alone so she agreed. Myah knew Shavon could be faced with the same decision. She only hoped Tracy had the same sentiments Shavon did.

CHAPTER 6

"I didn't know you like lobster."

"I didn't like it before now. You know women in this condition acquire weird taste buds," Shavon laughed but Tracy kept eating.

She noticed his lack of amusement and found herself feeling awkward. Dinner was relatively quiet. Neither one of them knew what to say. She wished that she could just hold him and make him believe that things would be all right. He wished it was all just a bad dream that would soon be over or had never happened. She decided to break the silence.

"Tracy, I'm not happy about it either."

Tracy continued to eat his shrimp. *'Why am I treating her like a stranger?'* he thought. *'It's not all her fault. It's your baby just as much as it is hers,'* he told himself.

"I know you're not, Shavon, but why us? I don't understand." He reached across the table and held her hand. "I wanted to call you last night," he said.

"Why didn't you?"

"It got kinda late. Besides, I didn't know what to say to you." Tracy continued. "I really needed you last night."

Shavon squeezed his hand. "Tracy, promise me you won't let this put a strain on our relationship."

Their eyes met. Anyone passing would know that they had deep feelings for one another.

"Is everything all right?" the waitress asked.

"Yes, Ma'am," Shavon assured her.

Tracy noticed the waitress had been very friendly and seemed to be sincere in her efforts to please them. She had a pleasant smile and a very pleasant face, he thought. He pulled a few dollars out leaving it on the table for her.

"Hey, man. What's happening?" said a voice behind them. Tracy turned to see Darryl.

"Hey, man, what's up? Where have you been?"

"Oh, I've been out of town for a couple of weeks. I went to see my old man. I don't know if I told you about it but he got married and I went up there for the wedding."

"How is he?" Tracy asked.

"Couldn't be better," Darryl looked behind Tracy.

"Excuse me for being so rude." He leaned in and kissed Shavon on the cheek. Darryl liked Shavon a lot. He was very happy for Tracy and he knew Tracy was happy too. She was the best thing that ever happened to him Darryl observed. "How are you, Miss Shavon?"

"I'm fine, Darryl. How are you?"

"I'm great." Darryl then directed his attention to the young lady standing behind him. "Shavon, you remember Rachel?"

Rachel smiled, "Hi, Shavon. It's nice to see you again."

Shavon returned her smile.

"It's nice seeing you too."

Rachel was shorter than the girls Shavon was used to seeing Darryl with. She was a little more 'healthy' too. Rachel was of a medium brown complexion, medium length hair, top heavy with a small waist and full hips. She stood 5'4 tall. She had a pretty face and a very outgoing personality. She was certainly different from most girls Darryl dated.

He dated many women but this one had been steady. Darryl was 6' 4" with a very light complexion. Darryl's mother was white and his father was black. Shavon was used to seeing him with high-yellow women with hair down their backs. Usually they were about 5'7 and slender.

Darryl seemed to enjoy his personal life and was envied by many. But Darryl would only admit to Tracy that sometimes it got boring. He got tired of women who liked him because of his popularity and good looks and did everything he asked. Tracy knew that if Darryl saw the same girl three times, he had become bored again with his lifestyle and needed to slow down for a while. He understood Darryl because he had been that way himself before he met Shavon. Darryl looked back at Rachel.

"And you remember Tracy, of course."

"Yes, I do." The two of them exchanged greetings.

"Why don't you two join us?" Darryl asked.

"Thanks, man, but we're on our way out. Maybe we can all get together and go skating next week." Instantly Tracy was slapped with the reality of Shavon's condition. He felt bad and tried to compensate. "Or maybe to a movie."

"Yeah. A movie sounds better," Shavon commented without looking at Tracy.

"Okay. It's a date. What's today? Tuesday? Let's go next Tuesday."

"Sounds good to me," Tracy agreed as he met Darryl half way for a handshake. As they walked away Darryl yelled to Tracy, "And you take good care of Shavon!"

Shavon and Tracy sat on the small couch in Mark's apartment making small talk. Neither one of them knew where to begin.

"How's your grandfather?"

"He's doing really well now. He's a little weak but he's much better."

"So, when will your mother be back?"

"Late tomorrow."

Tracy scratched his head. "So, how's school going?"

"Fine, Tracy. And besides, you already asked me that once today."

He knew that she was hinting that they should get to the point. Tracy drew in a deep breath and walked to the window while putting his hands in his pockets. He then turned toward Shavon who was now looking at the floor. She was as nervous as Tracy. *I just wish he would say something so we could get it over with*, she thought. Tracy had similar thoughts. *I wonder what she's thinking. I wish I knew so I could have some idea of where to begin.*

Neither one of them could look into each other's eyes. Shavon watched as he began to pace. He was terrified and she could see it. She expected he would be hurt and disappointed but it seemed to have affected him more deeply than she had known. She leaped from the couch and embraced him from behind.

"Tracy, I'm sorry," she whispered.

He blinked a few times to keep the tears from falling.

"Do you wanna get married, Shavon?" he asked nearly choking.

"No! Why would you say that? I don't want to change things between us. I want to do the right thing, yes, but marriage never entered my mind as the right thing to do. Yes! I do want to marry you but not now! I thought you knew me better than that." She turned away. "I don't believe this."

Tracy stared out of the window. "I'm sorry, Shavon, I just thought--"

"You just thought. Well, thanks a lot, Tracy. You make it sound like I want to tie you down. I want to marry you but when we're ready, not because were forced."

"No. That's not what I meant, Shavon."

"Yes it is." She grabbed her purse and headed toward the door.

"Wait Shavon!" She stopped in her tracks and dropped her head. He stood looking at her for a moment.

"I'm sorry. I just didn't know what to think. I'm so confused. I'm sure a lot of things went through your head too."

"Yes but never forcing you into marriage. That's what most men think of their women but I never thought you would think that. I thought I had earned more credit than that, Tracy."

"You have, Shavon. I'm sorry."

She could tell when she looked at him that his words were sincere. *Things just happened so unexpectedly. I can't really blame him for the way he's reacting,* she thought.

Tracy held out his hand and Shavon walked with him to the couch. They sat quietly for a few minutes. He held her as if it were his last time. She reluctantly pulled back. She knew what was on his mind.

"Tracy, it's really getting late and I think we both could use some sleep. I have school in the morning, you know."

"I know," he whispered as he kissed her wildly. "Mark will be gone for at least another 40 minutes."

"That doesn't give us very much time," she commented.

They smiled as they looked into each other's eyes.

"A little time is better than no time."

"You have a valid point, Mr. Gaines." She gave him a gentle hug. They both were relieved they had gotten the problem solved.

It was 9:30 p.m. when they reached the house. Shavon noticed her aunt's car was gone. Tracy put his arm around her and sighed, "Boy, I'm glad we got things settled.

Shavon smiled with relief, "So, when do you want to do it?"

"As soon as possible, Shavon. How long do you have?"

"I think we should let her get settled in first once she gets back."

"Let who get settled in first?"

"Mama, who else?" Tracy looked at her with a puzzled expression.

"I don't understand. Why would we let your mother get settled in first? She has nothing to do with this."

"Wait a minute," Shavon had the same look of confusion.

"There's no connection here, Tracy. I wanted her to get settled in before we tell her, that's all I'm saying."

"Tell her what?"

"What else?" she retorted. "About the baby."

"Why would we do that?"

"What do you suggest?" She looked at him incredulous of his ignorance. "That we let her figure it out when I can't fit my clothes anymore." Tracy felt bewildered.

"But, Shavon, you said--" He stopped.

"Said what?"

"Well, I thought we were gonna--" He paused again.

"Tracy, I wish you would finish what you're saying. Now what did I say?"

"You said you didn't want a baby either."

"I don't, Tracy, but we've got one now!" She opened the door and they stepped inside closing the door behind them.

"Wait a minute, Shavon. I thought you were gonna get an abortion."

"A what!!!" Her voice echoed off the walls and her eyes squinted as she looked angrily at him.

"But, Shavon, you said-- I thought--"

"Well, you thought wrong, buddy, because I never indicated I would do that because I wouldn't. So get it out of your head." Her voice began to tremble. "How could you even think such a thing? I thought I knew you." Her fists were balled tightly. She became very emotional and she could not control her anger. Tracy watched as tears streamed down her face.

He reached to comfort her. "Get away from me!" She pulled away as if a stranger had touched her. He saw hatred in her eyes.

"Just think about it, Shavon."

She attempted to control her anger, "Tracy," she said lowering her tone, "I suggest you leave." She said it slowly as she motioned her hand toward the door. She tried to maintain her tone but every word expressed more hurt and anger.

"Shavon, I love you."

"Don't say that! If you love me, you would love our baby too!" Tracy tried again.

"Shavon, it would be the best for both of us right now. I'm just getting started and you're still in school and--"

"Whether you like it or not, Daddy, you're going to have a baby," she said half crying.

His eyes were glassy now. He had completely misunderstood. But how? He didn't know but he did know he didn't want a baby.

"I can't afford a baby right now, Shavon." She looked at him with fire in her eyes.

"Well, I'll take care of the baby myself."

"How, Shavon? You can't even take care of yourself."

"Ooh. You rotten, selfish shell of a man! I wish I had never--" she stopped.

"Never what?"

He started toward her and grabbed her by the arm. She pulled her arm away and began running up the stairs. She tripped on a step and fell to the floor.

"Shavon!" He ran to her side and tried to help her up.

"Are you all right?" Seeing her fall sent his heart racing.

He was terrified. "Oh, God. Shavon, are you all right?"

Shavon lay there and trembled as she cried. "Just go home, please. Tracy, just go home." Shavon began to cry harder. "I hate you for this!"

"Shavon, please," he pleaded as tears dropped from his eyes. "At least let me help you up?"

"If you really want to help me, Tracy, get out!"

He stood staring at her for a few minutes but her anger nor tears, had begun to subside. She had hurt him deeply as he had hurt her. He didn't know what else to do. He turned and left.

As Shavon heard his engine, she could feel nothing but hatred for him now. She never thought the day would come when she would welcome Tracy's departure. She started to get up. "Oh!" She fell as she felt excruciating pain in her stomach. "Oh, no! Please, God," she cried, "Not my baby."

After she regrouped, she slowly crawled to the phone. She cried into the phone.

"Help me, Myah."

"Shavon!" What's wrong?"

"I need you, Myah. I need you."

When Myah arrived, Shavon lay on the floor unconscious.

CHAPTER 7

Dana looked at the doctor through worried eyes as Casey stood beside her.

"But, doctor, you say she's all right?" Dana asked frantically.

"Yes. She's just fine, Mrs. Robertson. But as I said, for both their sakes, I advise plenty of bed rest and foods rich in iron." Dana sighed.

Casey put his hand on her shoulder to comfort her. "Is the baby all right?" Casey asked the doctor.

"Yes, the baby's fine. Your daughter threatened a miscarriage but she was given an ultrasound scan, which was positive despite the bleeding and the pregnancy is confirmed. It's going to take at least three weeks to stabilize the pregnancy. She's no longer bleeding or experiencing abdominal pain but I'm going to keep her overnight just for observation."

Dana and Casey entered the room to find Shavon reading a childcare brochure. When she looked up and saw her parents, she stuffed it under the sheets.

"Hi."

"Good morning," her mother returned.

Shavon panicked. She had no idea of what Myah had told her parents. She would soon find out. Casey held an expression she didn't recognize. He leaned forward kissing her on the forehead.

"Hi, Daddy."

"Good morning, baby girl," he said with a slight smile of relief. Shavon felt a little easier.

Dana grabbed Shavon's hand putting her hand over it.

"How do you feel?"

Shavon smiled nervously, "Don't look so worried, Mama, I'm fine."

"You had a nasty fall, Shavon. Myah said you were unconscious when she got to the house."

Shavon tried to change the subject, "Hey, what are you are doing here? When did you get back?"

Dana sat down on the edge of the bed.

"I got in early this morning. Myah was asleep on the couch." She reached under the sheets and pulled the booklet out that Shavon had been reading. "Did you learn anything?"

Shavon lowered her head.

"Shavon, we talked to the doctor, he told us everything."

Shavon could see the disappointment in her parent's eyes.

"I'm sorry. I--I--"

Dana stood up and began to pace as her eyes watered.

"Shavon, why?"

Tears ran from Shavon's eyes as she lowered her head.

"Shavon, what are you gonna do now? You're still in school."

Shavon responded without lifting her head, "Pregnant girls finish school all the time, Mama," she said as she wiped her tears.

"The doctor wants you to take it easy for at least three weeks, Shavon. He thinks you need lots of bed rest. You can't go back to school for a while. Shavon, why didn't you come to me with this? Why did you feel like you had to hide it? The doctor says you're more than two months pregnant. How long would it have taken for you to tell me, Shavon, huh?"

Shavon glanced at her father who watched Dana intently.

"Mama, I--"

"Shavon, I can't stand here and act as if I'm not hurt because I am. I never thought you would end up like this. You're too smart for this. Does Tracy know?"

"Yes."

"Well, what does he think? Is he ready to be a father? Of course not." Dana answered her own question, which relieved Shavon. She couldn't bear to tell her parents what Tracy thought of the situation. Dana sat next to Shavon putting her hands on Shavon's face and began wiping her tears.

"Sweetheart, I'm sorry. I'm disappointed and I am a little tired from my trip." She hugged her daughter. "I love you, Shavon. If I made you feel rotten, that wasn't my intention. I just want you to have more out of life." Dana sighed. "I'm sorry if I exploded but it's just a shock. First, your Grandpa and now this."

Dana kissed her on the forehead.

"We're going to leave now and let you get some rest. We'll be back in the morning," Casey added. He held Shavon's hand as he kissed her cheek.

"We'll continue this discussion tomorrow, young lady. Your mother is upset, but she's also right about everything she's said. We'll talk about it more calmly--me, you, your mother and Tracy."

Once again Shavon was hit hard with reality. *I'm not ready to see him*, she thought. *I don't even want to see him. I was wrong about Tracy. How could I have been so wrong? I thought he really loved me. He does,* she thought. *He has to. But he doesn't want to accept the baby, why? I don't understand. It's not the baby's fault, it's ours and he should be man enough to face it.* Shavon was deep in thought, and didn't hear the door open.

"Hi, Shavon. How do you feel?" Shavon jumped.

"Myah, you scared me half out of my wits. I'm okay, I guess. The baby's okay too."

Myah put her hands in the back pocket of her Guess jeans as she sighed with relief, "I prayed for you and the baby."

"Thanks, Myah. You should have prayed for Tracy too."

"Why is that?"

Shavon flipped through the brochure like she hadn't heard her friend.

"All right. What happened last night?"

Shavon dropped the brochure and said, "Myah, I'm still in shock. I just don't believe it." She rested her head in her hands. "Myah, Tracy doesn't even want the baby."

"Did he say that?"

"Yes."

Myah stared at her for a moment. This was worse than what she thought.

"First he had the nerve to think we would have to get married. Then to top that off, he asked me to consider an abortion. Myah, I was so out done. I never thought he would even think of such a thing. After all this time, I don't know him at all," she said as her voice trembled.

"He's just scared, Shavon."

"Well, I am too but the baby is here and we'll have to deal with it. It's not the baby's fault." Shavon brushed her bang off her forehead.

"Myah, I was really ugly toward him last night. In the heat of anger, I said some painful things."

"Shavon, do you think he might, well, you know, avoid you because of the baby?"

"No. I--I really don't know anymore, Myah. After last night, I think he's capable of anything."

Myah looked at her friend wondering if she should disclose what was on her mind.

"He probably hates me now. I really hurt him last night. I said some things I never thought I would say to him. I yelled at him and said I hated him."

"That explains it then," Myah said in a low voice.

Shavon looked up with wide eyes. "That explains what?" Shavon could see that Myah was reluctant to say. "Myah, don't keep anything from me," she demanded.

"Well, it's just that I called Tracy this morning--"

"And," Shavon urged.

"And he wasn't home."

"Of course he wasn't, he's at work."

"Shavon, Mrs. Gaines said he didn't come home last night."

Myah saw the look of panic cross Shavon's face. Shavon sat up in the bed. "He didn't?"

Myah shook her head. "That's what the lady said."

"Did she say where he was?"

"No, she didn't know."

Shavon expelled a deep breath.

"She thought maybe you would know. I told her where you were and gave her the room number."

"Oh, Myah, what if he's somewhere on the side of the road bleeding to death all because of me."

"Stop it, Shavon. I'm sure he's fine and he'll probably be here later, you'll see. Grab hold of yourself. Take a couple of deep breaths."

"Good afternoon," said an aide coming into the room.

"Good morning," Myah returned. Shavon stared as in a daze.

"We've got some breakfast for you, Ms. Robertson. How are you today?"

"She's just fine, maybe a little upset though but health-wise, she's okay," Myah answered.

"Well good. We have some hot oatmeal, toast, applesauce, fresh orange juice and milk."

Shavon repugnantly looked at the tray. "I'm not hungry."

"But you need your strength," Myah teased. "You're not just eating for yourself now. You have to think about the baby first."

The aide turned and left the room. Shavon looked in the bowl. "Ugh!" She looked at Myah who was smiling now. "Myah, are you thinking the same thing I'm thinking?"

"And what would that be?" she asked wickedly.

They looked at the bowl simultaneously. Myah picked it up while looking around and slid it under the bed.

"So what do you want from Wendy's?"

"You know me so well. If I didn't know better, I would say you could read my mind. I want a small frosty, no make it a medium and a double cheeseburger with everything. No, forget the onions. They might give the baby gas."

Myah put her hand over her eyes and looked between her fingers. "You are truly sick. You know that, don't you?"

"Who in their right mind would eat that paste, Myah?"

Myah pulled the bowl from under the bed.

"Wait a minute, Shavon, that's not oatmeal, it's stucco."

They began to laugh hysterically.

"Somebody wanna share the joke with me?"

Shavon looked up. Tracy stood there with flowers in his right hand. Everyone was silent. Shavon felt nervous as she glared at Tracy. She could tell he hadn't slept well last night. *He was still handsome*, she thought.

"Hi, Myah. How are you?"

"I'm fine."

The room fell silent again.

"I'd better get going," Myah said.

"Myah!"

"Huh?"

"What about my--"

"Maybe Tracy will do it for you."

"I owe you one!" Shavon yelled as Myah went out the door.

She felt a lump in her throat as her eyes focused on Tracy. When she swallowed, it was dry and hard and she was nervous with perspiration. Tracy felt it too as he eyed her. He walked toward her but didn't dare try to touch her. He remembered well what had happened the night before.

"Shavon, I owe you something. I'm sorry for what I said to you last night. I was really out of line, mostly scared I guess." He was afraid to sit down or get too close. Shavon was calm and he didn't want to do anything to change that. "I didn't mean for you to end up here."

He bit his lower lip as he looked around the room. He thought to say he loved her but kept it to himself. She had already told him he didn't.

"Are you okay?"

"Yes. I'm okay."

"Then why are you here?"

"Well, after I fell last night, I had some severe abdominal pains and I bled a little. The doctor said I threatened a miscarriage."

Tracy's eyes drooped with guilt. Shavon grabbed his hand.

"But it's okay now. I just need plenty of bed rest for a while."

He hugged her and tears came to his eyes. She held him close.

"Okay, if you want to keep the baby, that's what we'll do. I'm just sorry I didn't see it this way last night then maybe all of this could have been avoided. I know I'm not ready to be a father but I'll just have to learn."

"Tracy, I owe you something too. I said a lot of mean things to you last night. You know I didn't mean them."

"I do?" he raised his brows. She let out a small laugh.

"Well, not all of it." She broke the embrace and looked at him very seriously. "I know it's going to be hard to face such a drastic change but we have to. We're both going to be parents."

Tracy hated the sound of that but he would never say it. He responded by telling her he would try.

"Did I tell you my mother told me you were pregnant before you told me?"

"No, you never mentioned that to me. How did she know?"

"Did you have morning sickness, Shavon?"

"No."

"That's probably because I had it."

"You did what!"

"My mother said my father had it when she was pregnant with me too. I think they call it couvade or something. She recognized all the symptoms. I couldn't sleep. I gained some weight. I even vomited a few times. Mama said I got lazy too. I really didn't believe her so I forgot all about it."

"Better you than me," Shavon said laughing.

CHAPTER 8

It was comforting to be back in Shavon's good graces. Tracy knew he wasn't ready to be a father but he vowed to give it his best shot. It was the right thing to do.

Shavon's next two months were hard for her. She had threatened another miscarriage and was forced to drop out of school. This hurt her but she would only do what was best for the baby.

Tracy was still very much in love with her but found that he had become distant and had begun to spend more time working. He and Shavon never got out anymore because of her delicate pregnancy. It bothered him greatly but he knew it was just another sacrifice for their *mistake* as he so often referred to it.

"Hi, Tracy," Jim said as he peeked through the door. "How about some lunch?"

Tracy pushed himself away from the desk. "Not a bad idea, Pal. I could use some lunch. Who's driving?" Tracy asked.

"Oh, I thought I'd leave that to you."

"Oh, you did?"

"Yeah, you know how you just love to drive." Tracy smiled and pulled out his keys.

"All right, you win."

"Hey, what about some pizza?"

"Pizza, this time of day?"

"What's wrong with that, Tracy? It's time for you to change your eating habits, eat some junk food once in a while. You're too skinny."

"Ha-ha. You're not much bigger yourself," Tracy conceded with laughter.

"I know. That's why we both need it."

Jim looked across the table. He felt bad for Tracy. Though he had never gone through what Tracy was going through, he was well aware of how Tracy felt. Jim began whistling.

"Okay-okay, that's enough. I got the message," said Tracy. Jim held up his hand.

"Just a little companionship, that's all I ask."

Tracy swallowed a mouth full of pizza, took a sip of pop behind it, sighed, and then leaned backward. "I don't know if I can do it, Jim." Tracy put his hand across his mouth.

"What is it you have to do?"

"I have to be a good father and supporter."

"And what's so difficult about that?" Tracy put his elbow on the table resting his hand on his forehead.

"I don't know; I'm just scared I'm not ready for the responsibility. I'm too young."

"You weren't too young to make the baby, were you?"

Tracy drew a deep breath. "I've heard that before and I don't need to hear it from you."

"Okay, Tracy, but think about it this way. Wasn't your father there for you? He was there until his dying day for you. And if he could hear you now, what do you think he would say?"

Tracy shrugged his shoulders.

"I don't know, man. I'm trying to face up to things but I can't sleep some nights. Shavon and I don't do anything anymore. She's forcing me to eat like she has to eat whenever I go over to her place for dinner. It's just not me. And all she talks about now is the baby. I think about the baby too but it's not even here yet. She never really asks about me anymore. That used to be her first question when I saw her but, man, so much has changed between us. She used to read fashion magazines. Now she reads everything she can find on childcare. I think she's developed a library on child care literature."

Jim stared at Tracy thinking of how much credit he had given him for the man he was and now he couldn't believe his ears. Tracy continued shaking his head.

"I went to see her last night. Do you want to know what happened? I took the story I wrote for this month's issue. She skimmed it. She used to read them and give her viewpoint. I mean it's like, like I don't even matter to her anymore and it hurts, man. If she's like this in the fifth month, how's she going to be in her eighth and ninth month?"

"I think you two should talk it over like mature adults. I know things will work out but you both have to try! She's a very beautiful girl, inside and out and she loves you, Tracy. No matter what, you shouldn't question that. You should appreciate the fact that she's going to be a good mother for your child."

Tracy stood up. "That's part of it too. I know I said I didn't want the child but I feel like it's not mine anyway and she's not either. I feel like I'm out in the cold. The baby changed both of us. We don't know each other anymore. I just wish the "mistake" had never happened." Tracy got up and began to walk out.

"Wait!" Jim yelled. "What about your half of the bill?" Tracy expelled a short laugh.

"I drove."

The ride back to the office was relatively quiet. Jim knew how Tracy felt and he would never bring it up again. *Tracy's a very bright mature young man*, he thought. *He'll get through this by the time the baby's born. Maybe then he will learn to love his child.* No matter what, Jim would still be in his corner.

***

"Mama, was Tracy late with his rent again?"

"Neicy, we gotta be patient with Tracy. He got more responsibility now."

"But, Mama, the baby's not even here yet."

"I know, Honey, but he been payin' office visit co-pays and buyin' maternity clothes. Tracy says Shavon eatin' like a pig. He puttin money aside so to be prepared once the baby comes. It ain't easy raising a baby when you're so young, you know."

Neicy looked toward the door as Delaney came in.

"Hi, Ma. Hey Neicy."

Delaney went to the bathroom to wash his hands and came back into the kitchen. He looked at his sister.

"Did you tell her?"

"Tell me what?" Maria asked as she stopped chopping onions.

"Look, Mama," Delaney began. "Tracy is becoming harder and harder to live with. He listens to the radio half the night and you know how thin these walls are. I have to get up in the morning. A growing boy needs his sleep."

Maria looked back at Neicy who continued with complaints. "Mama, I never get to see the programs I like anymore. Every afternoon he comes in here like he's King or something and guards the TV like it's his. We sure argue a lot more than we used to. We can't agree on or talk about anything like we used to."

Delaney cut in, "He used to help me with my homework sometimes. Now he says, "Ask your teacher, that's what she's getting paid for."

Maria frowned as she listened to her children go on about her eldest son. She too had noticed a change. He never held conversations with her anymore and he had begun to dodge Shavon's calls, which slightly pleased her but she didn't like seeing him so withdrawn. She noticed he had started to drink more beer and eat less food but she didn't press the issue with him. Maria looked at her children again. She knew that Tracy was treating them unfairly, using them as punching bags. Maria

decided she would talk with Tracy but she wanted to give him time to realize what was happening around him, hoping he would see what he was doing to his family.
"Okay, we gon' give him a lil' mo time and if that don't work," she sighed, "Then I just gotta have a talk with em'."

Delaney finished his sandwich and headed for the door.

"Any homework young man?" Maria asked.

"Just that stupid science work. I don't see why it's so important to know the difference between granite and limestone anyway."

"Upstairs young man," Maria commanded.

Delaney marched reluctantly up the stairs. Maria found herself laughing. She remembered how much she hated science when she was Delaney's age. She took a bowl of sweet potatoes out of the refrigerator.

"You wanna finish these, Neicy?"

Neicy was shaken from her thoughts by her mother's words. "Sure, Mama." She went to the drawer and pulled out a knife and began to cut the potatoes into slices.

Maria noticed her silence as she reached across the table for the greens.

"So what you thinkin' bout? You havin' trouble in school, Neicy?"

"No, it's not me I'm thinking about."

"Oh."

"Mama, it's Tracy. I think this whole situation is confusing him a little. He's losing sight of himself and he's doing things I know he really doesn't want to do. Mama, I think that if he keeps this up, he's going to hurt a few people."

Maria looked at Neicy with a comforting smile. "He'll get over this, you'll see. Time heals all wounds," Maria responded referring to his difficulties at home.

"Mama, do you remember my friend, Eden?"

"What about her?"

"I saw her last week and she said Tracy has been going over there. He's been spending time with her sister. You remember Diane, don't you?"

"That tall, dark skinned girl that used to go out with Tracy? I reckon I do."

"Well, he's seeing her again. He spent the night with her once last week. Remember that day Shavon called twice? Well, that's where he was."

Maria dropped a handful of greens in a bowl. "Neicy, don't believe everything you hear, all right?"

"Whatever you say, Mama, but if it's true he's being very unfair to Shavon. It takes two, you know. I think he's angry with her for being pregnant. He forgot one small detail, it's his child too! Not hers alone."

"And what makes you so sure it's his child?"

"Oh, come on, Mama. Shavon wouldn't have anything to do with another man even if he was rich. Everybody knows how she feels about Tracy and that includes you!"

"Well, maybe she tried to trap him. You know how some young girls are. Maybe she's afraid of losing him and thinks this is the best way to keep em'."

"I doubt that very seriously. Mama, don't forget, I know Shavon and she has never been stupid. I really feel sorry for her right now. Tracy should be more understanding. I've tried to see myself in her position and it's just not fair. She loves him so much."

Maria kept silent. *If he had stayed with Sherry Witton, things would be different*, she thought to herself. Maria had begun to blame Shavon for her son's unhappiness. *Shavon knew what she was doing from the beginning*, Maria thought. And now her Tracy was suffering because of Shavon's trap.

Neicy put her hand on her mother's shoulder for consolation. "Mama, I know how you feel about Tracy being with Sherry but face it. It's not going to happen. He might be going through a few changes right now but I hope for everybody's sake that they'll pull through, especially for the baby. Mama, don't forget how many girls Tracy ran around with before he met Shavon. She changed him for the better. He was only out for what he could get. Sherry was nice but Shavon is too. And, Mama, just think, you'll have a grandchild to care for and I'll have a niece or nephew to be proud of. And Tracy's going to be a real father hopefully," she said trying to convince herself. "Maybe when he sees the baby, we won't be able to keep him away from it."

Maria smiled as Neicy hugged her. "Maybe everything will be perfect after all," said Neicy.

Maria laughed. "Maybe you're right." But Maria knew it wouldn't be any time soon. She could see that Tracy wasn't ready to accept the baby and all the responsibility entailed, she would pray.

CHAPTER 9

Diane quickly pulled up her mini skirt and buttoned her blouse as Tracy lay on the bed watching. She went to the mirror and began to comb her hair. Diane's hair was always neat. She was proud of her full, rich, coal black hair. She wore it in a short bob with a tapered neckline. Diane was 5'9" of dark brown complexion and very thin. Her legs were large for her leanness.

She and Tracy had been a hot item for a while in high school. Diane loved Tracy completely. No matter what he did wrong, she excused it. Tracy had her waiting for him many times without calling. He would always excuse himself by saying you're not my wife, Diane, and don't forget it! He had seen a lot of her off and on until he met Shavon. Diane was hurt but she was far from lonely. She had known many men before and after Tracy. Diane was a firm believer in using a man when she wanted something and she always got it, except when she wanted it from Tracy.

Diane walked toward the bed and leaned over and kissed Tracy. She smiled as she looked at him.

"What are you smiling about?" Tracy asked.

"You, Silly." She began to laugh.

"Oh, yeah. I never thought of myself as funny."

Diane sat on the bed beside him. "Well, me neither but my sister has been trying to find out who I've been spending my nights with and I thought it was kind of funny. Why don't you want me to satisfy her curiosity?"

"What's the sense?" he said as he jumped up from the bed.

"I don't see why we should hide it, Tracy."

"Okay, Di," he said as he grabbed her arm, "Now is not the time and it's none of her business anyway. Let's just keep it between me and you, okay?" Diane could see the seriousness in his eyes and knew that she would have to agree to keep him.

"So how much longer do you think you can take things the way they are?"

Tracy looked down. "I don't know. I just don't know."

"Well, how far is she now?"

"Six months and she's really mean too."

Diane detected sadness but she felt good knowing he was finally hers. She knew he still loved Shavon deeply but she hoped the baby would shatter that love by the time it was born. She smiled submissively and gave him a hug holding him close.

"Do I make you happy, Tracy?"

Tracy was silent for a moment. Before he responded, he tightened his grip around her waist. "Yes you do, Diane," he whispered. "Happier than I've been in a long time."

***

As Dana sat in the living room, she found herself staring at the swan Shavon and Tracy had bought her at Christmas. *It's beautiful*, she thought. *Those two, what a couple*. Dana began to think of how happy they were at Christmas in comparison to their so obvious distance over the past months. She wished Tracy had been more enthusiastic about the baby but she partly understood his position. *He's still young,* she thought. *A job of such magnitude was beyond his teenage comprehension*. She knew that things were hard for them but they had to work it out alone.

Shavon started down the stairs as the phone began to ring.

"Hello.

"Hi, Mama, how are you? Good. How's daddy? Oh, I'm fine Mama."

Shavon heard more clearly as she came near. "She's okay. She's able to do a little more than she could before. Oh, I don't know. They don't seem to be as close as they used to be. I don't think he's ready to accept the baby yet. Mama, he's so young and the baby seems to have put a strain on things for them. Shavon's handling it pretty well, I guess but--."

Shavon turned and walked back up the stairs. She was hurt by the way things had turned out between her and Tracy but she was determined to hide it from her mother. She knew what her mother felt about Tracy before the baby but now she felt embarrassed for him. She had begun to think he didn't love her anymore. She felt fat, ugly and unwanted.

She sat on the bed and thought of how her last conversation with Myah had gone.

"Look at me, Myah. I'm fat and ugly. No man would want a woman like this."

She remembered Myah's argument of how everyone thought she was even more beautiful pregnant and that it was all in her mind. Myah's argument could not avert her feeling of unattractiveness.

The following month was long for Shavon. She and Tracy had seen less of each other than they ever had. He had begun to cancel plans on a regular basis using his work as an excuse. His 20th birthday was spent at Shavon's in front of the TV set. He had long since stopped offering to take her out to dinner or anywhere else. Whenever they went out, it was at Shavon's request. He never invited her to his house anymore. He had begun to hint about bills he had to pay; her car note, his car note and insurance, rent and the list went on.

Shavon had noticed a complete change in Tracy. She was sure she had lost him. She no longer asked him if he would like to do things. She knew she had been short with him occasionally but she believed that was due to her condition. And that wasn't enough to change him so drastically.

Dana noticed Shavon had begun to look worried and tired. She often stopped in the middle of a sentence and stared before she remembered what she was trying to say.

Shavon sat near the window at the dining room table playing with her hair.

"I say it's time for a haircut, young lady," Dana said with a warm smile.

"I think I'll keep it this time. I haven't worn it this long since I met Tracy." She smiled. "He likes it long."

The mere mention of his name had begun to hurt. She absently lowered her head. Dana began to braid Shavon's loose hair.

"You wanna talk about it?"

Shavon remained quiet as Dana continued.

"I want you to know that I'm here for you, Shavon. That's all."

Shavon began to tremble. Dana reached for her hand.

"Mama, he's seeing someone else."

Dana stood and listened as Shavon cried gasping for breath to tell her about Tracy.

"How do you know that, Shavon?"

"He doesn't come over much anymore. If I tell him I need something, he'll bring it by and stay for an hour or two and then leave," she swallowed then continued, "He never says he loves me anymore."

Dana leaned over and put her hands on Shavon's shoulders shaking her slightly.

"That doesn't mean he doesn't love you anymore, Honey. He's just confused, that's all. And it doesn't mean he's seeing somebody else. It just means--"

"But he is. I know it."

"How do you know, Shavon. Did he tell you himself?"

"No, Myah did."

"How does she know?"

Shavon began to cry again. "She saw him with her."

"It could be a good friend, someone he can talk to. Especially with the way things are going between you two right now."

"How many good friends do men take to motels, Mama?"

Dana's heart stood still. "Is that what Myah told you?"

"Why is he hurting me like this? I love him so much. He hates me for being pregnant and I know it."

"That's not true, Shavon. It may be hard for him to accept but maybe by the time the baby's here, he'll--"

"I doubt it," Shavon said quickly.

"Shavon, talk to him. Have you tried that? It's not all his fault, you know. You haven't been the best company for him. Maybe if you talk to him and try to come to an understanding--"

"I don't know Mama, I've lost hope."

"Shavon, just try it. It certainly won't make things any worse."

Shavon tossed and turned all night. She dreaded her talk with Tracy but knew it would be the right thing to do. She imagined the conversation. *Yes, I want out. It just can't work. I tried but I don't love you anymore.* Those words would hurt her more than anything she could ever imagine. But if he did want out, all she could do would be to accept it.

Shavon waited until she thought Tracy might be home before she called. All day she thought about what she would say to him. She was truly confused about the man she thought she knew so well. She had never imagined they would grow so far apart. Today she had many memories of the past two years. She thought about times she had been angry with Tracy and refused to talk to him. It seemed he was always the one who gave in. Tracy would do everything he could to get back in good graces with her.

She remembered their anniversary dinner and the walk they had taken. She remembered what he had said about forgetting her would be forgetting himself. There was certainly an awful lot of that these days. She had always been sure of where she stood but not anymore. She thought about how happy they both had been those first two years. It seemed to Shavon that everything had gotten lost somehow and there was little hope that things would ever be as they were.

***

"Hi, Neicy. How are you?"

"Hi, Shavon. I'm just fine. How are you and the little one?"

Neicy caught Shavon off guard. Shavon thought the family disapproved of her pregnancy. Not that it mattered to her but she didn't expect them to be happy by the way Tracy had been acting.

"Oh, oh, we're just fine," Shavon responded scratching her head.

"I haven't seen you in a while, Shavon. Why don't you come over for dinner tonight?"

It was obvious to Neicy by the way Shavon stammered that she didn't know what to say.

"I bet you're pretty big now. How far are you?"

"Seven months--and yes I'm fat," she said with laughter.

It felt good to Shavon to know that someone in Tracy's family cared enough to ask about the baby. She found herself feeling better about the baby than she had for a while.

"Can I speak to Tracy?"

"He's not here, Shavon," Neicy said hating to be the bearer of bad news. She felt the tension in Shavon's voice as she responded.

"Oh. When he comes home, would you tell him to call me?"

"Okay, Shavon, sure will. And don't be a stranger, Shavon."

Shavon smiled for the first time that day and it felt good. She suddenly felt down remembering what Neicy had just told her. *He's with her*, she thought. *I may not even see him tonight.*

Shavon told her mother that she would be taking a nap if she needed her. She began to think about what she would say to him. She obliterated any thought of divulging what she knew about the other woman. She only hoped it wasn't serious.

Shavon went to the closet and pulled out the dress she had designed and planned to wear to her prom. She thought of how she would miss going and all the other things she would miss out on after the baby was born. It bothered her immensely that she would not wear her most beautiful creation for a once in a lifetime occasion to the prom.

She smiled as she remembered how happy Myah was when she offered it to her for the prom. It made more sense to her to see it on Myah rather than in the closet. She slowly lied down and turned over to get comfortable when she heard a car pull into the driveway. She doubted that it would be for her. The only person she wanted to see was Tracy, and she knew it wouldn't be him.

"Shavon! You've got company."

When she reached the top of the landing, she heard Tracy's voice. She stood at the top of the stairs.

"Need some help?"

"No, I can make it." She spoke with cheer in her voice.

"I thought you might wanna go to the show."

Shavon tried not to show her surprise.

"I would love to."

Dana listened from the kitchen. *What a beautiful thing*, she thought.

Shavon and Tracy enjoyed the movie. He knew love stories had always been her favorite and today, he felt a strong urge to make her happy. He felt better about being with her today than he had for some time. He held her hand tightly all through the movie, which pleased her greatly. She felt something different about his attitude toward her. Tracy noticed that for once in the past four months, she didn't discourage his eating popcorn but joined him and it felt good. Shavon turned several times during the movie to find him watching her with obvious adoration.

Tracy started up the car.

"You enjoy the movie?"

Shavon smiled. "You know I did. I'm a sucker for love stories."

"I haven't forgotten." He returned her smile as he reached for her hand.

"So, you wanna get something to eat, Shavon? I know you're probably starving ."

"Sounds good to me."

At dinner, Tracy noticed that Shavon appeared to be a little preoccupied. He could tell she wanted to talk about something whenever she toyed with her fork and nervously shook her right leg. He leaned backward.

"You want to get if off your chest, Shavon?"

She looked at him with a slight smile. "That noticeable, huh?"

He smiled back, "Yeah, that noticeable."

"Tracy, I want to know what's going on with us. I don't know anymore. We hardly spend any time together. And most of the time when I call you, you're not there and you don't always return my calls like you used to. Tracy, I don't mean to complain but things are completely different. We've never been so far apart."

Shavon watched him closely. She had no idea what he was thinking or what he might say and she was scared.

"I must have disappointed you in some way but I don't know what I did. Maybe it's because of the baby, I don't know. It just might be me. Tracy, I'm sure you feel a drastic change in our relationship and even in yourself."

Shavon looked out of the window. She knew what she would say next would be harder to say if she were looking at him.

"I've started to think you don't love me anymore since I'm so fat and unattractive."

"Shavon! Don't say that. You're as beautiful as you were when I met you. The baby didn't change the way I feel about you, nothing has."

"Well, what is it then? Don't you know how distant you've been?"

He looked downward. "Yes, I know I've been distant. But do you realize that today was the first time in four months that you didn't criticize what I ate?"

Shavon's eyes widened with ignorance. "I wasn't aware that it had bothered you so much when I said something about what we should eat. I didn't know I was forcing you. I thought you enjoyed salads and vegetables. What else bothers you?"

Tracy didn't want to hurt Shavon but he continued. "Remember how you used to ask me about my stories, nearly demanding to see them?" Shavon dropped her head. "Well, you hardly pay attention to them anymore."

"But, Tracy, I read one about two months ago, didn't I?"

"Yes, but you only read one in the last few months. You used to tell me what you thought about them. You don't do that anymore either and it hurts. I miss it, I need it. You don't even ask me about me anymore. You always talk about the baby. It seems that the baby is your only concern. I feel as if I've been shut out completely. It could be jealousy, I don't know. I'm not sure what it is exactly but I do know that the responsibility is a part of it too. Shavon, I know it's my responsibility too but things are going to change forever and I can't seem to prepare myself."

He knew what he was saying was crazy but it was the way he felt. There was a long pause before he continued. " Shavon, it really tears me apart when you talk about the baby non-stop, you neglect me."

Shavon sat across the table hating herself for making him feel uncared for. She had taken for granted that he knew she still loved and supported him. She had become so wrapped up in what was good for the baby that she had unknowingly pushed Tracy to the side. She could understand why he had turned to someone else. She had not been there for him. Shavon looked into his eyes.

"Tracy, why didn't you tell me this before?"

He looked away shaking his head, "I don't know, Shavon. I guess I didn't know how to. I told you I would try to accept this and I've failed. That's unfair to you and the baby." He leaned back and took a long look at Shavon. "I refuse to believe you feel ugly."

"Well, I do. If you were fat like this and I stopped coming to see you, you would feel ugly too."

"Well, maybe," he conceded as he reached for her hand. "I love you, Shavon and nothing will ever change that."

They stood outside the car and held each other for a few minutes. For the rest of the night, they talked only about each other. Shavon didn't mention the baby. She knew what Tracy needed and she would be there to give it to him. She was relieved that he had not done as she had imagined he would and broken things off. She said a silent prayer of thanks for the way things worked out.

"Shavon, before we leave, I wanna be honest with you."

She knew that what he had to say was serious. She braced herself.

"I've been trying so hard but I'm not doing so well."

"What do you mean?" Shavon was almost certain he would admit to being with another woman and she couldn't bear to talk about it.

"I'm trying to accept the baby but I don't know how. I'm really confused. Sometimes it's like a nightmare and it scares me. I'm no example for a little kid. I don't even have patience with kids. I can't stand to be around them for more than an hour."

Shavon eyed him but reluctantly kept her thoughts.

"Shavon, help me. I don't know what to do. I feel so lost. I know it's my baby but honestly, Shavon, I haven't felt any love for it yet. I don't know if I ever will. I want the baby to be healthy and all but I don't feel like it will be mine. I don't feel a fatherly connection. I don't know if it's because we've drifted apart or not." Tracy saw a tear drop from Shavon's eye. He hugged her tightly.

"Shavon, I love you and I want to love the baby too. Don't hate me," he whispered.

"I don't hate you, Tracy. I don't know if the way I've been acting has made it harder for you or not but I'm going to do everything I can to make things easier for both of us, then maybe things will fall into place."

Shavon and Tracy spent the rest of the evening at his house. Everyone made bets on who the baby would favor most. Tracy relaxed and joined in the conversation and Shavon was pleased. She noticed that Tracy's mother had been nicer to her than she had ever been. Shavon was puzzled but nevertheless, she was happy. Neicy pulled out some old photographs of Tracy as he was growing up and kept everybody laughing with childhood events. Maria noticed that Tracy had totally relaxed and seemed to be himself again and for once, she felt grateful to Shavon. *I guess she is best for him,* she thought as she smiled at them.

The next two months went very well with Shavon and Tracy. They saw each other nearly every day. They were enjoying each other as they had always done. Tracy felt better about the baby. Feeling the baby moving on a regular basis had begun to give him a fatherly joy. He even began talking to the baby as Shavon had done all along. Things were better all the way around. Nothing could have made things better.

CHAPTER 10

Myah sat on the end of the bed as Shavon went on and on about all the nice gifts she got from her friends at the baby shower Myah had given her.

"Thank you, Myah," she said putting her hand on her stomach.

"We're going to need all the help we can get, won't we?" She looked at Myah with relief. "Just four more days, Myah."

"How much weight have you gained?"

"About 35 pounds."

"Wow! I hope all of it belongs to the baby," Myah said laughing.

"Me too," Shavon said as she giggled. Shavon looked at her friend and smiled.

"Myah, I'm sorry. I was so wrapped up in myself these last two months that I didn't get the details about the prom."

"Oh, it was really nice. Everybody asked about you. They all wanted to know where I got my dress. Girl, I got so many compliments on your dress. And I looked like a queen in it. You should have seen me." Shavon smiled as she listened to Myah praise herself.

"Oh, Robin and Sharon said they would try to make it to the baby shower but I guess something came up. And you remember Michael, don't you?"

"How could I forget? He stared at me from September to January last year. I'm not likely to forget him for a long time."

"Well, he said to tell you hi. He wanted to visit you but I told him about Tracy and the triplets."

"Triplets!" Myah fell off the bed laughing.

"Don't jinx me like that, girl. One is enough for me. Myah, I'm going to need your help. You have a little brother and I'm sure you know a lot about how your mother took care of him."

"Well, I think you should just rely on your mother for this one, Shavon."

"Oh no, Myah. Godmothers have to do all they can to help out." Shavon tried to raise herself and felt a pain.

"Oh, Myah!"

"Take deep breaths, Shavon."

She held her stomach for a few seconds and the pain went away. Twenty minutes later, she felt another. "Myah! Call Mama!"

Dana was home in 15 minutes. Shavon laid on her mother's bed as the pains came more quickly. Finally, Dana took her to the hospital.

***

Tracy drove home thinking about how he had ended things with Diane. Diane was a nice girl but Shavon would always come first. He remembered Diane's anger the last time they had met. "Look, when things get bad again, don't crawl back to me. I'm through with you once and for all, Tracy Gaines!"

He tried to tell her how sorry he was that he had let her get so emotionally involved with him but he reminded her that he had never made any promises. Diane had told him she never wanted to see him again, that he was only capable of using people and apparently cared about no one other than himself. Then she slammed the door with so much force, his ears were still ringing. Tracy cared about Diane and he felt bad about what he had done. But what he felt for Diane couldn't touch what he felt for Shavon.

Tracy walked in the house and his mother greeted him in the living room.

"Shavon's in the hospital."

"What happened?" He was terrified.

"I reckon the baby is on the way."

Tracy got all the information and went straight to the hospital. He smiled as he drove. *My child*, he thought exuberantly. When he arrived, he met Dana in the lobby. They sat and talked for hours before Dana suggested he go home and that she would call him when the baby was born. Tracy told Dana he wouldn't miss it for the world. He stayed and comforted Shavon as much as he could. She gave birth that evening at 10 p.m.

***

"Good morning," Tracy said as he entered the room.

"Hi. Did you see the baby yet?"

"No. Not since last night. I came straight in here to see how the little mother was doing."

"Oh, I'm just fine. How's the proud father?"

"My eyes might be red from lack of sleep, but proud I am." He leaned over and kissed her.

"Don't look too close. You're seeing the real me now," she said hiding her face.

"I know and I love every inch of you. Shavon, I never thought I would be this happy. I called Darryl at 3 a.m. and told him about our son. I woke up the whole house. I ran around the house yelling, "I have a son. I'm a Daddy. I'm a Daddy! You should have seen me." He held her hand as he smiled. "I love you so much and I'm so proud of you."

"I love you too, Tracy." She tightened her grip on his hand. I'll be right back. I'm going to the nursery."

When Tracy came back, Dana was in the room.

"So, who does he look like to you?" They asked simultaneously.

"I don't know. He wasn't there."

"Maybe they're checking him over." Dana said.

"Shavon, have you seen the doctor this morning?" Dana asked.

"Not yet."

A nurse came in with the baby. Shavon sprang with joy as the nurse came near. Tracy stood by Shavon's side.

"He's beautiful."

"Not beautiful," Tracy corrected, "handsome, just like his daddy."

"His eyes are a little puffy. Why is that?" Tracy asked the nurse.

The nurse smiled, "The doctor will be back in one hour from now. He'll answer any questions you may have. In the meantime, I'll let you have a little time with him and you can figure out a name for the little one."

They agreed to name him Terrell Ray Robertson. Dana was so happy to see them this way. Everything had worked out fine after all. Shavon and Tracy argued about who the baby favored most. Tracy thought he had his complexion. Shavon thought he had her nose and Tracy's eyes and her mother's mouth.

Dana left the both of them with their new born son saying that she would return later. Not long after, the doctor walked in on the happy couple. A nurse had just left with little Terrell so she could bathe him.

"Hi, Doctor."

"Good morning, Ms. Robertson. How are you feeling today?"

"Just a little tired. We saw the baby a little while ago." She realized she had neglected to introduce Tracy to the doctor. "I'm sorry. This is Tracy, the baby's father."

"I'm Dr. Garrett," he said with a smile. Tracy shook hands with the doctor.

"Dr. Garrett, we noticed the baby's eyes were slightly puffy. Is that normal?"

Dr. Garrett looked at them for a moment dreading what he had to tell them. "No, Tracy, it's not. We performed an emergency karyotype and skin biopsy. Your son's karyotype revealed a trisomy 21."

Shavon and Tracy looked at each other.

"What's that?" Shavon asked beginning to feel a bit nervous.

"Ms. Robertson, I'm afraid your son has Down Syndrome."

"So, what does that mean exactly?" Shavon asked with tears in her eyes. She felt her heart sink as soon as the words poured from the doctor's mouth.

"Your son was born with an extra Y chromosome. In short, one of the symptoms is mental retardation."

Shavon looked back at Tracy who asked, "But how?"

"We don't know how or why it happens. It affects about one or two out of every 100 babies born." The doctor paused with apprehension. "Along with Down Syndrome he has a congenital malformation of the heart which will eventually require surgery."

Tracy could see that Shavon was decimated and went to her side. He held her as the doctor continued.

"The disorder is not severe, therefore, surgery can be put off until early childhood but the problem must be corrected in order for him to live a normal life."

Shavon began to tremble as she stared at the floor, unconsciously digging her nails into Tracy's arm. She could not believe what the doctor was saying. Shavon started out whispering.

"No. Tracy, tell him he's wrong. He's talking about another baby, not ours. Tell him to leave, Tracy."

"Shavon, stop it," he said quietly touching her face.

"No, Tracy. No! Make him go away. He's wrong. I saw the baby with my own eyes, he's normal."

The doctor took a step toward Shavon. She flinched.

"No, Tracy. Keep him away. Keep him away!" she screamed.

Tracy tried to control Shavon but couldn't. She began kicking and screaming, "No! Not my baby. No! No! No!"

Dr. Garrett sent for a nurse and Shavon was given a sedative. After she went to sleep, Tracy walked absently out of the room. He felt a stab of pain as he thought about what the doctor had said. Mentally challenged and a bad heart. This couldn't be happening. He felt a pain like never before.

He bumped into people as he left the building but he never acknowledged it. He walked around aimlessly for a while before he got into his car. He had not driven far when his tears came down in full force. He fought to keep his eyes and focus on the road but the scene in Shavon's room kept playing over and over in his mind.

He looked up just in enough time to see a truck coming directly at him as he was ran a red light. Tracy quickly tried to turn the wheel but the force from the impact caused him to spin out three full times before he hit the side of an old brick building.

CHAPTER 11

When Tracy awoke he was in a hospital bed. As he gathered his bearings he felt an overwhelming soreness in his head. Then he remembered the accident and everything that had happened before.

"Oh, my head," he mumbled as he reached up touching the bandages. He lay there for ten minutes before a nurse came in.

"So, you're finally awake, huh?"

"Unfortunately. What's wrong with my head?"

"You were in a car accident. Do you remember that?"

"Yes, I do."

"I'll get the doctor for you."

Tracy laid his head back praying that she would bring some pain medication when she returned.

"Hi, young man. I suppose you want to know why you're here?

Tracy gave a positive nod.

"You're lucky to even be alive, Mr. Gaines."

"That bad, huh?"

"Your car is totaled. From what I hear if it weren't for the name on the car, you probably couldn't tell what make it was. Fortunately, you do remember the accident."

"Yeah. That's a good sign, right?"

"Yes. You've got a slight concussion but your CT scan was good. It could have been a lot worse, young man."

"Is that all that's wrong with me, Doc?"

"I'm not sure yet. How do you feel?"

"I'm in a lot of pain."

"That's understandable. Move your fingers and toes for me. How many fingers do you see?"

"Two."

"Good."

The doctor helped Tracy to raise his legs one at a time.

"They said you ran a red light."

"Well I guess it's true. Hey, when do I get out of here?"

"I want you to stay overnight. I'll discharge you after I take a look at you in the morning."

"Doc, can I get up? I need to make a phone call."

"No. You should stay put. There's a phone in the desk beside you. I'll send the nurse in with something to ease your pain. In the meantime, take it easy."

Tracy called Dana and told her about little Terrell's condition. "Shavon's pretty broken up, Dana. They had to sedate her." He began to cry. "Why us?"

"Tracy, where are you now? I'll come and get you. I don't think it would be wise for you to drive right now. You're too upset. Are you still at the hospital?"

Tracy cleared his throat and tried to calm himself as he told her.

"What!"

"Yeah, they say it was pretty bad but I only have a slight concussion."

"Oh God, Tracy. Why didn't you call someone?"

"I had to be alone, Dana. It really hurts. I'm really worried about Shavon. We were both happy about the baby but she carried the baby all those months and now this."

"I'm on my way, Tracy."

When Dana arrived Tracy was watching the traffic from his window. She could tell that he had been crying really hard. His eyes were red and he looked extremely tired. When he looked at her, he could see that she had been crying also. She hugged him.

"How are you?"

"Better. Did you see Shavon?"

"Yes. She's still asleep. I guess she was pretty heavily sedated."

"Did you see Terrell?"

"Yes."

"And how did he look to you?"

"I don't know, Tracy. Normal I guess."

"But he's not, Dana. He has Down Syndrome," he said shaking his head. "I just don't understand what made him that way."

"I don't know, Tracy. It's nothing you and Shavon did."

"Don't you see, Dana," he said frowning. "I imprecated this whole thing. If I had accepted the baby in the first place, maybe we would have had a healthy baby."

"That's not true, Tracy. You know that nothing you could ever say would alter your baby's health. I know it's tragic but it's not your fault. These things happen."

"Look, Tracy. Terrell would still have Down Syndrome if you had accepted him from the very beginning. Tracy, I know it's going to be hard for us but we're going to have to be strong about this. We have to help each other. It could have been worse, you know. What if we had lost him or maybe they said he only had so long to live?"

Tracy shook his head in agreement.

"Tracy," she said as she placed her hands on his face. "That would have just about killed us. I wish he had been normal too, but he's not. We just have to learn how to help him and give him plenty of love."

Tracy hugged Dana as tears fell from his eyes. "Do you think Shavon is going to blame me?"

"Of course not. She's much smarter than that. No matter how hurt she is, she would never blame you for something that wasn't your fault. Tracy, stop thinking such negative thoughts."

"Dana, I just feel so helpless. I don't even know what to say to your daughter."

"I'll be here for the both of you, Tracy. But, I'm sure you'll be able to handle things when you get your head together."

Tracy forced a smile, "Maybe you're right, Dana." He motioned for her hand. "Thanks," he whispered.

Dana rose and went to the door. "I'm going to see Shavon." She saw the expression on his face and knew what he was thinking. "Don't worry. I won't tell her you're here. Call your mother, I'm sure she's wondering where you are."

"Thanks," he whispered faintly.

Dana went to the nursery first to see Terrell. She couldn't hold back her tears. She silently prayed, "Please help us, God. He's just an innocent child. Help me to be strong for them."

Dana got herself together before she went in to see Shavon. Shavon laid there staring at the ceiling.

"How are you, Sweetheart?" Dana said as she walked toward her.

Shavon continued to stare off into oblivion but Dana noticed the tears that fell from her daughters eyes. Her heart broke for her. This had to be the hardest thing that either of them had ever had to deal with.

Dana sat on the edge of the hospital bed and moved a stray hair out of Shavon's face. "Tracy told me everything. I know it hurts, baby, but we can't change things."

Dana went on talking as Shavon sat silent. Nothing that anyone could say would make this better for her. She zoned back in as her mother said, "Shavon, did you hear me, honey?"

"I heard you, Mama," she said to pacify her mother. She turned over to lie on her stomach. "I'm really tired, Mama," she said abruptly.

Dana looked at her with deep concern. *She's just in shock*, Dana thought. *She'll be all right in the morning*. Dana leaned over and kissed her on the cheek. "I'll be back in the morning, Sweetheart. You get some rest." Shavon's eyes closed but she never said another word.

Dana talked to the doctor and he explained that Shavon was suffering from a mild case of depression.

"I'll send someone from the Down Syndrome Support Group to talk with her. She'll probably feel better in a few days. Her depression appears to be mild so I wouldn't worry about it right now. I think she'll be fine."

Shavon didn't say or eat much for the rest of the week. Most of her talking was to her newborn son. She cried each time they took him away from her. On the fifth day, she felt much better. She laughed a little with Myah and ate better than she had been eating. Myah saw that Shavon was in better spirits and tried her best to keep it that way.

"Oh, I forgot to tell you," Myah said grinning, "You look like hell! It's been a while since you had a comb in your hair or makeup on your face. And by the way, I'm getting so sick of that sorry looking ponytail."

Shavon laughed as she reached for a mirror, "You know what, Myah?"

"What?"

"For once you're right. I could use an overhaul of everything."

Myah left and returned with curlers and makeup. When she finished, Shavon looked like herself again. When Tracy arrived, he was very relieved to see Shavon in such a good mood.

"One hundred percent better," he said as he walked into the room.

Shavon smiled with delight. “Hi, Tracy,” she said giggling. “Did I look that bad?”

“Ummm…yeah!” he replied jokingly. She put her arms around him.

“I miss you, Tracy.”

“I miss you too,” he said with sincerity. “I need you,” he added.

“Ok, I’ll see you guys later,” Myah said. Tracy and Shavon continued to stare at each other.

“Um um, I guess I’ll be leaving.” She said it again only louder this time.

“Good-bye, Myah,” they said simultaneously.

The couple spent the rest of the afternoon enjoying each other.

CHAPTER 12

In the following days, Shavon and Tracy talked about what they thought was best for Terrell. They read everything they could and talked to medical professionals and a support group. They began to worry that they would not be able to take good care of him like an older, more experienced couple would. The thought of all the potential therapy and the condition of Terrell's heart worried them. They often felt like two scared children. They knew what they decided would affect the rest of their lives.

They briefly thought of adoption but decided there was no one better than little Terrell's own parents to love and take care of him. The mere thought of letting Terrell go was too painful for either of them. No matter what it took, emotionally or financially they were determined to make it through this.

Shavon and Tracy knew they had to be careful not to smother Terrell because of his condition. They began to learn to care for him through consultations with specialists. Often times they would find themselves in low sprits as Terrell was ill frequently. Because their families had showered them with the utmost love, encouragement and support, they finally overcame their constant worrying. Shavon often found herself stifling little Terrell but with the help of Tracy, she overcame that too.

"I can't help it, Tracy," she would always say. He would always remind her that confinement was hurting much more than anything.

As time went by, Tracy had begun to see that his money wasn't stretching as far as he had initially estimated. He had begun allocating money for Terrell's expenses in Shavon's 4th month of pregnancy but it wasn't enough. They never dreamed there would be so many procedures that insurance wouldn't cover.

Tracy hardly saw any of his money anymore, and there was very little he could do to help Shavon; as he was so accustomed to doing. Shavon missed Tracy's special gifts and surprises but they never once regretted their financial inability because of their son's condition. They both knew that having Terrell was the greatest gift God had ever given them.

Their families were also affected by Terrell's condition. In the beginning, Neicy found his condition hard to accept. She had often imagined (prior to his birth) that she would later take him places and do things the average healthy child would do. Accepting his limitations didn't come easy. She too worried about doing the right thing for him. She often worried that something would go wrong when he was in her care. But the more time she spent with little Terrell, the more she forgot his handicap. He was a complete joy to be with.

***

Tracy sat in the living room telling Darryl about his job offer. "I've been thinking about it for a long time, man. I don't want to leave everybody but the bills are really getting to be a problem. I need a car of my own. Shavon has really been generous with hers, since the accident."

"I am sure she doesn't mind. You two really seem to be happy."

"We are."

"Did you talk to Shavon about it?"

"No but I think I'm going to have to. We can't go on too much longer with so little money. Her parents help a lot but I want to take care of everything. I don't want them to feel as though Shavon and I can't handle our responsibility." Tracy reached in the bassinet and picked up his son. "But I know I'll miss them terribly." He began to rock Terrell in his arms. "I love you--you know that," he said touching Terrell's nose.

"Tracy, how long do you have before you have to make a decision?"

"Since they've fallen behind schedule that gives me another month or so. I really think this is the best thing for the three of us. If I go to New York, they're going to give me a car. After I've completed my training, I can marry Shavon and take her and Terrell back with me. That would be about a year from now but I think we can hold out."

"I'm sure glad you and Shavon pulled through all of this."

"It was hard, man. You should have seen us. When we initially got the news about Terrell's condition, it was really a mess but we came through it. Shavon's back in school with a half year left to go. She graduates in June."

"Tracy, I've been meaning to ask you what happened with Diane?"

"I told her I still loved Shavon and that I was going to make an honest effort with her."

Darryl laughed, "Poor Tracy."

"Why poor me?"

"Man, Diane loves you so much that she hates you," he laughed again.

"How would you know?"

"The last time I saw her she asked me about my friend, the creep. According to her, man, you dropped her like a cold piece of chicken."

Tracy laughed, "She said I used her. I guess I did though. She was there when I needed her. But one day I looked at her and I kept seeing Shavon. I started feeling guilty because Shavon and I had been so distant. I knew who I belonged with but I just lost sight of everything at that time. But anyway, I told her I didn't want to go on betraying Shavon or her. Since I couldn't be with her completely, I didn't think it was a good idea to be with her at all." Tracy bent down to put Terrell back in his bassinet as he laughed again. "Man, she was so mad. She slammed the door in my face."

Darryl laughed again as Maria walked into the room shaking her head. She picked up the guys empty cups that were on the end table and walked back out. He was well aware of how Tracy's mother felt about Shavon by what she didn't say.

Tracy looked at Darryl, "Do you remember Sherry Witton?"

"Your childhood girlfriend?"

"Yeah."

"Do you know that my mother still wants us to get back together?"

"Are you serious?"

"Yes, I am."

"She and Shavon don't get along?" Darryl asked.

"Yeah, they get along just fine. Mom likes Shavon but she loved Sherry and the prospective future for her son with that construction company Sherry's father owns."

"I can see it now," Darryl said raising his hands up and looking into the distance. "You and Sherry, walking down the aisle together. 'Do you, Tracey take this woman to be your lawfully, wedded wife?' I can see her parents and your mother smiling."

"And me running faster than I did in the fifty-yard dash," Tracy said as he laughed.

By the end of the week, Tracy decided he had to tell Shavon about the job offer. She didn't take it as well as he thought she would.

"Oh, Tracy, I don't want you to leave us."

"I don't want to go either, Shavon. But we need all the help we can get. Terrell needs a lot of care and we both know it's going to be that way from now on. Baby listen, there are a lot of things you could use too, you know. Your parents have really been great but I won't feel right until I get things in hand."

Shavon hugged Tracy with all her might. "I know what's best but I just love you so much. I don't want to be without you for a minute."

"Well, let's get married next week," he said.

"Don't be silly, Tracy," she said laughing. "I can wait. I don't want to be separated from my husband."

"It would only be temporary, Shavon."

"That's okay I'll wait."

Shavon threw one o of the pillows on the couch at Tracy and ran up the stairs. Tracy ran close behind her. When she reached her bedroom, she grabbed a pillow as quickly as she could. When Tracy entered the room, she attacked him with her pillow. After he got his balance, he snatched a pillow from the bed and hit her back. Shavon drew back and hit Tracy again moving swiftly to avoid getting hit back. He drew back to hit her and fell over the bed. She hit him four times before he regrouped. When he did, he chased her around the room.

Dana heard loud laughter upstairs as she came in the house. When she reached Shavon's room Tracy was throwing his pillow at Shavon. Tracy was so embarrassed when he missed and hit Dana. Dana stood in the doorway with her hands on her hips. Tracy covered his mouth which he realized was hanging open.

"Mom, I'm so sorry."

Shavon giggled as they both watched for Dana's reaction.

"What's so funny?" he asked elbowing her in the side as his golden brown complexion blushed in red.

Dana slowly bent over and picked up the pillow and began beating both Shavon and Tracy. After it was over, they all laughed about how much fun they had.

"This place is a mess," Dana said gasping for breath. She suggested they all go out for dinner because everybody was too exhausted to cook.

She enjoyed dinner with Shavon and Tracy. They dreaded his leaving but it had to be done. Two weeks before Tracy left, he gave Shavon an engagement ring to assure her that he meant every word he said.

"You can't afford this," she said.

"I know but you deserve it. Besides, I don't want anyone putting a claim on you while I'm away."

"Never," she responded with a passionate kiss.

CHAPTER 13

The first week apart was hard for them. Tracy was homesick and lonely for Shavon. She missed him in the day and dreamed about him at night. Before the week was out, they had received letters from one another. As soon as Tracy settled into his apartment, he called her and expressed how much he had missed her and his son.

"I'll be up there next month," he had told her. "Are you still wearing my ring?"

"I only take if off to do the dishes," she answered.

"How's my son?"

"Your son?" Tracy laughed.

"Oh, that's right. You did have a little to do with his existence."

"Well, our son is just fine but he said he misses his daddy a whole lot."

"Oh, did he?" Tracy said with raised brows.

"Yep, but not half as much as his mother does."

Tracy told Shavon all about his apartment and what he had seen since his arrival in New York.

"I wish you would have come with me," he told her. It was no secret that she wished she could have gone. She looked forward to his visit.

The weeks flew by and before she knew it Shavon was meeting Tracy at the airport. She carried Terrell Ray in her arms. She and Tracy had missed each other desperately. It felt good to hold her and his son again. Shavon could see that Terrell had missed his daddy too. On the way home Tracy talked about what he had experienced in New York.

"I like it better now. I guess the reason I didn't before is because I missed you and Terrell so much. How's school?" he asked.

"School is fine. I've been trying to balance my time between my homework and Terrell. Your mother and sister help out a lot."

"How's Dana?"

"Oh, she's fine.

"How's her new friend?"

"He's okay. He was over last night for dinner."

"Poor Shavon," he said.

She smiled, "I don't even think about Mama and Daddy getting back together anymore. But I have to admit when I first saw him, I was disappointed. He's a very nice man and Mama seems to be happy with him."

"You think they might get serious, Shavon?"

"Probably. He looks like the type."

"Yeah? And what type is that?"

"You know…your type."

"My type? How did I get in this?"

"He's really generous, Tracy. He's so considerate. I know he's always dying to be alone with Mama but he always asks me if I would like to come along."

"Do you ever go?"

"Sometimes."

"You tag along," he teased. "But I'll fix that as soon as possible." Tracy kissed Shavon's cheek as she pulled up to his mother's house.

Everyone acted as if Tracy had been gone for years. Maria prepared his favorite foods throughout the weekend. Shavon and Tracy spent Saturday evening alone which they enjoyed thoroughly. By Sunday, they dreaded being separated again but it was time for Tracy to go.

"Maybe I'll be able to come back next month," he had said.

The following month, Tracy went home for a weekend to once again enjoy the family and friends he had missed so much. He and Shavon had begun to write every three weeks instead of every week as they had been doing. He continued to call every two weeks and visit monthly. He was also home for Shavon's graduation in June and again in August for Terrell's first birthday.

Complexity of the job and money constraints began to lengthen the time between visits. Five months had lapsed since Shavon had last seen Tracy. Things were getting to be more complex and he was also needed to work on the weekends. Tracy enjoyed the work but knew that the pressure was building at home. He kept a picture of Shavon, himself and Terrell on his desktop to keep him going until he could see them again.

He was staring at the picture of his family when Karen, the administrative assistant walked in, "Hi, Tracy."

"Hello, Karen. What brings you here this morning?"

Karen dropped in the chair in front of Tracy's desk.

"Well, there's a dispute about some of the material that was ordered for our department. Whew! It's just a mess, boss. I wish you would tell Carl something. I really don't think he knows what he's doing and he won't listen to me."

Tracy smiled as he looked at Karen. Karen was 22 but looked to be about 18. She was only 5'2 with the heart of someone 6 feet tall. She was a light-skinned black woman with red hair which most of her friends thought was a Revlon dye job. What was most intriguing about her was her beautiful almond shaped eyes. Tracy was well aware of all the men in the office who had tried to get close to her without success.

Karen had been hired as an administrative assistant for Carl Gray. Carl had made sexual advances toward Karen three months after he employed her and she refused. From that moment on, they were on opposite sides of the bridge. Whenever Karen had problems with her boss, she went to his boss. Tracy really appreciated her diligence and often aided her when she came to him with a problem. He was very aware of the potential for a sexual harassment suit and tried to field any problems between the two of them. She was very conscientious about the good of the company and always had a valid reason for complaining.

"What is he doing now?"

"Well, he's certainly not doing his job. He has been out of the office more than he has been in and all this week, all he's done is fuss at everybody else for not doing what they were never told to do in the first place. When I tried to tell him that they hadn't been assigned to that particular job, he started blaming me. The man has a serious problem, Tracy. I know he's the boss but people can only take so much, myself included. If you ask me, he's having problems at home." Karen flared her nostrils and drew a deep breath then continued. "And that's where he should leave them."

"Don't be so hard on him, Karen."

"It's not me, Tracy, it's him. You know how I operate. I don't complain unless we have a real problem and right now it happens to be him. I'm not picking on him, Tracy. I really do like Carl," she paused with a smile throwing her eyes to the ceiling. "Sometimes." She and Tracy laughed together.

"You're probably right, Karen. I know how hard you work to keep your department together. I'll talk to him. I'm sure he doesn't want to lose you." Karen smiled as she removed herself from the chair.

"Thanks, boss."

Tracy powered his computer up from sleep mode and began to stack papers on his desk.

Karen stuck her head back in the door, "I'm going to lunch in a few, Tracy. Would you like to come along?"

Tracy continued to compile his papers and answered without looking up. "Oh, thanks, Karen, but I've got a luncheon meeting with the administrator. Don't really want to go though. But I will, I shall, I must."

Karen smiled slightly disappointed, "That's okay. Maybe another time."

"Oh shoot, I'm late!" he said looking at his watch. Tracy rushed pass Karen before she could turn around to leave out of his office.

She stood there feeling rejected again. She looked toward the picture on Tracy's desk. "Look at the happy family," she mumbled.

Karen felt very threatened by Shavon. She knew Shavon was the reason Tracy always turned her down for lunch and she was determined to get him. She often found herself daydreaming about him. She was very grateful to Carl for making such a mess out of things because each time things really got out of hand, she had a good reason to see Tracy.

She often imagined herself alone with him. She would introduce him as her fiancé in a crowd as she dreamed. "This is my fiancée," she would say. "You know, the man I spend all of my time with." She would be so proud to be seen with him. He not only had the looks, he had the personality, intelligence and respect of all his employees. Karen admired him for being such a young, black and gifted individual. She appreciated his talent as well as his charm. To Karen, it couldn't get any better. *All I have to do is hook him. But not too fast, I don't want to scare him away or crowd him. I'll do it slowly*, she told herself.

She had many dreams about Tracy but knew he never really looked at her in any way other than from a business perspective. But she was determined to get him no matter what it took.

***

Tracy sat across the table from Clifford Turner absorbing details for his department. Clifford was known to be very stern with his employees. He often made them do things over and over again until they were flawless. But Tracy found that outside of business, he was an all right kind of guy. Tracy considered him a well-organized businessman. He also noted that when Clifford asked for something, he got it.

"Tracy," Clifford swallowed then continued, "I'll be honest with you. I think you are coming along pretty well. Your organizational skills are fast improving. But I have one complaint."

He drank some of his soda. Tracy watched as he talked. Clifford was the healthiest white man Tracy had ever seen. He had green deep-set eyes and dark brown hair that had begun to recede. Tracy guessed his weight to be about 300 pounds. Tracy knew very little about Clifford. He had heard that Clifford was married and tried several times to picture how his wife might be.

"Last month, 'Mama's Dream' didn't make it to the printer. A lot of people were upset about it. I'll be frank with you. If it happens again, someone will be looking for a job. I came down hard on Joseph. He tried to excuse himself by saying he had you on the job but I didn't take that for an excuse. When plans are fouled up, my boss comes down hard on me and it goes down the line."

"Yeah, I know," Tracy mumbled.

Clifford laughed as he read between the lines.

"Well, to get to the point, Tracy, you're going to have to be harder on your production crew. If they need a little push, give it to em'. I've been in this business for 25 years and it doesn't pay to be soft-skinned. If you have to fire some people, fire em.' You've got to do whatever it takes to do your job no matter who gets hurt. You see what I'm saying?"

"I understand thoroughly, Mr. Turner."

"And drop the formalities; call me Cliff."

Tracy nodded with a smile.

"Whenever Joseph comes down on you, nine times out of ten it's because he's getting the heat from me so stay on your toes. By the way, Tracy, we've had unfavorable response to your artist. Tell him to perk up or he's gone. I've seen better art work from fourth graders."

Tracy looked at Clifford in surprise but said nothing. He didn't see anything wrong with Michael's work but what the boss said went. The thought of firing someone made him a little apprehensive. He never wanted to be in the position to determine if someone would be employed or not but there was no way out. He had to make a decent living for Shavon and Terrell and he would bare it for them.

Clifford concluded the meeting telling Tracy how pleased he was with his ability to come in and learn so much about the business. "I think eventually you'll make an excellent director," he told Tracy."

As Tracy drove home, he reviewed what he and Clifford had discussed. He thought about the artist. *What am I going to say to him? He has a family to support*. He began to imagine the conversation. Excuse me, Michael, but if you don't perk up--pack up." *Oh how cruel.* He dreaded the inevitable.

The following day Tracy set up a meeting for himself and Michael Steer, the artist. When Michael entered the office, he greeted Tracy with a smile and a warm handshake.

"Hi, Tracy."

"Hello, Mr. Steer. How are you?"

"Fine. How are you?"

"Can't complain."

"Good," Michael responded. Michael sat down as he searched Tracy's face for an indication of what the meeting was about. "So, what did you want to talk to me about?"

Tracy swallowed, "I wanted to talk to you about your work."

Michael sat up in his chair, "What about it?"

Tracy's eyes met his. *Spit it out-you're the boss*, Tracy thought. He looked back at Michael who was now on the edge of his chair. "I have to ask you to do better."

Immediately Michael took offense, "Better? I do a dammed good job. What do you mean better?"

"Well, certain people--"

"What people?" Before Tracy could respond, Michael was up with his finger in Tracy's face.

"Let me tell you something, boy. I don't know who you think you are but let's get something straight. You're just a supervisor and you don't know anything about what I do. You probably can't make a good circle. Where do you get off telling me I can't draw? I've been drawing professionally most of your life!"

Tracy stood up, "I'm going to ask you to calm down. Look, Michael, I think you're doing a fantastic job but--"

"But what? You got a friend you think might be better?"

"Now wait a minute," Tracy said expressing his disconcertion over Michael's last comment. "That's not necessary. I'm telling you for your own good."

Michael sighed heavily. "What you trying to prove? You think you got power to fire me?"

Tracy was furious but maintained his composure. "Look, I don't have to prove anything to anybody. I'm only trying to be straight with you. You want your job, don't you?"

"Look kid, I know more about this business than you do. I could do my job and yours too if I had to."

"Mr. Steer, you're blowing this conversation out of proportion."

"I don't think so," Michael snapped. "You're trying to tell me I can't do my job. You got a little training and it went to your head. You think you know it all, don't you?"

Tracy thought to tell Michael that Mr. Turner had given him the order but kept it to himself. *I can't let this man think just because he's older, that he can push me around*, he thought. *I'm the boss*, he reminded himself. He didn't believe what he had heard as he gazed at Michael with disbelief. He had heard enough. He sat in his chair, crossed his legs and responded to Michael's question.

"No Michael, I don't think I know it all. But I do know this. One, I'm not a boy; I'm grown man and you will treat me as such. As far as wanting to fire you goes, I didn't plan to but if you don't improve and if you ever speak to me in that tone again, I will."

Michael rolled his hateful eyes on Tracy and walked out of the door. Tracy couldn't believe what had just happened. Michael had never once given him or anybody a problem and he was only trying to help him. He never knew Michael would react that way. He regretted that he was the bearer of such bad news. He knew that scene was probably the beginning of many more. He just hoped that if he had to do it again, he wouldn't have to deal with someone as obstinate and spasmodic as Michael Steer.

He thought about the scene all week. It hurt Tracy to lose a friend but he tried to deal with it. He knew it was better to lose a friend than a job. He wrote Shavon a long letter explaining what had happened and how it had affected him. He felt as if Michael didn't have the least bit of respect for him as a supervisor and that he would have to be firm about his orders or he wouldn't have anybody's respect.

The rumor spread quickly that Tracy's position had gone to his head. Everyone feared he had turned against his own and forgotten who he was. Michael never spoke anymore when Tracy came in. He only made eye contact when Tracy spoke to him directly. This bothered Tracy greatly but he couldn't give in. He had already tried to explain once. He felt that if he went any further, he would be begging.

The next few weeks were exasperating for Tracy. Almost everyone around him was trying to stay out of his way. He began to feel lonely. He knew Michael had said something but he had no idea what it was. Tracy had one remaining friend. He could always depend on Karen. She would peek in his office at least once a week to share a funny joke to help him get through the day.

He was expecting to see Karen when his door opened, but was surprised when Joseph walked in the door.

Tracy rose from his seat and shook Joseph's hand.

"The production crew has improved significantly, Tracy. What did you say to them?"

"I called a meeting and told them it was mandatory to expedite production techniques. I explained that production was unsatisfactory and I brought up the missed deadline from last month. They in turn explained why things were slow."

"And why was it?" Joseph asked.

"They didn't have the appropriate apparatus so I had the buyer order some new equipment. The old equipment was worn out and slowed things down considerably. Also, I had consultations with our nonproductive employees and gave them incentive by asking them to do research on the best equipment for our company. The response was great. They came up with some very powerful suggestions."

"Good, I'm pleased. You handled that in a very considerate manner. I probably would have gone down there and threatened the whole department."

That moment had been the most relaxed moment he'd had with Joseph in two months.

"I'm going to be out of the office for the rest of the day. So if any urgent situations arise, just call my secretary. She knows where to contact me."

"Will do," Tracy responded. "Oh, Joseph, I need to inform you before you leave about the Duplicating Department."

"What about it?"

"We need another copier. We have quite a few employees in production who use it religiously and time is of the essence with the majority of them. They don't have time to stand in line, because of other pressing work. We need to get another copier in there as soon as possible. The only one they have access to breaks down a couple of times a week. That would be another obstacle that would alleviate our production problem."

"Yeah, I agree."

"I also took a look at the budget as you suggested and I think we can save on printing paper. I've been in touch with the printer and they suggested another type of paper that would be more economical and equal in quality. They'll be sending samples which I will send to your office for review."

"Tracy, you work out the details, document them and send me a memo or something. I'll review it and pass it on to Finance."

"Of course," Tracy said as Joseph turned to leave the office. "I'll have it ready within a week. You have a good afternoon."

"You too, Tracy," Joseph said as he walked out of the door with his briefcase in hand. He quietly admitted to himself that Tracy was doing a good job as a supervisor. He would never admit that he was against promoting Tracy to this position. He briefly recalled Tracy's first few months as his assistant. He often remembered it as a period of disaster. Tracy couldn't make any decisions. Joseph laughed out loud as he remembered how Tracy panicked about every little problem and apologized about every little mistake he had made. Now Tracy was on top of his game. He participated in the management meetings making suggestions on how to cut costs and save time, which greatly pleased management.

Joseph remembered one incident in particular. After one of the management meetings was over, Tracy immediately excused himself and left the room. Marcus, one of the senior V.P.'s, looked at Joseph and asked why he hadn't come up with what Tracy suggested, being that he was the more mature and experienced man?

Joseph hadn't told Tracy but he was glad to have him as an assistant and felt very confident with his ability to run the department. No one knew Joseph was priming him to take over his position. He was ready to retire. He and his wife had always dreamed of opening their own family style restaurant and with a successor like Tracy, that dream was well in reach.

CHAPTER 14

The next four months went by slowly for both Tracy and Shavon. One day after shopping all afternoon, Shavon walked into the house with Terrell in her arms with Myah following close behind. Myah dropped the packages she carried for Shavon.

"What you gettin' Tracy for Christmas?"

"I don't know yet but I'll tell you one thing, I might have to take a part time job this Christmas. Tracy sends me enough money but it only covers the expenses for Terrell. I really don't have any extra. Terrell's at the doctor's office so frequently for ear infections or colds, it gets kind of expensive. I made a few outfits for some of mama's friends so that I'll have some money for my little man here," she said rubbing his nose with hers. She continued as she removed his snowsuit. "I saw a sharp double breasted black suit I could get for him."

"Why not make it?" Myah asked.

"I really don't have time. I have to work with Terrell a lot and take him to his therapy sessions. He seems to be coming along pretty well but he needs all the time I can give him."

Myah watched Shavon as she took off her boots.

"Shavon, you really do need some rest, you know."

"Myah, I could really use a break but everybody has something they have to do. They don't have time for a baby."

"What about Tracy's mother?"

"She and Neicy have part-time jobs and it's too much for me to ask Mama. She helps out all the time. Besides, I'll have a break in about two months. I'm going to New York to spend a week with Tracy. They're having an anniversary party for the new division and he wants me to be with him. I'm so proud of him, Myah. I know it's hard for him to be away from everybody because it's hard enough for me being away from him. He's really been good about things. He doesn't complain in his letters anymore about wanting to come home to me and Terrell. From what he says, he's doing better than ever. He's assisting the director now."

"That's great, Shavon."

Shavon set Terrell down in his playpen and moved into the kitchen. "I'd better get some dinner on. Mama's going to be here in a couple of hours. She has helped me so much and so have you, Myah. I haven't forgotten the times you sat with Terrell for me. I really appreciate all of your help. What would I do without family and friends?"

Myah smiled, "I'll always be here for you, Shavon. You know that."

"I know and I'll always be here for you too."

After Shavon got settled, she fed Terrell and laid him down for a nap, then put dinner on.

"I miss Tracy so much. I miss going to the show with him, watching TV with him, talking to him every day and I even miss eating dinner with him. I guess I just miss him period. I will be so glad when these next two months are over. I'll be staying with him for a whole week. Aunt Florence is going to keep Terrell through the day and mama will keep him at night. He's going to spend the night with Mrs. Gaines Saturday and I'll be back to pick him up Sunday. So you see both of us are going to have a big week ahead of us."

"Don't you talk to Tracy once a week anymore?"

"Well, sometimes I do but the phone bills were getting to be a bit expensive. But for the most part, he calls every two weeks. He's really working hard from what he tells me. I'm surprised he calls as much as he does."

"Shavon, why didn't you just marry him and go to New York?"

"Myah, if I left here there would be no one to take care of Terrell when I need it. I could never trust a stranger. I think he needs the feeling of being well loved and nurtured by both of our families instead of just his parents. I would have to find new doctors for him." She sighed. "I really don't want to do that. Tracy told me he wouldn't have a lot of time to spend with me when I'm there and I think that would be a terrible way to start a marriage, don't you?"

Myah shook her head in agreement. "I guess so with so many challenges already there."

"Myah, I feel that if our love is strong enough, we could get married anytime since we'll always be together anyway."

"Yeah, I guess it would be a little difficult for you two right now."

Shavon walked to the stove and stirred her chili beans.

"I just want him to get well situated. Later on, he'll be able to take off just about any time he wants to. I can wait. I'm in no rush."

"Oh, you have it all mapped out, don't you," Myah said as she giggled.

"Well, you know what I mean, Myah. He'll have someone to give his load to as the company expands. I want a full time husband. If I marry him right now, I won't have a husband at all. I think Terrell needs all of us right now. If we were married, I would be in New York without a job, and without help with Terrell."

"I guess you know what's best for you but I would have to be with my man." Myah told her. "You remember how I used to be about Ronny? I took whatever time from Ronny that I could get."

"I remember," Shavon said. "You were one step away from being a stalker." They laughed.

"I know. I was all in, wasn't I girl?"

"Yes, you were," Shavon said as her laughter subsided.

Myah held up her right index finger. "Ahh, but in the end he fell in love. Need I say more?" Shavon grinned at Myah.

"No. I think you've said enough."

As the girls ate dinner, Dana rushed in bringing with her a breeze of 20-degree weather.

"Hi, Ms. Robertson."

"Hi, Honey. Mmmm, it smells good in here."

Shavon noticed her mother looked very hurried.

"Hey, Mama, you staying for dinner?"

"No, Honey. I'm having dinner with Steve and I'm late. Where's Terrell?"

"He's in your room sleeping."

Dana rushed to her room, kissed her grandson on the cheek, picked up a few things and left again.

"Gee, that was fast," commented Myah.

"I know. Mama's pretty content these days. She spends a lot of time with Steve and I'm glad she's got somebody nice."

"That's great, Shavon. She deserves every bit of happiness she's getting."

"Everybody's in love with somebody," Shavon said as she reached for the crackers. She dropped her head unknowingly.

"And you and Tracy will be together soon too. Probably by the end of next year," Myah said with encouragement.

"Yep, probably so. You know he's been gone nearly a year? I really think about some of the things we've done and all that we've been through. I really appreciate him. He's my world. Just when I had given up hope, he came through."

"What do you mean?"

"You know, when I was pregnant. It was really heartbreaking but we made it through. And now look what he's doing. He's given up so much willingly that is, for a baby that a year and a half ago he didn't think he'd ever love. I could never love anybody else. Tracy is the only man for me. Mama says I should start going out with my friends but I really don't want to. I told her I would think about it though."

"Why did she suggest that? Doesn't she know you and Tracy plan to get married?"

"Yes, she knows but she said she felt that way for Daddy once. He had been everything to her and now look, they're divorced. She said you never really know how things will turn out. She tells me not to cut myself off from my friends, especially since Tracy's away. Myah, there have been so many times I wanted to call him and say let's get married but it's not right for us yet. And you don't know how many times I cried when I was writing to him. I had to throw the letters away because I had smeared them with tears. I can't let him know how I feel or he'll pressure me into marrying him now. Maybe Mama's right. Maybe I should get involved with all of my old friends. Things will probably be better if I do. Right now, I'm home all the time and I really don't do much to keep my mind occupied, Tracy does. He has his job, his manuscript and whatever else he does. But I'm here all day long." Shavon paused. "Did I tell you that one day about two months ago he called me at three in the morning?"

"No! Was he drunk? He must have been out of his mind!"

"He called to tell me he missed me. It's hard for both of us but we can withstand it a little while longer, I guess."

Myah looked at her friend and could only admire the strength that she exuded. 'Don't know if it could be me,' she thought to herself.

That night after she had put Terrell down and was about to lie, down the phone rang.

"Hi!" Tracy spoke with excitement.

"Hi, to you too."

"You all packed?"

"No! We've got another two months to go."

"Oh, that's right," he said followed by a small chuckle. "I miss you, Shavon. I can't wait to see you." He blew a few kisses through the phone. "You know what I'm going to do to you when you get here, don't you?"

"I can only imagine," she said with a devious smile.

"How's my son?"

"He's just fine. He's sleeping right now. We had a little outing today."

"Oh, yeah? Where did you two go?"

"We went to the mall to do a little Christmas shopping."

"What did you get for me?"

"Nothing, yet. I don't know what you need."

"You," he answered softly.

"I'll take care of that when I get there," she responded. "Tracy, I wish you were here right now."

"I do too, Shavon. But just think, in two months, we'll have six and a half days together. I don't know if I'll ever be able to make up for lost time but I'm certainly going to try."

Shavon sat on her end of the phone smiling. She missed him so much.

"Are you blushing, Shavon?" Tracy asked as he began to laugh.

"You know I am. I can't wait to see you."

Tracy was silent for a moment. "Shavon, I love you."

"I love you too, Tracy."

CHAPTER 15

The next two months seemed to drag by but all Tracy could think about was the upcoming visit from Shavon. He couldn't seem to keep his mind on his work.

The day finally came when he could pick up the love of his life. When she arrived, he met her with some flowers and a loving smile, which only matched hers. They gave each other countless, affectionate hugs and kisses. It seemed it would never end. They held each other tightly saying how much they loved and missed one another. Finally, they remembered where they were. Shavon looked around.

"Tracy, everybody's looking at us."

"Well, let them look," he responded giving her another kiss.

"I've missed you so much, Tracy."

"Me too," he returned.

"Well come on, let's go."

On the way to his apartment, Shavon filled him in on what everyone at home was doing. She held his hand all the way there.

"And Myah's going to beauty school."

"She is?"

"Yes."

"So who finally told her?" Tracy asked as he laughed. Shavon looked at Tracy with a half smile.

"I'm gonna let you get away with it this time because I'm glad to see you." He laughed again.

"I'm only joking. Myah's a nice looking, skinny girl. I like her a lot." He pinched Shavon's cheek causing her to smile. "Can't you take a joke?"

"I'm sure Myah wouldn't be able to take it," Shavon said as she repeated the joke trying to keep from laughing.

"So, how's she doing?"

"Oh, she's just fine, Tracy. Everybody's fine. I meant to ask you, does Darryl have another girlfriend?"

"I don't know."

"Don't you keep in touch with him?"

"Well, I haven't talked to him in about three months. I don't know who he's going out with."

"Well, I saw him with some new girl. I just thought you might know."

"No, I don't. Stop being so nosy."

Shavon smacked Tracy on his right thigh and laughed as he yelled out in pain.

"I wasn't being nosy. I was just a little curious, that's all."

He put his arm around her evading another swat of her hand.

"You know you have to make up for that, don't you?" Shavon giggled.

"Yep, and I'm looking forward to it."

There was a long pause.

"Tracy, your mother's angry with you."

"Why?"

"She said she hasn't talked to you in almost three weeks."

"Well, three weeks is certainly not a lifetime."

"It is to a mother, Tracy. They want to talk to their kids every chance they get."

"I don't think every three weeks is so bad, especially considering my finances. You know Mama. Whenever I call she talks about when we were kids. Especially the time I was in the second grade and Charlene Griggs chased me home."

Shavon laughed.

"I guess she feels like she lost her baby."

"Yeah. I guess," he said quietly

"Shavon, how are things going with Terrell?"

"He just had a check up and his heart seems to be okay but the doctor said he still might need the heart operation in a year or two."

This was the first somber moment of the conversation. They both looked sadly at each other.

"I'm so afraid of that operation. Tracy, he's so young."

"I'm scared too," he whispered. "Maybe by the time he's two or three he won't need it."

"I wish that were true, Tracy, but we both know that there's a good chance he'll need it." Shavon looked around as they drove through the crowded streets.

"So, this is New York, huh?"

"Yep, sure is. The city that never sleeps. How's he coming along with his therapy?"

"He's doing really well." Shavon became excited. "He's learning how to feed himself now. You should see him."

"I will, Shavon. Whenever somebody at work mentions their children, I think about Terrell Ray. I've missed you and the little bugger something awful."

"He misses you too."

"Did he tell you that?"

"Well, not in so many words, but--"

"Then how do you know?"

"He gets pretty excited when I show him your picture." Shavon looked at Tracy's profile and began to shake her head with a content expression.

"What?"

"I think I've got the most handsome man in the world." Tracy blushed putting his hand up to his face.

"You think I look the same?"

"Yep and I wish Terrell had your eyes."

"And I wish he had your dimples, Shavon."

"Yeah, me too. Do I still look the same?"

He paused for a moment.

"No. You don't look like you used to."

Shavon didn't know how to react to his reply so she said nothing. He leaned in and kissed her. "I didn't think it was possible but you look even more beautiful."

Shavon looked around the apartment. "It's small but it's cute. You know what you need?"

"What?"

"You need some pictures and plants. That would make it look a little livelier."

"Okay. Maybe you can pick some out for me tomorrow."

"Well, it's about 5:30 p.m. What do you want to do tonight?" Shavon walked into the kitchen as he followed.

"I thought I'd take you to dinner."

"No, Tracy, not tonight. I have waited for three months to spend time with you and our first night together won't be in public. I plan to cook for my baby."

He smiled, "You always did take good care of me, didn't you?"

"Un-huh and I'm not going to stop now. I can't let a few miles pull us apart."

"Me either," he said as he reached to give her a hug.

Shavon prepared a succulent roast with buttermilk biscuits and mixed vegetables. After dinner, they talked about everything. He discussed in detail his likes and dislikes about his job and she talked about her life at home with Terrell and her mother. It seemed as if they were getting to know each other all over again. It was exhilarating for both of them. Tracy had expressed to her how sorry he was that she couldn't get started with her career. He suggested that once he got on his feet financially, he could pay someone to take care of Terrell so she could go to school.

They cuddled on his cozy love seat to watch TV. His fingers began to flow through her long, soft hair as he kissed her. Once again he felt the warmth of the body that he had missed so desperately. She felt his heart beating faster as he touched her. She responded by calling his name. He took her hand and led her to the bedroom.

They felt as if they were making love for the first time. They were absorbed by each other's passion. Again and again their passion ignited as they stepped inside of one another's love. They whispered to each other all through the night of their lingering feelings. He asked her once again to marry him. She answered telling him that they would talk about it later.

That was the first night they had ever spent together and they enjoyed each other thoroughly. Tracy had secret thoughts about Shavon leaving but brushed them away. He wouldn't let that spoil a night he had dreamed of for so long. Afraid to let one another go, they slept entangled.

Shavon was awakened by the sunlight coming through the blinds. She found herself tightly entangled with Tracy. She looked around the room until she spotted the clock. It was 10:30 a.m. Tracy was still asleep and she didn't want to wake him. She lay there imagining how it would be waking up with him every morning. "You're getting weak," she whispered with a smile.

As she watched him, she let her mind wander into what she thought was paradise. Finally, she tried to slide her arm and leg from beneath him to go to the bathroom but she couldn't move. She tried again but he was too heavy. Finally, she decided to tickle him. With her fingers at his sides, she began to tickle him. Tracy jumped quickly. When he opened his eyes, she was laughing hysterically.

"Ugh! What happened to you? You look terrible," she said.

"What's with the early morning humor?" he asked.

"Well, I was trying to get up because--"

Tracy began to tickle her.

"No!" she yelled. "Stop! Stop! I've gotta--"

Tracy laughed louder. "Who looks terrible now!"

"Me! Me! Please let me go."

He flipped over pulling her on top. She fought unsuccessfully to get up.

"I've gotta--" Shavon couldn't hold it any longer.

Tracy felt her slowing down. Suddenly, he felt wet.

"What's this?" he asked as he looked down.

Shavon looked at the ceiling.

"That's what I was trying to tell you, numbskull."

Tracy jumped up out of the wet bed.

"I didn't know you still did that. If I had, I would have gotten you up in the middle of the night to go to the bathroom. No more water after six o'clock for you, young lady," Tracy looked at her and laughed hysterically while Shavon stared at him with a blank expression.

Shavon glared at him as she turned to walk into the bathroom. "That's alright, go ahead and laugh," she said angrily slamming the door.

"I am!" he yelled.

Shavon yelled to him from the bathroom, "Well, you're not only gonna have a wife, you're also going to have a bed wetter!"

"Uh, Shavon," Tracy said rubbing his chin, "About that proposal--"

Shavon quickly turned on the shower to smother her laughter.

"He hasn't changed a bit. He's still my Tracy."

The next day was exciting for Shavon. Tracy took her around the city, showing her where he spent much of his time. He took her to his office. She was impressed. She was so pleased with how well he had done. It gave her a thrill to see him at work. The office was large and luxurious. He had modern furniture, his own assistant--the works.

"What do you think?"

"Tracy, it's just too much. I love it!"

He took her to lunch and later they went shopping and found a couple of portraits, a fig tree and a centerpiece for the dining room table. They laughed and talked about just about everything all day long. By 9 p.m., they were exhausted and they retired to bed early.

By the third day, Shavon felt as if she were right at home. When Tracy got off, they took a long walk and discussed their plans for the future. The rest of the day was spent relaxing. Tracy sent out for pizza and they watched TV until 10:30 p.m.

"I feel like I'm on my honeymoon," he told her.

The following day was spent preparing for the anniversary party. Tracy worked late that night only seeing Shavon on his lunch break. She busied herself throughout the day by reading Tracy's unfinished manuscript, which she enjoyed very much. Whenever she thought he had done his best, he did even better. His talent never ceased to amaze her.

All week long, Tracy came home to find that Shavon had cooked dinner and the apartment was immaculate. He noticed that her little touches had drastically improved the overall appearance of his apartment. They both hated to see the end of the week nearing. Friday evening Tracy took Shavon shopping and bought her a two-piece skirt suit.

"It's beautiful. They really dress here, don't they?"

"Yep and this would be the perfect place for you to start out. But some of this stuff is so outlandish, it's ridiculous. You're as good as they are, if not better."

"Thanks," she said modestly.

"Don't thank me, it's true."

"Well, I do feel good about my work. Maybe one day I'll be a famous designer."

"Move over, Vera," Tracy said with laughter.

"And speaking of talented people, I read that manuscript you're writing and it's fantastic!"

"You really like it, Shavon?"

"I sure do. Sounds like a bestseller to me. I can't wait until you finish it. Where are you going to send it?"

"I don't know yet."

"It's a winner, Tracy, I'm telling you. And I wouldn't say that to be complaisant either. You just watch."

"If you feel that strongly about it, it must be pretty good," he said. "You've always been a pretty good judge about things of that nature."

Shavon and Tracy kicked off their boots and fell on the sofa where they slept the rest of the evening.

Shavon awoke from noises in the street and realized that she and Tracy were late for the anniversary party. They bathed and got dressed as fast as they could. Everyone was there when they arrived. Tracy introduced Shavon to numerous people, but Shavon could only remember one name, Karen. Shavon could tell by the way Karen spoke and abruptly walked away that she wasn't very pleased to meet her. Nonetheless, she didn't feel the least bit intimidated by Karen. She noticed Tracy had talked to Karen briefly and walked away. It was obvious to Shavon that Karen wanted more. Shavon was confident that what had happened last year with that other woman wouldn't happen again, because she would make sure that she was there for him.

They enjoyed the party immensely. Everyone was saying what a handsome couple they were. Shavon observed that Tracy was well liked and respected by his employees and co-workers. After the party, they returned to his apartment where he opened a bottle of champagne. They toasted to his accomplishments with the company. The anniversary party, made Tracy feel even better about his job. He told Shavon that his goal was to go even further in the company. Her wheels were turning as he talked. She was very pleased and proud of what he was doing, especially after all the praise she heard at the party. But if he kept moving up, where would she fit in? Would he have time for their son?

Saturday was a day for complete relaxation. Tracy was off and enjoyed every minute of it with the woman he loved. He and Shavon laughed and talked and played charades for the better part of the day. After dinner, they lied on the sofa and watched TV until Shavon noticed he had become quiet.

"What's wrong?"

"Nothing," he answered as he slowly closed his eyes. She admired his perfect black lashes and full brows.

"Then, why are you so quiet?"

"I guess I'm just all talked out."

"You've never run out of things to say, Tracy. I remember when we first started going out. You talked so much," she giggled. "Mama asked me if you were nice. I said 'yeah, Ma, but he sure talks a lot. There's never a dull moment with this guy.'"

She laughed behind her story. Tracy didn't respond. She felt a sense of rejection. She tried again to make him talk but he wouldn't. She tried to make him laugh. Again, to no avail. She extricated herself from their embrace and went to the bedroom. Tracy watched her as she left but still said nothing. He suspected she had gone to get something out of the room. Ten minutes later, he realized she wasn't coming back. He peeped in the room and she was in her gown lying on the bed.

"I thought you came to get something."

"No, I just didn't enjoy my company."

Tracy opened the door all the way.

"What do you mean?"

"Just what I said."

"Shavon, what's wrong with you?"

"Nothing. At least that's what you told me a little while ago after you went into your own little world." Tracy sat down on the bed next to her placing his hand on her back which was facing him.

"I'm sorry. I wasn't really in my own world. I was just thinking about tonight being our last night here together." Shavon was silent for a moment.

"Shavon, did you hear me?"

"Well, since it's my last night, I would think you would do anything to make it the best, not push me away."

He tugged at her shoulder, "Shavon, look at me."

She reluctantly turned over. He eyed her from head to toe pleased she had lost all of the weight that she had gained from her pregnancy.

"Did I tell you that you look beautiful in that gown?"

She pulled away.

"Okay, Shavon, I didn't mean to make light of things."

"Well, that's just what you did."

"Shavon, stop being so obstinate. You're nothing but a big baby."

"Oh, I'm a big baby but what you were doing was understandable. I didn't come up here to be ignored and rejected by you."

"I know you didn't but Shavon, why do you have to leave anyway?"

"Tracy, we've been through all this before."

"Shavon, I can't help it. I want to be with you and our son."

"I want to be with you too, Tracy, but let's get ourselves together before we get into something as serious as marriage. Besides, I think the best place for Terrell Ray right now is a place full of people who love him. Here, he would only have me and you--sometimes. He needs more. Don't forget our son is handicapped. He needs more attention. He needs to be around all the family he can. I can't do it alone."

Tracy laid down beside her.

"You might be right, Shavon, but I need you and Terrell with me. Don't you think he needs his father?"

Shavon lowered her head with guilt. She began to stroke his sideburns slowly as she spoke in a placid tone, "Yes. He does need you and I promise within the next year or so, we'll be together."

"That's a long time," he said in a voice filled with sadness.

"Not really. I know I'm going to love you forever. I'll always be around."

"Me too," he said as he kissed her.

"Maybe you can stay for one more--"

Shavon rolled on top of him and kissed him quickly as she laughed.

"No more talking," she whispered.

"No more," he returned.

CHAPTER 16

The drive to the airport was depressing. They tried to make small talk, which didn't go over very well. Once they reached the airport, Shavon got in line to check her bags. Tracy held her hand tightly.

"Tell my mother hello and kiss my son for me."

As the line moved up, she fought back her tears.

"Keep the line moving," the attendant screamed as everything and everyone around them moved in a hurry. They would have waited in the line forever if it was up to them.

Tracy looked at her sadly.

"Shavon--"

"I know; me too."

They hugged tightly once more before she disappeared through the tunnel. Once seated, Shavon wiped away the mist in her eyes. She convinced herself all the way home that they would be together again soon.

In the months that followed, Tracy developed an even better understanding of the operations of the company. There were very few questions he couldn't answer and very few things he couldn't do.

With Joseph out of the office, that left Tracy in control eighty percent of the time. Sometimes he found it to be a headache. Other times, it was the best thing that ever happened to him. Tracy worked with the writers, giving them tips he had used himself to enhance his creative ability. He too learned a lot from them.

Throughout the year, the company made changes in personnel. Some of the writers were replaced along with Michael Steer, the artist. Tracy hated to see Michael go but it had to be done. He had not improved to the satisfaction of the editors and Tracy was given orders to fire him. That was the worst part of his job. Michael had been so furious that he started throwing things around Tracy's office. Tracy's assistant called security and Michael was thrown out.

The company's financial status slowly increased. The better things got, the harder Tracy worked. Joseph depended on Tracy implicitly now. Tracy didn't realize he had put all of his energy into his work, hardly making plans for anything else and that included seeing Shavon and Terrell. He still missed them and thought of them a lot but he didn't have time to be with them anymore.

He had gotten a raise, which impelled him to do even better. He was now very happy about his financial status, as he watched the bills drop substantially. Shavon was very happy about the bills being paid too but she wanted to see Tracy more often. He would say he would try to get away but he couldn't promise. She became frustrated insisting that he had become married to his job.

"Well, I wanted to marry you but you didn't want to get married. If you and Terrell were here with me, I wouldn't have to keep myself so busy," he argued.

"Well, I'll tell you what, workaholic, Terrell and I will be up there next weekend."

"Good," he said happily. "Your ticket is on the way."

When Shavon and Terrell went to New York, she was as overjoyed to see Tracy as he was to see her. Seeing Terrell was exhilarating. He had grown so much in a little over a year. Tracy felt good being with his little family again.

Two weeks later, Tracy pried himself from his desk for a weekend with his family. Maria was thrilled to see her son. It was approximately two years since he had moved away and she was still wishing he could transfer back to Detroit. Two years felt like a lifetime to her. She gave a small dinner party for him Saturday evening. She invited Shavon, Dana and a couple of his friends.

While he was there, Tracy spent as much time as he could with Terrell. Maria was pleased to see Tracy spending time with his son. She knew he loved Terrell but she often worried how he went months without seeing him. Judging from what Shavon had told her, they didn't talk as often as they once had, either.

Maria and Neicy waved as Tracy walked out of the gate to board the plane.

"I miss him already," Maria said sadly.

"You should be used to it now, Mama."

"I guess you're right." She looked around as Neicy drove.

"Mama, do you think Tracy has changed a little."

"Yes." Maria answered without looking in Neicy's direction.

"I think he has too." Neicy frowned. "It seems to me that all he really talks about now is that company and his job. I got tired of hearing about it. At first, I wanted to hear everything because I'm so proud of him but he talked about it incessantly the whole weekend. If I got tired of it, I know Shavon did. If I were her, I think I would have let him talk to himself."

"Neicy!" Maria was exasperated. "Don't talk about your brother like that!"

"Mama, it's true. I think everybody noticed it. Why are you defending him?"

"Ain't nothin' to defend. I admit it. He done changed. It seems like that job means the world to him."

Even more than his son," Neicy whispered. Neicy cleared her throat. "Mama, Tracy is crazy about Terrell but I think he should come home a little more than he does."

"I can't argue with that, Neicy. I think he should too." Maria paused then continued. "I guess part of his distance involves money too. Now Terrell's betta I care."

"Yeah, you're right about that, Mama. He certainly is. He has the best of everything, and I'm grateful for that," Neicy said.

"We all are."

"But I'll just say this, Mama. I hope he won't let his position totally consume him because the bottom line is, Shavon can't be the mother and father and neither can we."

Maria continued to look out of the car window as she listened to Neicy. She knew that everything Neicy had said was true but he had turned himself around once, maybe he would do it again.

Tracy began attending seminars which taught him about building a more productive organization by building successful teams. He lectured on how a company could profit on high achievers and in turn make things more beneficial for them. He had talked of how a good team environment fostered creativity. Most of all, he was proud of Classic Magazine, Inc. and his enthusiasm spread.

Clifford Turner gave Tracy permission to enforce his idea to start monthly meetings where employees were paid for ideas that helped to improve operations. Everyone began to feel good about going to work. Some of the strict, unnecessary regulations were negated. Employee raffles took place bi-weekly and a TV/VCR was put in the lunchroom for employee entertainment. Employees who had six consecutive months without an absence were rewarded. Many changes had been made and the employees were gratified.

Tracy was now consummately dedicated to his job. It had been over a year since he had seen his family and friends. He often thought of them but there was just so much to be done at the office. Joseph had taken an indefinite leave of absence to open his restaurant. Tracy was promoted to the position of director. His new position not only meant more money to send Terrell to a good school but it also meant traveling, which he yearned to do. He was soon taking trips for business related purposes to California, Wyoming, Florida, Idaho and more.

He had talked to Shavon three months back but he had become so busy that he thought of home less and less as time passed. Myah had written him about a surprise birthday party for Shavon. He called Myah saying he would be there with bells on but never showed up. He felt bad but he had gotten a last minute call for a business trip and he felt obligated, business came first.

The loneliness became overwhelming and he began dating a friend of Karen's. Karen had introduced them to show her friend who this fantastic guy was she was so determined to be with. When Tonya saw Tracy, she forgot all about Karen's friendship. She could see that Tracy was also attracted to her. Besides, she knew he wasn't interested in Karen anyway. Karen had invited Tracy to dinner once, which he enjoyed but he just wasn't interested in a personal relationship with her.

When he met Tonya his eyes lit up. Karen was furious with Tonya but Tracy never knew it. Tonya was 5'8" with a medium brown, flawless complexion and high cheekbones. She looked like she could have had Indian relatives. Her face was round and had a child-like, candid look about it. Tracy viewed her as a perfect figure eight.

He felt slightly guilty because of his thoughts of Shavon. Then he reminded himself that the woman he wanted to be with didn't want to be with him completely. Tracy had had uncommitted relationships with a few women over the last two years, but he had grown tired of the loneliness. For weeks, he fought with the dilemma of dating one woman. He even called Shavon to deter his temptation. He finally came to the conclusion that the loneliness was too much for him to deal with. Finally, he called Tonya and they began to see each other on a regular basis. He found her very comforting on lonely nights but he reminded her from time to time that there was someone at home that he was waiting for.

As time passed, they became closer and Tracy asked her to move in with him as weekends weren't enough. He enjoyed having someone to come home to after a hard day's work or after a business trip. Tonya was always ready to cuddle up and be close to Tracy and he loved it. She knew she had lost a long time friend in Karen but as long as she had Tracy, it really didn't matter.

***

With the encouragement of her mother, Shavon had begun going out with her old friends. At first, she didn't feel right about it but after being without Tracy for so long, she too became lonely. She had met a few guys when she went out with her girl friends but ended up comparing them all to Tracy. She allowed herself to become close to Christopher Johnson. Christopher was crazy about Shavon but the feeling wasn't mutual. He tried his best to impress her but she wasn't enthused. She thought he was really nice and attractive. His muscular build was quite alluring but she found him to be boring. He had practically begged her to be his lady but she continued to put him off constantly talking about Tracy.

Shavon closed the door behind herself after stepping into Myah's house.

"What are you doing?"

"What does it look like?" Myah responded.

"I'm trying to put the hem back in my skirt."

Shavon burst with laughter.

"What's so funny?" Myah asked in a very obnoxious tone.

"Myah, look at the hem for a minute. What do you think is wrong with it?"

"Nothing, yet. I'm not finished with it."

Shavon laughed again. Myah drew a deep breath and fell back in her chair.

"What's so dammed funny?"

Shavon could see that Myah was aggravated by her ridicule.

"Okay, Okay." Her laughter subsided. Shavon lifted the skirt from the sewing machine as Myah watched with curiosity. "Do you see this?" Shavon turned the skirt over. Myah wrinkled her nose urging Shavon to expound her point. "This is the outside." Shavon then reversed the garment. "And this is the inside."

Myah began to laugh at herself after she realized she had sewn the hem from the wrong side. She threw the skirt to Shavon. "Here! You finish it. This is your department anyway!"

After Shavon finished the skirt, she and Myah sat in the living room with a bottle of wine.

"Shavon, I'm really getting serious about Ronny. We don't argue like we used to. Maybe he's maturing."

Shavon giggled as she took a sip of wine. "No offense, my friend, but are you sure it's not you who's maturing?" Shavon laughed again. Myah reached for the bottle and refilled their glasses. "So, you think you might want to marry Ronny?"

"Yeah, I guess I do. Ronny has really stuck with me. It's been over three years now.

"I know," Shavon agreed.

"It seems like we're getting closer every day."

"I'm happy for you," Shavon said with a warm smile.

Myah felt cold as she realized what she had just done. '*How could I be so insensitive*?' she thought. She could only imagine how Shavon must have felt after her remark. It had been more than a year since Shavon had seen Tracy and she didn't need to be reminded of his absence.

"So, how have things been going with you and Chris?"

Shavon studied Myah's face a moment. She was well aware of what Myah was trying to do.

"About the same. Myah, he's so boring. Sometimes when he's talking, I put my head on his shoulder, not because I want to be close to him but because he puts me to sleep and that's the only way I can cover it up."

Myah laughed, "He can't be that bad, Shavon."

"Nope, he's worse."

Myah tried to suppress her laughter but couldn't.

"Do you know how many girls would die to just hold a conversation with that guy?"

Shavon gave Myah a slight smile as she answered, "No. But I know one girl who wouldn't."

"Shavon, that's really not fair. You are so mean."

"What's not fair? What should I do--lie to him?"

"No. I suppose not. But be nice, Shavon. He's in love, poor thing." She looked away and back at her friend again.

"Shavon, if you don't like him, why do you continue to see him? You've had your choice of quite a few."

"Well, he's the only one that wasn't a sex fiend."

Myah giggled, "What's wrong with sex fiends?"

Shavon rolled her eyes to the ceiling, "I don't believe you asked me that, Myah." Shavon took a few seconds giving her response a second thought. "I take that back. I believe every word of it."

Myah turned on the radio.

"Oooh! This is our song she said after humming a few notes. "Don't you and Chris have a song?"

"You can't be serious. If we did it would be called, *What a Boring Couple.*"

Myah laughed hard as Shavon continued. "And you should hear him asking me to be his lady," Shavon said as she threw her head back. "Myah, I know I was wrong but I laughed in his face."

"Um, um, um. You are something else, girl."

Suddenly, Shavon's laughter ceased. "He says, he's here and Tracy's not."

Myah was quiet for a moment. For once, she was at a loss for words. She hunched her shoulders. "Shavon, I just don't know what to say. I really find it hard to believe that you and Tracy have drifted so far apart."

"I know, me too. He's always so busy. I was really upset when he missed my party but I finally got over it. But do you know, I haven't talked to him in three months? If you think that's bad, I haven't seen him in over a year."

Myah shook her head.

"Myah, I wish I had married him when he asked me."

"It's not too late, Shavon. You and Tracy are still engaged and very much in love."

"I know I am but he doesn't ask me to marry him anymore. Myah, his job seems to take precedence over everything. I've competed with other women before but not with his job!"

"He has really changed, Shavon. He used to put you first. This is not like Tracy at all."

"Yeah, I know. Out of all the things Tracy has done, this is the worst. I still can't believe he's put his job before his family this way. I know he has ambition but he has cut everybody out of his life. He hasn't talked to his mother for more than four months. Whenever Terrell and I go over there now, neither me or Mrs. Gaines want to mention him. I might ask her if she's heard from him but that's about it. Whenever we do talk about him, she gives me this funny look. And Neicy just shakes her head. I think they feel bad for his behavior. He surprised all of us, especially me." Shavon expelled light laughter to camouflage her pain. She rose and grabbed her coat.

"Where ya' going, Shavon?"

"I got a date with Mr. Boring."

"Have a good time!"

CHAPTER 17

Another year quickly passed as Tracy continued to be a workaholic, absorbed in his work and his new love. He sometimes felt guilty and had told Tonya a number of times he should call his family more.

"I don't want them to think that I've forgotten about them."

"Don't you miss them?" Tonya asked twirling her hair around her finger as she watched him loosen his tie and take a seat next to her.

"Yeah but after so long, it gets easier. I used to wish I could go home all the time but now things have really changed, especially on the job." Tracy leaned back on the sofa. "I really enjoy what I do. There's a sense of excitement that I just can't explain."

"I know," Tonya said with a bit of unpleasantness in her tone.

Tracy looked over at her with a frown on his face, "What do you mean by that?"

"Nothing," she said lighting a cigarette.

Tracy stood over her and folded his arms, "If you have a gripe, I would appreciate it if you would share it with me."

"Just forget it, Tracy." She leaped to her feet and went toward the closet.

"Where are you going?" He watched as she put on her sweater.

"I don't have a problem, Tracy, you do."

He grabbed her arm. "Talk to me, Tonya."

She drew a deep submissive breath before she began, "Tracy--"

The phone rang. He looked at it as it rang, hesitant to answer it.

"Well, aren't you going to answer it or should I? It might be your mother." Tracy knew Tonya would never answer the phone. They had an agreement and he was sure she would stick to it.

"Hello? Hi!" He spoke with exuberance as he sat on the edge of the couch oblivious to Tonya and her attitude. When he did remember, he turned around and she was gone.

As he talked to Shavon, he went to the window and watched Tonya walk numbly to her car. He was somewhat surprised that Shavon had called him at home. She was accustomed to calling him only at the office because the office was the only place she could ever catch him. The sound of her voice stirred emotion in him.

"I was going to call you today, Shavon."

"Well, what happened?"

"The day's not over," he replied. He could tell that she was exasperated with him.

"Shavon, are you angry with me?"

"Oh, Tracy, I just wish you would call more often. It's so hard to reach you."

"I know, Shavon. And if you are mad, you have every right to be. I don't know why I haven't called. I think about you and Terrell all the time."

"We think about you too, Tracy. I want you to know that I'm still wearing your ring." A wave of guilt followed Tracy's smile.

"Shavon, I love you," he said in a hoarse voice. She was silent as she thought of her joy and pain with him. "I'll always love you," he added.

"I know, me too. Until I die," she whispered. A moment of silence fell between them before she spoke again.

"Tracy, I have some bad news."

"What! Did something happen to someone in my family?" he asked frantically.

"Yes, it's Terrell. The doctor says it's time for the heart operation. It didn't correct itself as he had hoped." Her voice trembled. "Tracy, I'm so afraid for him."

Tracy sighed and slowly sat down, "When?"

"Sometime within the next three weeks. He's so young. In four months, he'll be five."

"I know," he said sadly. "I hope he's strong enough."

Shavon tried hard to compose herself, "I'm really worried, Tracy."

"I know, Shavon. When do you want him to have the operation?"

"I wish I could say never but I think the sooner, the better. The longer we hold off, the worse it could be for him."

"Get an appointment as soon as you can. I'll take that week off."

"Okay."

"What's today?"

Shavon looked around the room for a calendar. "Wednesday the seventh."

"Try to get an appointment for mid-May."

"Okay." Shavon put Terrell on the phone. "It's Daddy, Sweetie."

"Daddy!"

"Hi, Terrell! How is my little man? Daddy misses you so much." Terrell's vocabulary was limited. He was still unable to speak clearly but Tracy understood every word.

"Come see me, Daddy!

"I miss you too, Terrell and I'll see you soon. I promise. You keep being a good boy for Mama."

"I be good boy."

"Daddy knows, Terrell. Daddy knows. I love you, son."

"Love you, Daddy."

"Kiss Mama, for me."

Terrell puckered his little lips and Shavon leaned in for a kiss. They talked a couple of minutes more then Tracy said good-bye.

"Bye-bye."

Shavon took the phone, "He kisses just like you."

Tracy laughed, "Is that a good thing?"

"Yes. There's nothing sweeter than a kiss from the two of you."

"You're the best, Shavon."

Tracy was teary eyed. "Call me first thing in the morning and let me know so that I can make the adjustments here, and Shavon?"

"Yes?"

"Try not to worry too much. It's not good for you or him right now."

After he hung up the phone, he unbuttoned his shirt and walked toward the bathroom. He ran a tub of hot water and slid in. He thought of nothing but Shavon and Terrell as he bathed. "Oh, God," he mumbled while biting his lips. When he climbed into bed, he felt scared, hurt and lonely. He looked at the empty space next to him where Tonya usually lay. It was 10 p.m. and she hadn't returned. He thought of how he needed her tonight but knew he really wanted Shavon.

Tracy lay awake until 11:30 p.m. before drifting off into a deep sleep. He began dreaming he was in an operating room with Terrell. There was a medical team of five standing over him shaking their heads as they worked. Suddenly, the head surgeon put his instruments down, pulled off his mask and began walking away. Tracy stood there crying and holding his dead son. He felt himself yelling Shavon's name. He woke up and found that he was shivering with fear. He turned over for comfort from Tonya but he was alone.

Terrell was ecstatic when Tracy arrived, "Daddy, Daddy!" He ran toward Tracy.

Shavon leaped from her chair, "Stop it, Terrell!" she said crossly.

Tracy's eyes met hers, "It's okay, Shavon," he assured her as he reached for his son. Shavon turned and went into the kitchen. Dana followed her.

"Shavon, you have to remember he's still a child."

Shavon covered her eyes. "I know, Mama, and that's the worst part of it."

Dana hugged her, "Well, Tracy's here now."

"Thank goodness," Shavon mumbled.

Tracy walked into the kitchen with Terrell in his arms. Dana excused herself. Tracy watched Shavon for a moment then walked toward her with Terrell still in his arms. The three of them kissed and hugged tightly.

The following day Shavon and Tracy sat in the surgical waiting room nearly ten hours while Terrell underwent surgery. Dana and Casey had just gone to the cafeteria for coffee. Shavon looked at Tracy nervously but managed a smile. This was the first time in years she had seen him in a jogging suit as opposed to a suit or jeans.

"I didn't know you even owned a jogging suit."

He smiled, "Is that some kind of a put down?"

"Of course not. I like the way you look in your jogging suit."

"You like the way I look in everything."

"You are so conceited, Tracy."

"Well, it's true isn't it?"

"You know it is," she admitted. He held her hand.

"Did I tell you, you look good in everything too? Even that red you're wearing." Shavon looked down. She was wearing a navy blue sweater dress.

"What red?"

"The red in your blood shot eyes." She punched him in the stomach.

As they were laughing, she saw the doctor coming up the hall. She touched his hand and nodded in the direction he was walking. They rose together.

When the doctor approached them, he was smiling. "You two look terrible. You really should go home and get some sleep." They both ignored his suggestion and he continued, "The surgery was a success and he's in recovery right now. He'll be there for a couple of hours then he'll be in ICU." They smiled with relief. "He's asleep but you can see him now."

Seeing Terrell this way brought tears to their eyes. They were so grateful his life had been spared. After leaving the operating room, Tracy reminded Shavon of how much he wanted them with him. She reminded him of how leaving Detroit would be bad for Terrell.

The following week went quickly. Tracy spent as much time with Terrell as he could. He visited Terrell twice a day until it was time for him to return to New York.

Tracy sat in his empty apartment working on the last chapter of his manuscript. He tried calling Tonya twice that week but there was no answer at her ex-roommate's apartment. He tried calling her job but each time he called, someone would tell him she wouldn't be in for the week.

Tracy spent the next two weeks in Detroit with his family. He needed to be near Terrell Ray to know that everything was all right. He couldn't rest easy until he and Shavon got an okay for Terrell's release from the hospital.

When he returned to New York, Tracy finished the last chapter of his manuscript and sent it to Selmar Publishing Company for consideration. He figured it would be some time before he heard from them but it would be well worth it if he did. Selmar was one of the most reputable publishing companies around and he felt good about his manuscript. He hoped they felt good about it too.

CHAPTER 18

Tracy stood bewildered as he stared at the last person he expected to see, in the doorway. He didn't know what to say to Tonya. It had been nearly three weeks since he had last seen her. She too looked bewildered.

"Hi, Tracy."

"Hey, Tonya. You can come in if you'd like."

After she went inside, they both sat feeling like strangers. He had no idea of what to say. He was afraid that if he said the wrong thing, she would leave again. Tonya felt it would be best to let him talk first. She wasn't sure of where she stood after walking out on him. She was slightly surprised to find him so receptive to her presence.

"I tried to reach you a number of times but people on your job would only tell me you wouldn't be in. So after a week passed and you didn't return my call, I figured you didn't want to see me anymore. I finally stopped calling."

"Tracy, I needed some time alone, that's all."

"Tonya, why did you walk out without telling me what was wrong?"

"Well, I started to, remember?"

"I don't mean to start an argument or anything, Tonya, but I think that was really unfair."

"I know, Tracy. That's why I came back. I thought maybe you would be willing to hear it now."

"Go on," he urged. He hoped she wouldn't bring up Shavon's name.

"Tracy, it seems to me that for too long now, all you've had time to do is work. We don't do anything anymore. I know your job is important to you but if we want to be happy together, something has got to change. You cancel out on the plans we make and sometimes you come home and go straight to bed because you're tired. We haven't been to dinner or lunch in about six months. Why? I'm trying to understand you but I don't," she said pulling out a cigarette.

"I thought you said you stopped smoking."

She lit it. "I did. But whenever something's bothering me, I start up again."

Tracy pulled the cigarette from her fingers. "Tonya, I didn't realize I had been neglecting you so. Why didn't you say something before now?"

"I wanted you to realize it yourself."

"I'm sorry." He hugged her. "I'll give you more time but you might get tired of me."

"I doubt it," she said as he kissed her.

Tonya didn't know it would be so easy but she was very relieved that Tracy had accepted her back with open arms.

The following month was August and Tracy went home to spend time with Terrell for his birthday. He was so proud of Terrell. He had turned five and would be starting school in September. During his visit, he noticed Shavon had done extremely well with teaching their son. Terrell was so polite and well mannered. He felt guilty that she had been both parents but she would marry him if she wanted things to be any different.

Three months later, Tracy received a response from Selmar Publishing Company explaining how impressed they were with his manuscript. They set up an appointment to meet with him about publication. Tracy and Tonya were thrilled. They celebrated before he even got a contract with Selmar.

Tracy called home and told Shavon. She was overwhelmed with joy and not the least bit surprised.

"See. What did I tell you? Oh, Tracy, I'm so proud of you!"

Shavon blew kisses through the phone and Tracy returned them.

"You had so much faith in me, Shavon."

"Why, of course," she said with gaiety.

"Tracy, I have some good news too. I'm working now."

"Oh, yeah!"

"Yes, and it really feels good."

"Where?"

"For Sims department store, as a seamstress."

"Good, Shavon. I'm so happy for you." He paused momentarily and smiled. "Look at us, we're both achieving our aspirations. Shavon, I know it's not exactly what you want but it's a very big step in the right direction."

"Yes it is," she agreed. "I'm starting school too, Tracy. It's going to take longer because I'm only going part time."

"Part time is better than no time," he told her.

His words of encouragement meant the world to her.

Ironically it was nearly six months later in the middle of May when Shavon heard Tracy's voice again.

"Hi, Shavon!"

"Hi," she answered with excitement.

"How are you?"

"I'm fine. How are you, Tracy?"

"Oh, things are just great, Shavon."

"I guess so," she said sarcastically. "You don't return our calls anymore?"

"Shavon, I'm sorry. I intended to but I've really been working hard. I've been intensely dedicated to my novel."

"Oh! How's it coming?"

"Shavon, I think within the next eight or nine months, it will be in book stores everywhere."

"That's great, Tracy!" Even though she was frustrated with him it was hard to not feel the excitement from his accomplishments.

"How are your classes coming, Shavon?"

"Oh, they're going really well.

"I've found that I have greater amenities than I was ever aware of. I've been thinking a lot about getting my own business established after I graduate. My teacher really gives me a lot of encouragement."

Tracy's mind drifted as Shavon talked. He thought of how they both had taken a step into a long desired dream. He was disappointed that they couldn't share their happiness face to face. She had her new job and classes to attend and he couldn't dare ask her to take any time off.

"Shavon, that's fantastic. I know you'll do well when you get yourself established."

"But look at you, Tracy. I know that once your book is published, all of your old friends will be calling to find out if it's really you. I can see it now. Your name is going to be on everybody's lips."

"Shavon, stop counting chickens. Half of them won't remember my name."

"That's not true! You were so popular. I can't help it. I know a winner when I see one."

Tracy abruptly ended their conversation, "Shavon, I can't talk now. I'm on my way out. I'll call you tomorrow. Love you. Bye."

Shavon stood there holding the phone as she heard the dial tone. "Boy, he must have literally had one foot out of the door when he called."

Tracy hung up just as Tonya was coming through the door. "Hi," he said moving away from the phone.

"Hi, Tracy. You're home early today."

"Well, I have a few things to talk about with my publisher."

"Oh." She tried to hide her disappointment. She had hoped it was to spend time with her.

Tracy jumped to his feet throwing his arms around her. "Tonya, I know I haven't been here much lately but as soon as all of this business with my book is over, things will be back to normal."

"I hope so," she whispered

***

Shavon was walking on air. She beamed as she talked to Christopher. He was still boring all right but anything he could say since she got a job as a seamstress sounded fine to her. "You ready?"

"Yes!"

"Shavon, I want tonight to be special for you. I'm so proud of you. Most people don't start out with such good jobs. The average person starts out in a restaurant being over worked and under paid."

"I know," she agreed. "That's the same thing Tracy--" Shavon looked at him feeling bad for what she had said.

"I'm sure the show has started by now, Ms. Robertson."

"Yeah, let's go," she responded. Shavon hated it when he got so formal. That always meant he was upset with her.

She held his hand throughout the concert trying to make up for what she had said earlier. She hoped she hadn't spoiled his evening. After the concert, Chris took Shavon to dinner. He hardly said anything for the rest of the night. When he took her home, she tried to tell him how much she had enjoyed his company but he cut her off, telling her he couldn't take it anymore.

Shavon went gloomily into the house hating herself for ever mentioning Tracy's name. After all, she was with Chris. The following week, Shavon didn't hear from Chris. He thought about her day in and day out but he would never let her know it. He was tired of playing second fiddle. He wasn't sure if he stood any ground at all where Shavon was concerned but avoiding her to conciliate her was certainly worth a try.

All week, Shavon found herself wondering if Chris would ever speak to her again. She knew she had been wrong before but this time it slipped. Prior to the concert, she didn't care how mad Chris had gotten when she mentioned Tracy. Tracy was her fiancé, near or far and that was final. But now things seemed to be changing.

Shavon laid her *Fashion Extraordinaire* magazine on the coffee table as she thought about Chris. *How can you let him get to you this way? He's just a friend. You're not serious about him. Tracy's the only man for you, you know that.* "But Tracy's not here," she mumbled. "And I do have to admit that lately Chris has been a little more interesting."

She thought back to their last date. When she had tried to kiss him goodnight, he had turned to her cheek and slightly kissed her goodnight. She was very disappointed but she knew she had induced his attitude.

"Shavon, I think you're falling for this man," she admitted to herself. "No you don't, wait for Tracy. It might be sooner than you think." Shavon looked at the phone. "Then again, it may be years before you two get married, maybe never. Chris isn't so bad. He's smart, handsome, loving and well-built," she said with a giggle.

She reached for the phone. "Hello, may I speak to Chris? Oh, okay. Well, would you tell him to call Shavon? Thanks."

Shavon stayed home for the rest of the day but never received a call from Chris. The following day, Chris returned her call.

"Hi, Shavon."

"Hi."

"My brother told me you called."

"I just called to see what you were up to," she said. There was a pause in conversation.

"What are you and Terrell doing today?"

"He's going over to his grandmother's house in about an hour, why? Did you want to do something?"

"Would you like to see a movie?"

"I'd love to."

"It's a date then. I'll pick you up tonight at seven."

Shavon smiled widely as she hung up the phone. She never dreamed she would be happy to see any man outside of Tracy but she was. For once, she looked forward to her date with Chris.

Chris noticed that Shavon had seemed considerably interested in him tonight. His first inclination was to think she was trying to make up for her inconsiderate remark, but she seemed to be closer to him. She appeared to be more conscious of his presence than she had ever evinced.

After the movie, they stopped by Chris' place to check on things. Chris had always been careful about the people he chose as friends but he had taken his younger brother in temporarily. His brother wasn't as choosy. Shavon loved Chris' house. She admired him for being so together. He was a master electrician and good at just about anything he set his mind to.

He had a sparkling gray Mercedes, that all of his friends envied him for and a motorcycle, which Shavon had enjoyed throughout the past summer. She admired him for owning a home. All of her other friends either had apartments or stayed with their parents. Chris had done so well to only be 27 years old.

Shavon felt good being with him tonight.

"Would you like a drink?" he asked.

"Something light, please. You know I'm really not a drinker." Chris laughed.

"Well, would the lady care for some Asti-Spumanti?"

He flashed a beautiful smile. Her mind drifted with thoughts of him as he spoke. She had never really paid attention until tonight but she found herself seeing him in a different light. Her eyes widened when she realized her mind had wandered.

"Yes, I would. Thank you."

She thought of what Myah had said months back. Now she understood what Myah meant about Chris. As they conversed, she drank one glass to his two. He began talking about his childhood. She found the stories of how he got in trouble in school hilarious. He told her about how he had once quit a very promising job to become a singer. What she found to be so funny was that he was the only one who enjoyed his singing.

"But all that was before I grew up."

"I know you grew up after that."

"Quick, fast and in a hurry! Everybody started telling me what a fool I was. Then, one day I woke up and didn't have anywhere to go. I had pushed my practical goals aside. My mother had threatened me so many times. She kept saying, 'you'll be out on the street, boy!'"

Shavon laughed, "Well, to have been such a degenerate, you sure pulled yourself out of it."

"I wanted a good woman," he said as he looked into her eyes. "A good woman needs a good man, nothing less."

Shavon blushed as he grabbed her hand.

"You are so beautiful, Shavon," he said as he continued to stare into her eyes. He began running his hands through her hair. He leaned over and kissed her forehead then pressed his lips against her hair.

"I love the smell of your hair. And it's so soft," he whispered. He slowly began kissing her lips. She yielded to the softness of his kiss. He slowly slid his arms around her thin waist holding her tighter and urging her to respond. She returned his embrace as he slid her down on the couch until he was on top of her. She felt a rush of desire going through her but couldn't give in.

"Chris," she whispered. He continued kissing her. Shavon felt his hands roaming her body. "Chris, don't!" She knew she didn't want him to stop but she couldn't go through with it. She belonged to only one man in such a consummate fashion. He began unbuttoning her blouse.

"Chris-- We can't," she whispered. He continued to touch her making it harder for her to resist. She stopped fighting him and he began unzipping her jeans. She began to squirm.

"No Chris! I can't."

"Why not?" he asked in a whimper.

"I can't, Chris. I just can't."

Chris stopped in his tracks and sat up. The light was low but she could tell that his beautiful black skin was flushed with anger.

"What is it, Shavon? Why do you always fight me so? Why did you resist? I know you want me too, don't you?"

Shavon pulled herself into an erect position and proceeded to button her blouse.

"I--I don't know what you want me to say, Chris."

He stood up. "Why won't you just be honest?"

Shavon dropped her head. She knew she had hurt him. Once again she felt that she had made a mess of things.

"It's Tracy, isn't it?"

Shavon looked up in surprise.

"Chris, please."

"Well, he's the reason, isn't he?"

"Chris, don't do this. We're talking about you and me, nobody else. It's just not right for me now."

Chris sighed, "Will it ever be right for us, Shavon?"

She looked up sympathetically wishing that moment had never happened.

"Forget it, Shavon. Come on, it's getting late."

Shavon felt uncomfortable on the way home. She knew she had lost him but she could only do what her heart allowed. She didn't bother to apologize before going in this time. She got out of the car and went inside, never looking back.

Shavon awoke with the same thought she had before she went to sleep. She thought of last night's incident with Chris and made herself believe that if Tracy had time for her, last night would never have happened. "Shavon, you're getting weaker," she told herself. "Tracy has been gone too long." She looked at the photograph of her and Tracy at his prom. "Tracy, I love you. I don't want to be with anybody else but I'm starting to care a lot for Chris. I wish you were here."

She picked up the phone and dialed Tracy's number. She was relieved to hear his voice but it turned out to be his answering machine. Shavon left a message hoping he would return her call immediately. She had bathed and began dressing when the phone rang. She caught it on the first ring.

"Hello."

"Were you waiting for my call?"

"Chris?"

"Yes it is."

"Hi."

"Shavon, I was wrong last night. I shouldn't have come on to you like that. I hope you're not angry with me."

Shavon was flabbergasted, "Chris, it's not all your fault. I shouldn't have let it go so far. I knew I couldn't take it any further."

"No, Shavon, it wasn't your fault at all. I know how you feel about Tracy and I shouldn't have expected anything more than what we already have." She smiled as he talked.

"I don't want to pressure you into anything. I want it to happen when you're ready, if you're ever ready. And that's a chance I'm willing to take because you really mean a lot to me."

"You are really something you know that," she said with a smile.

"Yeah, but I just hope I'm enough."

"Do you have any plans for next Saturday?" she asked.

"Only to be with you."

From that moment on, Chris and Shavon became closer.

Chapter 19

Tracy's promise lasted nearly a year but now Tonya wondered if she would be better off alone, she already felt she was. Sometimes when Tracy came in he was so exhausted, he went straight to bed. Tonya was finding it harder and harder to be patient but she continued to endure it.

The next year seemed to have flown by. Shavon had become completely involved with Chris. She was tired of being alone. Outside of a "thinking of you cards" and a couple of missed messages, she hadn't heard from Tracy in over a year.

Things had really gone well with Tracy's novel. Shavon was right; it was an excellent book to all who read it. Tracy began to go away for weeks at a time leaving Tonya at home. The only thing he was interested in was his writing career. He had taken a leave from his job at *Classic Magazine, Inc.* and became more involved with writing. Tonya sat home many nights thinking about what Tracy had said. She kept hearing and envisioning the scene over and over again.

"Tonya, this is my life. Don't take that away from me. I live for this."

"I understand," she told him. "But I would love to be a part of it all too. I know it makes you happy, Tracy, and I want to share it with you. Open up, Tracy, please."

Tonya remembered his expression. He was really sincere about making things better between them but there was so much in the way, his career and most of all, Shavon.

Tonya endured Tracy's neglect two months longer. June 10th, Tracy called his apartment to tell Tonya he would be on the 10 a.m. flight but there was no answer. When he arrived in New York, Tonya had a long letter waiting for him. She explained how she tried to understand him but couldn't. She told him how she loved him more than any other man she had ever known. He could see that when he got to the bottom of the letter, she had been crying. He forced himself to read the rest of the letter. Her last statement was the one that hit him the hardest.

Tracy, I'll never love anybody like I love you but you'll never love me the way you love Shavon. You never said you loved me with sincerity. Tracy, if you really love Shavon, and I know you do, you should be with her no matter what it takes before it's too late.

Tracy stared into space as he dropped Tonya's letter. He found what he read hard to believe. What did I do wrong? He asked himself that question over and over again. *I don't understand*, he thought. *She knew how important it was for me to be a successful writer. I don't believe it. Why would she want to deprive me of that, it's my life.* He thought of Shavon. "That's where you're wrong, Tonya," he said defensively. "Shavon really loves me and she will always be there."

Tracy was exhausted the next morning. Everyone could tell that something was definitely wrong. He felt really bad about the way things had ended with Tonya. He had hurt her badly and never really knew it until she was gone. He didn't bother to look for her. When Tonya was angry with him, she had always covered her tracks well. He knew this time, it was final.

Tracy became totally dedicated to his writing career. There was no one to go home to so most nights he didn't. He began a new manuscript, which kept him very busy. From time to time, he thought of what Tonya had written in her letter about him never loving anyone like he loves Shavon. He called Shavon but there was no answer and he chose not to leave a voicemail message. He believed in her love implicitly and he knew she believed in his. He agreed with Tonya about his love for Shavon.

***

Shavon picked Myah up from the beauty salon. As they drove home, they talked about Chris.

"Shavon, I knew you would finally come around." Shavon smiled.

"You didn't know anything."

"Well, I had an idea."

"But, I'm telling you, Myah, at first he was just a nice person. You know-- someone to pass the time with."

"But now," Myah urged. Shavon giggled.

"He's really special to me."

"Special! Is that all? He takes you anywhere you want to go. He does anything you want to do. He keeps Terrell sometimes when you have things to do. He even picks him up and spends time with him as if he were his father. You've gotta admit, some guys wouldn't even consider doing so much for another man's child. He loves you and Terrell! Shavon, you couldn't ask for more than that."

Myah noticed Shavon had become reticent. "Shavon, are you still thinking about Tracy?"

Shavon sighed and pushed her hair behind her ear, "You know I'll never stop loving him."

"Shavon, I thought after you had become so physically involved with Chris that you finally got Tracy Gaines out of your system."

"Nope. I love him just as much as ever."

"Shavon, that's not fair to Chris."

"Life's not fair, Myah!"

Shavon tried to compensate for the negative tone she used with Myah. "Myah, I'm really crazy about Chris and I have a certain amount of love for him, but he's just not Tracy. He makes me feel good but not as good as Tracy. I know I haven't seen Tracy in nearly two years but I'm still hoping things will work out. He loves me and Terrell too much to let go completely. I'm not excusing him for neglecting us but Tracy will always be my one true love. I can't explain it but we understand one another! Whatever stage he's going through, sooner or later, it's going to end."

Myah abruptly changed the subject. She knew that nobody could change Shavon's mind about Tracy. She also knew Shavon hurt inside but continued to hide it because of her love for him.

"So, how's your mother enjoying her honeymoon?"

"She's really happy, Myah. I think Steve has really been good for Mama. I'm glad they got married."

"How did your dad feel about her remarrying?"

"He tried to hide his feelings but I could tell he was hurt. He has always wanted Mama back but he knew she would never truly trust him again. When I asked him how he felt about it, he just hugged me and said, 'If your mother is happy, so am I.' Myah, I swear I saw a tear in his eye."

"That's too bad, Shavon. But like he said, if she's happy, I'm happy."

"Yeah. She called last night to tell me that she was having a good time in the Bahamas. They're going to Vegas to do a little gambling before they return. Steve has been there before but it will be Mama's first time and she is so excited about it." Myah turned on the radio.

"Shavon, you think things might change a lot in your household?"

"Maybe, Shavon said. "For one thing, I think a newlywed couple should live alone. Daddy said I can move in with him but Mama and Steve said they want me and Terrell to stay right where we are."

"So, what are you gonna do?"

"I think I'll stay with Mama. It would be hard for Daddy to get used to having me and Terrell around the house. He wouldn't have any privacy. And besides, Mama wouldn't feel right if I moved out."

As Shavon lay next to Chris, she thought about her mother and Steve.

"What are you thinking about?"

"Mama and Steve."

"What about them? Aren't they happy?"

"Yes, they're very happy."

"Then what's the problem?"

"Chris, I feel like a burden to them. They should be able to start out alone, not with a 22-year-old daughter and her son."

"Your mother wouldn't have it any other way, you know that, Shavon."

"I know. She already told me that. But Chris, I feel like we're in the way and I'm really not ready to get my own place. I just don't have the money."

Chris rolled over on his back, "I've got a suggestion."

"What?"

"Why don't you and Terrell move in here?" Shavon laughed.

"I thought you would come up with a way to help me make more money, Chris. Don't be silly. If I feel like a burden with my own mother, how do you think I'll feel with you?"

"Shavon, I'm in love with you and I want to share everything with you and Terrell."

"Chris, I really appreciate all you've done for me and Terrell. You're the best. But please don't ask me that. You know I could never do that."

"Shavon, I'm sorry but I need a better answer than, I can't."

"Chris, I don't want to live with a man."

"Well, there's an alternative for that too." He paused before he continued. "Let's get married?"

Shavon stared at him for a long moment trying to find the slightest hint of frivolity but he was serious. She thought of Tracy but she knew she couldn't tell him the reason for not wanting a commitment with him.

"Chris!"

"Shavon, you say you love me. It is true isn't it?"

"Of course it is, Chris, you shouldn't doubt that."

"Well, why can't we get married?" Chris moved next to her putting his arm around her shoulders. "Shavon, I want you to be my wife. Just say yes. I would love to be a father to Terrell."

Shavon was thrown by his fatherly remark. She hated the sound of that. She was one second away from telling him he would never be Terrell's father. *Terrell has a father*, she thought.

Before she could speak, Chris began, "Shavon, we can get married whenever you want to. What about October. It's just a month away."

"No! Chris. I love you but we can't get married." Shavon saw the pain in his eyes and tried to make him feel better by explaining in detail why she couldn't marry him. Chris didn't know that she was only telling him half the truth.

"Chris, if Mama hadn't gotten married, you wouldn't be asking me this. I don't want to marry you under these circumstances. I don't want to marry you because I need a place to stay. I'll get my own place before I let that happen." She hugged him tightly. "Chris, you mean so much to me."

"Just not enough to marry," he said sadly.

"Not right now." She held him and thought of Tracy. She knew she could never marry him. She had taken Tracy's ring off for him but it didn't change the way she felt. Her heart said more than wearing Tracy's ring could ever say.

CHAPTER 20

Dana rushed in the house. "What happened, Steve?"

"It's Terrell. He's had a heart attack."

"What! Where is he?"

"I called the EMS and they took him and Shavon to the hospital. She asked me to wait here for you."

"Oh, Steve," Dana began to cry. "Is he all right?"

"I don't know." He held her trying to comfort her. She abruptly broke the embrace.

"I've got to get to the hospital."

"Of course you do, Sweetheart. I'm coming with you."

"Did anybody call Casey? Of course not," she said answering her own question. "Shavon didn't have time." Dana called Casey before she and Steve rushed to the hospital.

Dana and Shavon sat in the waiting room hugging and crying.

"Mama, I don't know what to do. Where's Tracy? He should be here. Did you call him, Mama?"

"No, Baby, I didn't even think to call him but I called your father."

"Oh, good," Shavon responded nervously.

"Shavon, call him now."

"Let's see. 272- It might be 272-43-"

Steve and Dana sadly watched Shavon as she paced. Shavon repeatedly sat down and jumped up in a matter of seconds.

"Oh, Steve," Dana cried. "It hurts me to see her this way. Look at her. She's so scared and confused. I wish I knew Tracy's number."

"It would certainly help matters," Steve commented.

Shavon panicked as she saw Dr. Marcus coming toward her.

"Mama," she cried squeezing her mother's and Steve's hands. Dana's eyes filled with tears when she saw the expression on the doctor's face.

Dr. Marcus explained that Terrell was in the Intensive Care Unit and that things didn't look good for him. He needed a heart transplant.

Shavon and Dana stood in the room and watched Terrell as he slept. Shavon hardly said a word. Tears streamed down her face but she remained calm. The nurse spoke in a low voice.

"I have to ask you to leave now," the nurse said. Dana stepped back.

"Come on Shavon."

"No, Mama, I want to stay a little longer."

"I know, Honey, but--"

The nurse inconspicuously signaled to Dana that she would give them 10 more minutes. Dana stood there a few moments longer then left Shavon to be alone with her son. Dana watched Shavon as she left the room.

Casey rushed in to comfort her. She embraced him.

"Daddy, he's so weak and I can't help him," she cried.

"I know, Baby. I know. The doctors are doing all they can until they can get a heart." Casey's eyes were misty. He knew what could happen to his only grandchild.

Shavon seemed to be in a daze. Dana looked at Casey wondering if he noticed it too. Casey put his arm around Shavon as they walked.

"You okay, Honey?" Dana asked.

"I'm fine, Mama."

She spoke so calmly that Dana was slightly worried.

"You sure?" Casey asked.

"Yes," she whispered.

After an hour in the waiting area Dana suggested they go home and get something to eat. Honey, Terrell's going to be sleep for a bit. Let's go home and give Tracy a call and get something to eat."

As they sat at the dinner table, Dana and Steve watched Shavon play with her food.

"Shavon, you've better put something in your stomach," Steve told her.

"I guess I wasn't hungry after all."

Dana cleared her throat, "So, what did Tracy say?"

"Nothing," Shavon spoke without looking up.

Dana and Steve looked at each other with puzzled expressions.

"I don't under--" her mother started.

"His phone is disconnected."

"Disconnected?"

Shavon answered calmly, "Yes."

"Did you call his mother?" Steve asked.

"Yes, that was the only number she had."

"What about his job?"

"He took a leave of absence Mama. I wrote him a letter," Shavon said getting up from the table.

"Where are you going?" Dana asked.

"I'm going to mail the letter."

"Honey, I can do it."

"No, Mama. Thanks but I'm fine. I'll do it."

Shavon, Dana, Steve and Casey returned to the hospital later that night. Shavon was alone in the room with Terrell.

"Hi, Baby," she said as he tried to smile. "Mama knows you're hurting so just lie still."

Shavon leaned over and kissed him on the forehead and began rubbing her hands through his hair.

"You are so handsome." Terrell blushed.

"And you're pretty, Mommy," he whispered.

"Thank you, Terrell Ray."

"Mommy, I'm tired."

"I know but you can take it because you're strong." She wanted to cry as she forced the words out. "You're six years old now."

Terrell gave a faint smile, "Yep. I'm six."

She squeezed his hand. "My little Terrell," she said trying to remain strong for his sake.

"So, did you eat dinner?"

"Yeah."

"What did you have?"

"Soup."

"Did you like it?"

Terrell quickly shook his head no. Shavon laughed.

"I'll bring you a treat in the morning."

Terrell looked around the room.

"Mommy, take me home." Tears came to her eyes but she wiped them away. "Mommy, don't cry. I'm okay."

"I know but you know how we grownups worry about little people like you."

Shavon rubbed his face then dropped her smile.

"Baby, I don't know how long you have to stay here. I just hope it won't be much longer."

He frowned, "Me neither. He looked around the room again. "Mommy, where's Daddy?"

Shavon swallowed dry and hard. "He'll be here, Baby. His phone is off so I wrote him a letter. He should be here in a few days."

"I miss Daddy."

"I know, Babe. I do too. He'll be here before you know it. Don't you know that he loves us more than anything?"

"Will he come, Mommy?"

"He'll come, Baby. He won't let us down." Shavon silently prayed that Tracy would come soon. She and Terrell needed him.

Terrell's condition worsened as the week went by. He became weaker each day as they waited for a heart. By the beginning of the second week, Shavon had not heard from Tracy but she had convinced herself that he would come. She believed he could sense their need for him.

Wednesday morning after Shavon returned from the hospital, she opened the mailbox and found the letter she had written to Tracy. Shavon felt a stab of pain as she read the front of the envelope. *Addressee unknown. Return to Sender.* She found her key and opened the door. As she entered, she fell to the floor crying.

"No! No! No! Tracy, please, please come! We need you. Terrell's asking for you. Oh, God. Where is he?"

Myah sat and listened as Shavon talked and cried at the same time.

"Myah, he moved away and didn't call me. How could he do this to us, how? If he really loved us he would be here."

"Shavon, let me call Chris."

"No, Myah."

"Why not? It might be good for you to be with him right now."

Shavon sat down. "Myah, I hurt him badly."

Myah looked at Shavon quizzically, "How?"

"He wanted to be with me every day at the hospital. All I could think about was good ole' Tracy. Chris started acting like he was Terrell's father. I didn't want that because he's not, Myah. But he just forced the issue of being close to Terrell." Shavon paused and walked to the window. "He asked me to let him go in as Terrell's father. I had to draw the line somewhere. Myah, I told him no. I wanted him to see Terrell because I know he loves him but not as his father. I don't care how far apart Tracy and I have been for the last few years, he's still the father of my son."

Shavon bit her dry lips as she continued. "Then, he said something about me still loving Tracy. I couldn't deny that so I didn't. I told him I still love Tracy. He asked me if Tracy came back to stay, what would happen between us? Myah, I had to tell him the truth. I couldn't let him go on believing something that I don't believe myself." Shavon walked back and sat on the couch. "So, there you have it." She blew her nose. "But all I care about right now is my baby. Myah, he's got to hold on."

Myah sniffed and looked away. "I've been praying since he went in the hospital, Shavon."

"I know, Myah."

Later that night, Shavon had exhausted every option of getting in touch with Tracy. No one knew where he was living.

November 3rd, Saturday morning, Shavon and Neicy sat in the waiting room while Maria and Dana sat with Terrell. Shavon stopped in the middle of her conversation with Neicy when she saw Maria and Dana rush out of Terrell's room.

"Shavon!" Dana yelled.

Shavon rushed to Terrell's room. Dana grabbed her by the shoulders, "Shavon, listen. The doctor's in with Terrell now."

"What happened? Is he all right?"

Dana started to cry. Maria hugged Shavon.

"He gon' be all right." Maria fought to keep from breaking down as her tears streamed. Shavon tried to get pass Maria but Maria's healthy arms held her tightly.

"Shavon, no!" her mother yelled. "You'll only make things worse."

Maria watched Dana as she cried and shivered with fear. She realized Dana couldn't do anything to help her daughter.

"Let me go. I've got to be with my baby!"

Shavon broke free of Maria's hold. As she entered the room, she screamed, "Terrell! Terrell!"

Terrell Ray was gone.

CHAPTER 21

Saturday had been a very long day for everyone. Shavon spent the rest of the day sitting in the darkness of her room. Dana was worried about her and asked Steve to go up and talk to her. She only stared into space. All she could think about was Terrell's last words. "Mommy, where's Daddy?"

Dana and Maria made all of the arrangements for Terrell's burial. Shavon agreed to everything they suggested. Chris stood beside Shavon at the cemetery. Despite the way things had ended between them, Chris really loved Terrell. He stood beside her with tears in his eyes as he thought of all the things he, Terrell and Shavon had done. Afterwards, he and Shavon spoke briefly. Chris held her one last time then he was gone.

When Shavon got home that Wednesday afternoon, she said good-bye to Myah and returned to her dark room. She held up pretty well for the rest of the week, which made Casey and Dana sleep a little easier. The following week, Dana began to pack Terrell's clothes for the Goodwill. She heard Shavon humming in the kitchen. She sighed with relief. "Well, at least she's feeling finally feeling better," she whispered. Shavon walked into the living room as Dana folded a pair of Terrell's jeans.

"What are you doing with those? Shavon asked with a surprised expression.

"I'm packing them up for the Goodwill," Dana answered reluctantly.

"Why?"

"Well, I thought some other kids might be able to use them." Shavon took the jeans from her mother's hand.

"These are perfectly good jeans. Terrell can still wear these."

Dana's eyes widened with disbelief, "What did you say, Shavon?"

"I know he's a growing boy but he can still fit these." Shavon picked up a shirt her mother had laid on the couch. "This too. Mama, put these back. I can't afford to buy him any clothes right now."

Dana's mouth hung open "Shavon, are you all right?"

Shavon looked at her mother with an odd expression. "Me? I should be asking you that question." Shavon laughed and went upstairs with Terrell's clothes in her hand.

Dana stood in the living room dazed as if she had seen a ghost. She began to panic. "Oh, my God! What should I do? She couldn't possibly have meant that. Why would she say something like that?" she thought to herself.

Dana sat for half an hour fighting with her conscience of whether or not she should talk to Shavon. *If she really thinks he's still alive, she might become erratic if I tell her he's not. But I'm her mother, I've got to try*, she thought.

Dana formidably climbed the stairs to Shavon's room. Again she heard Shavon humming.

"Shavon, what are you doing, hun?"

"Nothing really. I was just about to call Myah."

"Oh," Dana mumbled wondering how to approach her.

"Honey, you didn't mean what you said about Terrell's clothes, did you?"

Shavon looked at Dana with a puzzled expression, "Mama, are you sure you're all right?"

Dana braced herself, "Shavon, Terrell's not here anymore."

"Mama, you make it sound so final. He'll be out of the hospital in a few days. Gee whiz!"

Dana cleared her throat, "Shavon, it is final."

Shavon backed up, "What do you mean by that?"

Dana went toward her. She continued to back herself into the corner.

"Shavon, do you remember what happened last week?"

"No. What?"

"Honey, you have to accept it."

"Accept what?" Shavon yelled. "Mama, you're scaring me, stop it." Dana watched her intently. She really believed Terrell was still alive.

"Shavon, Terrell's dead."

"No! He's not dead, he's not! I took him breakfast this morning. He told me how he didn't like the hospital food. Mama, go away." Dana reached for her hand.

"How could you say that? You're my mother."

"Baby, I know it hurts but we have to accept it."

Shavon became violent. "He's not dead, so don't you say it anymore. You don't love him. You never loved him!" Dana touched her wrist. Shavon pushed her away knocking her to the floor. As she stood up, Shavon yelled at her. "Don't come near me!"

"Honey, let me help--"

Shavon pushed her mother against the wall. Dana hit hard this time falling to the floor again. She couldn't get up. Shavon grabbed her coat and ran out of the house and up the street screaming. Liar! Liar!"

***

"Shavon, what happened--what's wrong?"

"Myah, I think Mama's going crazy!"

"Why? What happened?"

"I don't know, she's just talking crazy. She thinks Terrell's dead. I tried to tell her he's not but she won't believe me. Maybe she wants him to be. I really thought she loved him. She's his grandmother, Myah. How could she behave this way?"

Myah stared at her friend a moment.

"Myah, did you hear me?"

"Y-yes, I heard you." Myah could see that Shavon was already upset so she went along with everything she said. She hugged Shavon.

"She'll be okay, Shavon. I don't understand it either. She shouldn't have said that to you. Why do you think she would say such a terrible thing?" Myah asked hoping she would be shocked into acknowledging the truth.

"I don't know, Myah. Mama has never done anything like this before--never!"

As Shavon went on, Myah listened and watched. She was terrified. *She hasn't accepted his death*, she thought. *I don't know how to help her.* Tears came to Myah's eyes as she listened.

"Myah, you've got to help me. I can't go back there, I can't!"

"Okay, Shavon," she said nervously. "You can stay here as long as you need to."

"Thanks, Myah. You are really a true friend."

Myah forced a smile and hugged Shavon again. *I hope your friend is doing the right thing*, she thought.

Later that day, Shavon's father went to see her. He tried to tell her that Terrell had died. Again, she became enraged.

Afterwards, she sat talking with Myah.

"I don't understand what's wrong with them. Myah, you try and make some sense out of all of this. Why are they saying such terrible things to me? Myah, tell me they're lying."

Myah quickly remembered how indignant Shavon had become with her father. She knew that if she said anything other than what Shavon wanted to hear, Shavon would leave. She kept in mind that if she left, there was no telling where she would end up. She had nowhere else to go and she needed her.

"Yes, Shavon, they're lying," she heard herself say. She swallowed as she thought of the blatant lie she had just told her best friend. But she kept reminding herself that it was in Shavon's best interest. She knew that she was not qualified to make an appropriate decision but she made the best one she could.

Dana and Casey sat at the table discussing Shavon's problem. Neither one of them wanted to see her in a psychiatric hospital but she had become more violent each time she saw them. She still believed she saw Terrell each day when she went to the hospital. No one knew what she did once she got there but she always felt relieved when she came back. She continued to talk about Terrell on a regular basis. Dana and Casey dreaded the inevitable. Finally, Shavon was admitted to a psychiatric hospital. The doctor felt she would be better off away from her family.

For the first month, Shavon wouldn't talk to anyone. Whenever the doctor tried to talk to her, she would become indignant and argue that she didn't belong there. "Please, let me out," she would say. "I've got to take care of my son."

Shavon made no progress in her first three months. Though she talked a little more, she was still quite withdrawn. She refused to talk to her parents when they were given visiting privileges. She would only talk to Myah. She would ask Myah if she was taking good care of Terrell. There were days when Myah found herself totally exhausted. She thought of Shavon for hours at a time and often found herself emotionally drained. She thought of Shavon as a sister and seeing her this way hurt deeply.

She had always thought of Shavon as a strong-minded person. She never knew that Terrell's death would weaken Shavon's mind to the point where her sanity would diminish. Myah found herself thinking about Terrell as well. She began to see how a child could mean the world to its mother. She cried many nights for them. She felt that one reason the truth was so insurmountable for Shavon was because she had been the mother and father for her son. Shavon had been with him day in and day out for most of his life and his handicap had increased their closeness.

Dana and Myah sat in the living room with solemn faces. Myah shook her head. "I don't know. She seems to be her normal self but then she'll bring up Terrell. I don't know what to say to her anymore." Myah's eyes watered.

"I know, Honey, she's not improving. And the worst part about it is that she thinks me and her father are trying to hurt her."

"She still loves you though," Myah said sadly. There was a long pause of silence. "So, when are you and Steve moving?"

"In a month or so. His house has three large rooms and a pool, so it was an easy decision to sell mine. I hope that when Shavon comes home, she won't mind living there with us."

Myah smiled. "I'm sure she won't."

"Myah."

"Huh?"

"Do you ever mention Tracy when you and Shavon talk?"

"No, why?"

"Shavon has built up some pretty impervious feelings toward him. It would be best not to mention him. The doctor thinks it would be too much for her now or any time prior to some sign of improvement."

"Oh, I'll be very careful."
"Where do you think he might be, Myah?"
"I don't have a clue but I wish I did."

CHAPTER 22

Tracy sat in his new apartment conversing with his agent about his upcoming novel. "It's going to get better reviews. I can feel it." he said with enthusiasm.

"I don't doubt it," his agent agreed.

Tracy smiled, "Man, I did a lot of research but I'll have it ready in about four more months."

Matt picked up his glass of beer and drank down the rest.

"I'll bet your people are really proud of you."

Tracy smiled again, "Yeah, I think they are but I don't want to tell them about this one until I'm finished. It's like no other project I've done. I haven't talked to them in a while. I know I should call, especially since I've moved and all but I just put all of my time and energy into this project."

"Yeah, I know," Matt agreed. "And it's going to be well worth it."

Tracy stretched his arms in the air, working out the kinks.

"I think I might take off next month and go to Detroit. I haven't seen my family in almost two years, do you believe that?" Matt shook his head as he smiled. "I know it's a shame but I'll see them soon. I'll bet my son thinks I've forgotten all about him. I really miss him too." Tracy looked toward the TV where Terrell's picture set. "Maybe you'll get a chance to meet him and his mother soon."

"How old is he?"

"Six and a half."

"I remember when I was six, Tracy. I got whooped every day. My father swears I wasn't happy til' I got smacked for something."

Tracy laughed, "Well, my son has never really gotten into anything. He's a good kid. He's special needs."

"Oh, yeah?"

"He has Down Syndrome. I really should be there with him."

Matt agreed, "Yeah, this is the age he needs you most."

"I know. I think I'll call his mother tonight."

Matt stood up. "Well, I guess I'll hit the road. I've got some more business I have to take care of."

After Matt left, Tracy lied on the sofa and watched TV for a couple of hours. He remembered that he said he would call Shavon but put it off for the next day.

***

Dana closed the door to the empty house.

"Oh, Steve," she said staring at the house. "I've lived here for nearly twenty years. I kind of hate to leave."

"I know but my house is your house. Dana we're going to make some wonderful memories."

Steve kissed Dana's cheek as he put his arm around her. Before they pulled off, Dana took one last look at her house. As they made their way down the road, she remembered Shavon's fourth birthday and her first day of school. She saw a vision of Terrell sitting on the porch playing with his fire truck a year before he died.

"Oh the memories," she murmured as she slowly lost sight of her home.

***

Shavon sat talking with Theresa, another patient.

"I've been here for five months, Theresa, and I don't even belong here. This is just a waste of my life. I could be somewhere starting my career as a fashion designer and I'm locked up in here."

"Me too. I know I've had my down moments but I'm okay now."

Shavon looked at Theresa. She knew how insecure she was. She had heard many times of how Theresa had attempted suicide when things didn't go her way. In the brief time that Shavon had known Theresa, she thought of her as an extremely bright young lady. Shavon felt that Theresa had a lot going for herself and she couldn't understand why she would keep trying to kill herself. Theresa was very pretty. Her eyes were of charcoal black and extremely clear. Her full figure was very well kept and she spoke with the utmost intelligence.

"Tosha's coming up here in a couple of weeks."

"Your little girl?"

"Yeah."

"Is her father bringing her?"

"I don't know. He's still angry with me for jumping out of that window." Shavon studied her fashion magazine.

"Do you have anybody special?"

"No! Who told you to ask me that?"

"Nobody did, Shavon. I just--." Theresa watched Shavon as she jumped from the table and headed for her room. "Gee! It was only a question."

Shavon sat in her room and tried to erase her memory of Tracy as she so often did. I don't ever want to see him again, she reminded herself.

Tracy was right about his book. It was a hit and on its way to being a bestseller. He was thrilled that his dreams were coming true. When he finally composed himself, his first thought was to call Shavon. He knew it had been much too long. He briefly thought of how he had neglected to call as he had said he would months ago. He called her mother's house and found he had the wrong number.

"I could have sworn that was the number." He stood confused as he held the receiver.

Tracy was really excited as he drove up the street. He pulled in the driveway and noticed a strange car in front of the house. He smiled as he knocked. The door slowly began to open. He stared at the white kid who appeared in the doorway. He guessed the kid to be approximately fourteen years of age. *He looks awfully comfortable here*, Tracy thought as he tried to look into the house. The boy kept the door close behind him, careful not to reveal the inside of his new home to a stranger.

"Who are you?" Tracy asked.

"I'm Bill. Who are you?"

"I'm Tracy, Bill. Is Shavon here?"

"Shavon who? Oh, yeah. You must mean the black family that used to live here. Well, they moved some time ago." Tracy's heart jumped.

"Moved? When?"

"It's been nearly four months."

"Four months?" he whispered.

"Yep."

"Thanks." He walked numbly to his car.

Tracy's next stop was his mother's house. He had forgotten his key and no one was there. He went to see his best friend, Darryl.

Tracy sat down on Darryl's sofa.

"Man, where have you been?"

"Here and there, man. I've really been busy." Tracy told Darryl all about his novels and how much he had learned and experienced as a writer.

"Yeah, man. Things have really gone well for me. They really have." Tracy paused momentarily. "But what I wanted to ask you is if you know where I can find Shavon? Her and her family have moved and nobody's at my mother's house.

"No, man. I have no idea. But I'll tell you one thing, Tracy, if you had kept better contact with everyone, you wouldn't be looking for Shavon now. Before now, I hadn't talked to you myself in over three years."

"I know, I know. But man, I finally got my bestseller. It's called Innocent."

"Wow. That's cool. So you gonna hook a brother up?" Tracy laughed.

"Why did I expect that?"

"Well, man if you had kept in touch, I would have bought it as soon as I heard it was out."

"Yeah, but I'll keep in touch from now on."

"So, how long was it after the funeral did they find you?"

"Funeral?" Tracy's heart pumped rapidly. "What funeral?" Darryl sat back in complete surprise.

"Who died?"

"You mean nobody ever reached you? Oh, man."

Darryl's heart fluttered as his speech became stagnant. "Tracy, Terrell died of a heart attack six months ago."

Tracy sat on the edge of the couch in disbelief as he burst into tears. Darryl hated being the one to tell him but he had to know. He hated seeing his closest friend torture himself so.

"Tracy, where were you? Shavon tried everywhere she could think of and so did your mother." Darryl stopped when he realized Tracy hadn't heard a word he was saying. Tracy had begun beating the wall. Darryl tried to calm him but he kept saying how he should have been there and how Terrell needed him.

"How could I have been so self-centered?" he said as he fell to the floor. "It should have been me," he cried. Darryl tried again to console him by telling him that if he had been there, things would have still ended the same for Terrell. Tracy argued that his not being there made all the difference in the world. "I knew I should have been here," he cried. "Now look. My son is dead. You can't excuse my behavior, man. I have been so wrapped up in myself for so long. I never once forgot him, Darryl, I didn't."

"I know, Tracy, I know."

"But, he'll never know," Tracy murmured. There was another downpour of tears. "Why him? Why, Darryl? Why?"

Darryl watched Tracy as he cried like a baby. He had never seen anyone so grief stricken in his life and he didn't know what to say to make things easier.

After Tracy calmed down, he asked about Shavon.

"How is she?"

"I don't know, Tracy. I haven't seen her since the funeral."

"I've gotta find her," he said leaping from the couch. As he went to the door, more tears fell from his puffy eyes. He had never known a pain as deep as losing his son.

"Tracy." Darryl called to him sympathetically. "It's not your fault."

Tracy shook his head showing his gratitude for Darryl's solace.

"But they couldn't find me," he said as he walked gloomily out of the door. Darryl knew his friend was devastated and couldn't help wondering what would happen when he met up with Shavon.

CHAPTER 23

Myah stood there staring Tracy down. He could feel the odium in her stare. She could see how hurt he was from the redness of his face and eyes but it didn't matter.

"I don't believe you! You're not around when you're needed but when you're not needed, you're here with bells on."

"I'm not here to fight with you, Myah. I just need to know where I can find Shavon."

Myah laughed. "Oh and automatically I'm supposed to be subservient to you, huh?"

"Myah, please."

"Don't beg me, Tracy. You'd better beg Shavon for forgiveness."

"Myah, I know I was wrong for not being around like I should have been but you are not my keeper. Keep your degrading remarks to yourself."

Myah laughed again.

"Why are you so smug?"

"Smug? Me?" She smiled.

"Myah, stop playing games! Where is she?"

"Wherever she is, she's not waiting for you. Shavon hasn't mentioned you since Terrell died and she won't let anybody else speak of you."

Tracy felt a chill run down his spine as he let her words sink in. He could only pray that she was exaggerating.

"Are you going to tell me or not?"

Myah took a step away from him.

"And you think you got a negative reception from me. Shavon doesn't want to see you."

"What makes you so sure, Myah? It's not my fault that things happened this way. She wouldn't stop loving me for that. I couldn't prevent it. I wish I could change things, Myah, but I can't," he said sadly. Tracy thought about Myah's attitude toward him. "We're closer than even you could possibly know, Myah."

"Right," she said sarcastically.

"Myah, why are you so bitter?"

"Is that what I am, bitter?"

"Yes, you are."

"If your best friend was in a mental hospital and her so called fiancé could have prevented it, wouldn't you be hurt too!"

***

As Tracy drove to the hospital, he thought of Myah.

"I have hurt so many people," he whispered. He thought of how his mother must have felt. *She's probably hurt and angry with me too*, he thought. "You have been so selfish," he said angrily as he continued to wipe away the tears. "If you had been there, Shavon wouldn't be where she is. Forgive me, Shavon," he whispered as he drew near the hospital.

Tracy's heart dropped as he talked with Shavon's doctor.

"If she sees you, I'm afraid it may trigger a set back or maybe violent behavior. We can't let that happen, Mr. Gaines. The mention of your name upsets her terribly. I'm afraid she has a very strong hatred for you. She seems to be improving though. She has had a few dreams about your son. She says her dreams are sometimes sad. I think she'll soon realize what has happened. And you'll be glad to know that we're watching her very closely. Mr. Gaines, we can help her to deal with reality but we can't change the way she feels about you."

On his way to his mother's house, Tracy thought only of Shavon and Terrell. He remembered the day Terrell was born. He had memories of how happy he and Shavon had been. He now felt as if he had been torn in two. Terrell was lost to him forever and

Shavon was in a mental hospital hating him more each day. He felt like dying.

***

Myah sat in the living room with Dana.

"Maybe I was too hard on him, Ms. Robertson. Oh, I mean Mrs. Thompson. But I can't help feeling like he put Shavon there himself. We all know how she felt about him. She always told me he was her world. I really think if he had been there for her, it would have made her much stronger."

"I don't know, Myah. I wish things had been different too but I can't blame what happened to Shavon on Tracy. She might have been able to handle her adversity if he had been there but it's not his fault she couldn't."

"Maybe you're right," Myah said.

"Why don't you call him? I'm sure he's going to need someone after he talks to the doctor and finds out he can't see Shavon."

"Yeah, maybe I should."

Myah rose from her seat as she smiled at Dana. "Now I know where Shavon gets it." Dana looked at her with confusion. "You really have a kind heart. My mother would have put a contract out on him."

Dana laughed as Myah walked out of the door.

After dinner, Myah called Tracy. She had promised Dana that she would at least try to be civil toward him. Regardless of how she felt for him, he too had lost a son, and deserved some time to grieve.

"Did you see her?" she asked when he answered the phone, skipping over the pleasantries.

"No. The doctor thought it would be best if I didn't. But of course, you already told me that."

"Tracy, I'm sorry I was so ugly with you this morning."

"Don't be. You were absolutely right about everything you said. Myah, I failed her and Terrell." He looked toward the ceiling and sighed.

"Tracy, are you all right?"

"No, I'm not," he said followed by a slight laugh.

"Is your mother there?"

"No. They're all gone. It seems nobody really cares to be around me these days."

"Tracy, have you been drinking?"

"No, I wish I had but that wouldn't help anything."

"Come on, Tracy, stop feeling sorry for yourself."

"I'm not feeling sorry for me. I feel sorry for Terrell and Shavon. I hurt Shavon more than I ever thought possible. I've lost my son. A son I wasn't there for half of his life."

"Tracy, that's all over."

"I wish it were, Myah, but it's not. They needed me and I let them down. I don't think I can live this way. The guilt is so overwhelming. I should be with Terrell."

"Tracy, don't say that. What are you gonna do? Tracy, don't do anything crazy."

"Myah, this may be the best thing I've ever done."

"No, Tracy, don't say that. Shavon's getting better. She'll--"

"She'll only be bitter," he said. Maybe she'll be better off if I'm not here to hurt her anymore. Terrell's dead. Shavon hates me and there's nothing left."

"Tracy, don't do anything. I'm coming right over."

"Don't Myah," he said adamantly.

When Myah arrived, Tracy slowly opened the door.

"Myah, please."

"No! Tracy, I'm not leaving. Let me in!" She caught Tracy off guard and forced the door open. As she looked around, she saw a pistol on the table. She looked back at Tracy.

"Myah, you shouldn't have come."

"Tracy, I think I'm half responsible for the guilt you're feeling and if you kill yourself, I'll never get over that. And besides, Tracy, there are so many people who love you. If you kill yourself, you're killing a part of your family and friends too. And what makes you think you can make things up to Terrell after you kill yourself. How are you gonna reach him from hell?"

Tracy didn't respond as she ranted at him.

"You made one mistake but if you die because of that mistake, you will never be able to make up for it. You'll never get another chance. You can't just give up on life because you hurt a few people. I know it hurts but Tracy, you're stronger than that." Myah began to cry. "Tracy, please don't do this. Shavon is the only one really suffering right now but if you kill yourself, we'll all be hurt." She sniffled. "And who knows, when Shavon gets better, she might want to see you."

"I doubt it," he said despondently.

Myah got the phone book and immediately called suicide prevention. Tracy spoke with one of the counselors for nearly an hour. After he hung up, he talked and cried with Myah until he felt better. He greatly appreciated her help. He never thought he would be crying on her shoulder. Before Myah left, he hugged her and assured her that he wouldn't kill himself.

The next day, Tracy went back to New York.

CHAPTER 24

Shavon continued to improve. She began having more dreams and she was able to remember the bad one's when she awoke. She kept dreaming that Terrell was seriously ill. When Myah came to visit, she no longer asked if she was taking good care of Terrell but she still avoided talking about Tracy.

Two months later, Shavon began discussing what had happened with Terrell in her dreams with her doctor. She still thought he was only ill and she never remembered how the dreams ended. She would sometimes wake up in a panic but she felt it was because Terrell was ill.

On November 3rd, Shavon awoke screaming. Nurses rushed to her room and found her crouched in the middle of her bed. She had not quite awakened from her sleep. One nurse shook her, calling her name, "Shavon, Shavon! It's okay."

When Shavon finally opened her eyes she screamed, "He's dead! He's dead! My baby's gone!"

Shavon was unaware that November 3rd was the same day that Terrell had died exactly one year ago. Nurse Barton held her until she calmed down. She had finally come to the realization of Terrell's death. Again she mourned as if he had just died but this time, she was well aware that he was gone.

After a little over a year of psychiatric care, Shavon was released. She apologized to her parents numerous times for all the trouble she felt she had caused.

After a few weeks she called her former employer at the department store hoping he would let her have her old job back. He welcomed her with open arms. "I was wondering when you would be back," he had said.

Shavon had been back on the job for almost three weeks when her boss, Dave King, called her into his office.

"Is everything okay, Dave?" He gave her a warm smile.

"You're doing just fine. As a matter of fact, you're doing better than I knew you could." Dave pulled a sketchpad from beneath his desk. "Is this yours?"

Shavon looked at the pad with surprise. "Yes! Where did you find it? I lost it a few days ago."

"Someone found it in the lounge and brought it to me."

She was relieved. "I've been looking all over the place for this pad."

"Shavon, I took a look at your designs and I said to myself, now what on Earth is she doing sewing someone else's clothes? You really have a lot of talent. Why didn't you tell me you could do this?"

Shavon shrugged her shoulders. "I don't know. I never really thought about it, I guess."

"Shavon, I showed your designs to our fashion consultant. I hope you don't mind."

"No. No, I don't mind."

"Shavon, she would like to see more of your designs. Is that possible?"

"Sure, I have plenty at home. I can bring them in tomorrow."

"Great! I'll give her a call and set up an appointment for you to see her."

Shavon left the office with a smile on her face. After all the time she had spent in the past writing letters to different companies and waiting for responses, someone right at home was interested in her designs. She was so thrilled she rushed home and called all of her friends and told them about it. Everyone kept their fingers crossed that she would finally get an opportunity to start her career in the direction she had long dreamed of.

Shavon's optimism paid off. Melani took one look at Shavon's designs and offered her a position.

"Do you have any children?"

"No." She answered with deep regret. "Why?"

"I need to know if you're free."

"Free as a bird."

"No husband?"

"No. No one."

"I asked because we have a few locations where we could use you. Now, Shavon, this is a great opportunity for women like you because you haven't begun yet. It's not really a big step up. This job will mostly educate you and prepare you for your own business if you choose to have one. You must understand that you will be designing clothing, among many other designers, under someone else's name. The job pays pretty well and you will learn more working there than you could ever learn in school. There's nothing like the actual experience," she said as she patted her long, well groomed nails on the desktop. Shavon listened with interest.

"We have LA and New York." Shavon swallowed hard when she heard her say New York. Her expression revealed repugnance for New York.

"Do I have a choice?"

"Yes. You do." Shavon sighed with relief. "Or, you can stay right here but the other two locations need someone right now."

Melani could see that Shavon was undecided and offered her some time to think things over. She asked Shavon questions about herself as well as questions about her experience and knowledge of fashion designing. Shavon impressed her with an answer to every question. Before the meeting was over, Melani knew that Shavon had the potential of a great designer. Shavon rose from her seat and shook Melani's hand, thanking her for the wonderful opportunity she had given her.

"You're quite welcome, dear. I hate to see such talent go to waste." Shavon turned and walked toward the door. "Shavon?"

"Yes?"

"Have you ever thought about modeling?"

Shavon smiled pleasantly, "Not interested."

Melani laughed as Shavon walked out the door.

"I'll see you next week!" Melani yelled.

Shavon didn't sleep well for the next few days. All she could think about was what lay ahead for her career. She knew she had wanted this opportunity for such a long time but she found it hard to leave her parents and all of her friends. She reminded herself several times that it might be the best chance she'd ever get. She believed leaving Detroit might be good for her.

Three weeks later, Shavon found herself standing at the gate waiting to board a plane to California. "What am I doing?" she asked herself. 'I could stay here and work for Melani. *But I have a better chance for growth in LA*,' she thought. Shavon finally convinced herself that LA was the best place for her. Deep inside she felt she needed to get away and be alone to help find her way again.

She glanced around the station. "I never thought I'd leave Detroit," she whispered. She was nervous and excited all at the same time. She suddenly felt lonely. She thought of Terrell, "I wish you could be here, Baby. You will always be a part of my life." She smiled at the memory him.

"Do you always talk to yourself like that?"

Shavon quickly turned to the masculine voice behind her and found herself looking at the handsome dark brown face that she had once admired so deeply.

"Jerome Ware! How are you?"

"I'm fine. How are you?"

"I'm just great. What are you doing here, Jerome?"

"I'm going home."

"Home?"

"Yeah. I just came here to visit my parents. I'm living in Los Angeles now."

"Really? That's where I'll be living! I just got a new job there working as a designer and I'm absolutely thrilled about it."

"That's great! Congratulations!"

"Well, what are you doing with yourself these days?"

"I own my own accounting firm in Los Angeles."

"Wow. That's wonderful! I always knew you would do well."

Jerome smiled at Shavon's compliment, "I knew you would too."

For a moment there was silence.

"Well, since you'll be living in LA, maybe we can get together some time?" Jerome suggested.

Shavon could feel herself blushing. "Yeah. Maybe we can."

Jerome switched seats with the passenger next to Shavon. They talked and laughed about old times all the way to LA. She told him about the crush she had on him in high school and he admitted he'd had a crush on her as well.

Shavon's job was going well for her outside of the pressure of not being able to produce as rapidly as she had wanted. She often felt unsure as to how much capability she had as a designer. She would lay awake nights wondering if she had made the right decision.

'Is this really benefiting me?' she often asked herself. But she would always answer yes. She had been disappointed on occasion when her designs were rejected but it only impelled her to greater determination. As the months passed, she learned everything she could to better herself. And with the help of the more experienced employees, she began to realize that panic was her worst enemy. After she learned to relax and take things in stride, things began to fall into place.

CHAPTER 25

As time passed, Shavon and Jerome saw each other more and more. She learned that he and Cynthia had married but divorced because of her ultimate goal to be a high fashion model. Cynthia had gone to Europe completely dedicating herself and made it to the top.

Shavon looked at Jerome and laughed hysterically, "Well, go on big shot."

Jerome smiled sheepishly as he fought to stay on his feet. "I just have to warm up, that's all. Lady, do you know that I haven't been on skates in years?"

"That's not what you said when you were boasting last week about how you would smoke me out of the rink."

Jerome laughed.

"You can laugh if you want to," she said "but if you don't get off of that wall, I'll never let you live this moment down."

"I will."

"You'd better," she said as she laughed and skated away. Shavon skated around a few times then decided to look for Jerome. When she spotted him, he was trying to get up off the floor. She laughed so hard that she could hardly make her way across the floor to help him.

"Give me your hand, silly."

Jerome looked up to find Shavon standing over him with a red face and tears in her eyes.

"Okay, you win," he said laughing. He held his hand out for hers and the next thing he knew, she was on the floor beside him.

"Ouch!" she yelled. They sat for a moment and laughed at each other. Finally, they both had to be helped off the floor.

As Shavon crawled into bed, she reviewed her evening with Jerome. She always enjoyed herself with him but tonight was the most fun she had had in ages it seemed. She thought about her family and friends at home but she was glad to be in LA. She initially thought she could never be alone in another state without them. She missed her family terribly but flew home, sometimes accompanied by Jerome. She promised to keep in close touch and she did.

Shavon truly loved her job at Melani's shop but she began to concentrate on the plans for her own boutique. Jerome encouraged her as much as he could and gave her good management advice that he used to organize his firm. Shavon saw many pleasurable attributes in Jerome and she admired him greatly. He was the utmost assertive and it seemed to have changed her perspective on life for the better. She felt that running into him was the best thing that ever happened to her.

Jerome's family accepted Shavon right away. She felt as comfortable with his family as she did with him. They seemed to be getting closer all the time but she still wasn't sure exactly what she felt.

Shavon worked hard on her plans. Sometimes she would spend late night hours working while Jerome slept on the couch. The more she designed, the better she got. She was completely confident in herself now and knew her time was coming near.

"Hi, Shavon."
"Hello."
"How about lunch?"

"Oh, Jerome. I would love to but I was late this morning and I'm a little behind on my work, so, I think I'll just grab a sandwich or something."

"Well, how about dinner?"

"Okay, I think I can arrange that."

"Shavon, I don't want you to slave over the stove. I would like to take you out for dinner."

"Thanks, Jerome, but if I cook tonight, I won't have to be bothered with it tomorrow."

"Okay, you win. I'll see you around six."

Shavon was so tired that she fell asleep in Jerome's arms as he watched TV. Before he left, he softly kissed her cheek and stood there thinking about how happy she had made him. "I love you, Shavon," he whispered. Jerome left after covering her with a blanket.

The following day, Shavon awoke and found that she had slept on the couch. She called Jerome at work.

"Oh, Jerome, I'm sorry. I didn't mean to fall asleep like that."

"That's okay. I knew how tired you were."

"I'll make it up to you, Jerome. Let's have dinner tonight."

"Okay, but this time I'll be the cook."

"You're on," she agreed.

For the first time since they had begun dating, Jerome cooked dinner. Shavon felt very special. He had gone out of his way to please her. He lit a candle and put on some soft music. Moments later, he put dinner on the table. Shavon took one taste of his steak and nearly burst with laughter.

"Jerome, I'm sorry, but this steak is terrible!"

Jerome frowned first then laughed. "I know it is."

Shavon walked over and gave him a tight hug. "I don't care how bad the dinner is. You have really made me feel good. I want you to know that I appreciate it."

"I know you do." He paused before he continued, "I love you, Shavon."

She held him tighter as she felt her heart beating faster. She hadn't felt that feeling in a long time and she knew what it was. She returned his confession. Tonight was the first time they had ever admitted their true feelings for one another. In the beginning, Shavon was confused but now, her doubt had been replaced with certainty.

Shavon and Jerome stood on their toes in the stand. They both loved sports and they enjoyed cheering for their home team, the Spartans. Shavon couldn't remember the last time she screamed so much. She grew more hoarse as the game progressed but she felt it was well worth it when they won.

"That was a great game, wasn't it?" Shavon shook her head in approval.

"You wanna go over to my place and catch that movie you were talking about?"

Again, Shavon gave a positive nod.

"What's wrong, Shavon? Cat got your tongue?"

She cleared her throat.

"No. The Spartans do," she answered hoarsely.

"And you were a cheerleader once," Jerome teased.

"And--was--of---best."

Jerome laughed as she struggled to get out every other word. "Come on." He squeezed her hand. "When we get to my place, we'll fix you right up. All you need is me and a little lemon, whisky and honey.

As they watched the movie, Shavon noticed Jerome seemed a little reserved and preoccupied. She wondered what was wrong. She had never seen him that way. *I'll ask him tomorrow*, she thought.

The following day Jerome dropped by the shop to see Shavon but she was out on business. He couldn't wait so he left her a message. When she got back, the receptionist handed her the message.

"Thanks, Ann," she mumbled as she walked on.

Shavon sat down as she read the message from Jerome.

Shavon,

I'm sorry but I have to cancel out on the tennis game this afternoon. I'm flying to Detroit. I'll call you later.

Love,

Jerome

All day long Shavon wondered why his trip was so urgent. She went directly home after work and waited for his call. Jerome didn't call that night.

The following day, Shavon tried to find Jerome's parents' phone number but couldn't. "Oh, Jerome, call me," she kept saying. She worried about him throughout the day. "I hope everything is okay. Why won't he call me?" She barely got anything done at the shop. Her mind was on Jerome.

Much to her relief he finally called the following day.

"Hello."

"Hi, Shavon. How are you?"

"I'm fine. How are you?"

"I'm okay but it's not me I'm worried about."

"What's wrong, Jerome?"

"It's my kid brother. He's in a coma."

"Jerome! How? What happened?"

"We don't know, Shavon."

"Well, what is the doctor saying?"

"About the same thing he said last time."

"Last time," she said in surprise.

"He's been in and out of coma's off and on ever since he was 11."

"They don't know why?" she asked.

"No. They just tell us that only time will tell."

"Is the family okay?"

"Yeah, everybody's fine. We thought all that was over. He hasn't had an attack in nearly three years. Everybody's just surprised."

"And you say they can't find anything."

"Not a thing."

"Jerome." She said his name sympathetically.

"All we can do is pray that he'll be all right."

"I know."

After they hung up, Jerome felt better. "She's just so understanding," he had told his mother. "She offered to take some time off to be with us. I don't know what I would do without her."

Three days later, Shavon sat in her apartment as she heard a knock on the door. She looked through the peephole and saw Jerome. She quickly opened the door.

"Hi. What are you doing here? I thought you were in Detroit."

"Come here," he said. He hugged her tightly.

"I missed you," he whispered.

"I missed you too."

"How's your brother doing? Is he better?"

"No. Things haven't changed. He's still in a coma. I decided to come back because I couldn't do anything there but wait and worry. Sometimes he would stay in a coma for nearly a month." She kissed his cheek and softly hugged him.

For the next few days, there had been no change in Jerome's brother's condition. Jerome stayed by the phone when he could, hoping he would receive word that his brother had regained consciousness but the call never came.

Friday morning Shavon sat at her desk waiting for a call from Jerome. She tried calling him at home first, then at his office. After she was told that he wouldn't be in, she knew something was wrong and she went to his house.

Jerome's car was in the driveway. She knocked lightly but there was no answer. She walked around to the side window which was open. The house was quiet and dark but she could tell he was there. She returned to the front door, knocking harder this time and calling out to him.

"Jerome! Jerome, it's Shavon. Let me in. She didn't hear a sound. Jerome, please open the door." Jerome slowly opened the door and walked back inside.

"Jerome, are you okay?" He didn't say a word. He only stared downward. "Jerome, is it Gary?" He looked up with tears in his eyes and she knew Gary had died. Tears fell from her eyes as she put her arms around him. Jerome began to break down and she held him tighter.

"I understand," she whispered. He pulled away.

"Shavon, please. Just go. I need to be by myself."

"No, Jerome. I knew Gary too. It's not only your loss. I know just what you're going through."

"No you don't. He wasn't your brother."

Shavon could see that staying would only makes things worst. "Maybe you're right. I'll be at home. Call if you need me." Shavon turned to Jerome when she reached the door. Jerome only stared downward. He felt so alone. She was well aware of how he was feeling because of her own loss with Terrell but she had never told Jerome about her son.

Shavon worried about Jerome all night. She tried to wait until he called but couldn't.

"Jerome, how do you feel?"

"I'm fine. Just a little tired."

"Did you sleep well?"

"As well as to be expected."

"Have you eaten?"

"Yes, Shavon, I'm fine."

"I love you, Jerome."

"I know," he answered, "Me too."

"Would it be all right if I come over?"

"No, Shavon. I would be terrible company."

"That's okay, Jerome. I want to be with you. I know how you must be feeling."

"Okay," he agreed.

Shavon cooked Jerome's favorite meal to impel him to eat.

"No, thanks. I'm really not hungry." Jerome remained reticent no matter what she talked about.

"So when are the services?"

"The family hour is Tuesday at six and the funeral is Wednesday at ten."

"Does your mother need help with anything?"

"I don't know."

"Well, I'll just give her a call."

Shavon talked to Jerome's mother as he listened. "Okay, well I'm just glad you're okay. I'll see you Tuesday. Bye."

Jerome put his arms around her. "You are really wonderful," he told her. Then he went back to his silence.

"Jerome, talk to me. I hate seeing you this way."

"I don't have anything to talk about. I told you, I wouldn't be good company."

"I know but you're not trying to make things better."

"Shavon, he just died. I can't turn off my grief just like that."

"I know, Babe." She began to rub his shoulders as she remembered how she had reacted when Terrell died. She too had been quiet. And just like her, he had begun sitting in a dark room and she worried that he would end up as she had.

"Jerome, come on. Open up. I'm here to listen to--"

"Shavon."

"Yes."

"How many brothers and sisters do you have?" She dropped her head.

"Well, none but--"

"Shavon, I love you and I thank you for being here. You are really wonderful and I mean that from the bottom of my heart, but you couldn't possibly know what it's like to lose a sibling." He began to cry. "Shavon, he was my youngest brother. He had so much going for him. He was a good kid. You are an only child, you can't sit here and say you know what I feel. You don't know the half of it. I knew this wasn't a good idea."

She began to cry. "I was only trying to help you, Jerome, not hurt you. I'm sorry if I've been a burden but you're wrong about one thing, Jerome."

He reached for her. "I'm sorry, Shavon. You're not a burden. I didn't mean to imply that you are."

She backed up. "Jerome, you have to be strong, you can't let this misfortune take over."

"I'm not."

"Yes, you are, Jerome! I know the symptoms. First, you feel sorry for yourself then you close everybody else out. You sit in dark rooms, you won't talk. Then you'll pretend that things hadn't happened that way." She jumped from the couch and headed for the door as he watched. When she reached the door, she turned to him. "You're not the only one in the world who has lost someone that means the world to them. I've watched you and you have done just as I did two years ago."

He watched with astonishment as she wept and talked. "Terrell was my world and I didn't think I would make it after he died. I wouldn't listen to anybody and it seems you're leaning in that same direction. I had the hardest time accepting it. He was my one and only child."

She was overcome with tears. Shavon leaned against the door crying as he watched. He didn't know what to say. He had no idea that she had encountered such a tragedy. He led her back to the couch where they fell asleep in one another's arms for the remainder of the night.

Shavon took a week off and attended services with Jerome. She was there every step of the way. After a few weeks, everything was getting back to normal for Jerome. He had appreciated her support more than he could tell her. Her support made him fall deeper in love.

Shavon sat on the couch yawning. She stood up and stretched her arms.

"Well, I have a full day ahead tomorrow, Jerome, and you do too. So, why don't we just call it a night?"

Jerome stood up and Shavon's stretch turned into a hug. He broke the embrace. "Shavon, I have something for you."

He pulled out the most beautiful ring she had ever laid eyes on. Four months later, they were married.

CHAPTER 26

Shavon was reading the paper when Jerome came in the kitchen. He tucked his shirt in his pants and leaned over and kissed her on the cheek.

"Hi, Sweetheart," she said pleasantly. "How are you this morning?"

"I'm fine."

"Looks like we're in for a beautiful day."

"I know," he responded.

"I thought if I could get off a little earlier today, we could have a picnic in the park."

"That would be great. I like taking my beautiful wife out in public." Shavon smiled.

"And your beautiful wife loves being seen with her handsome husband."

Jerome leaned over her shoulder. "What are you reading about?"

"Nothing. I was just skimming this fashion article. I'm just trying to figure out how some of these designers come up with these eccentric outfits. I know a good designer uses imagination but I don't know what this designer uses."

He moved closer putting his arms around her neck. "Are you still thinking about opening your own shop?"

"Yeah, I'm still trying to work out the details. I need a catchy name and a good location."

"How do you think they'll react to your leaving, Shavon?"

"They'll be happy for me. I've been there for nearly two years now and everybody knows my own line has always been my dream."

Jerome went to the refrigerator and poured a glass of orange juice. He drank some and left the rest on the table for

Shavon. He leaned over her shoulder again kissing her on the neck.

"Do you know that in four months, we will have been married a year." Shavon smiled brightly revealing her dimples.

"Yes, I know."

"What are we going to do for our anniversary?" he asked.

"Maybe we can take a trip."

"Not a bad idea," he agreed. Jerome looked into the paper as he leaned further over her shoulder.

"Maybe we can go to--"

"Maybe we can what?" Shavon asked.

Jerome stared into the paper. "Is that the same Tracy Gaines I went to school with?"

Shavon's heart jumped to the mention of his name. Jerome began reading the article out loud. *Young, Black, Detroit born writer, Tracy Gaines is now gaining fame in the music business as well as the bookstore. Tracy has thus far been known as an adventure novelist with his current novel (Tracks) fast becoming a bestseller.*

"You remember him, don't you?" Shavon's breath was shallow but she forced herself to speak.

"Yes, he was on the team with you, of course I remember."

She reached for the glass of orange juice setting in front of her. She needed to calm her most obvious nerves as he began reading the rest of the article. Shavon handed him the paper and rose abruptly from her chair spilling the orange juice on the table. Jerome looked at her. She rushed to get paper towel. He watched her as she fumbled nervously.

"It's just orange juice, Shavon."

"I know, I guess my hand slipped."

He continued to read and she left the kitchen. Before he left for work, he went upstairs to find her lying down.

"What's wrong? Are you okay?"

"Yeah, I've got a slight headache but I'm fine, really." She reached for him. He moved closer giving her what she felt was a much needed hug.

"Let's make arrangements to leave work early and go on that picnic I mentioned earlier," she said.

"Okay, Sweetheart, I'll call you later." She held him tightly once again before he left. She found herself wishing he had stayed.

At the office, Shavon began to think of Terrell. The thought of Tracy entered her mind and she forced it away. Her anger toward him had not subsided.

Jerome and Shavon sat watching some children playing at the park as they enjoyed the breeze of summer air.

"You want some more wine?" she asked.

"No, I'm fine, thanks. She leaned over and kissed him.

"Why are you so quiet? Did things go bad at the office today?"

He looked around as if he were searching for words to start up a conversation. "Shavon, it really puzzled me earlier when you acted so nervous. At first I thought you really did have a headache but after I really thought about it, I realized what it was that upset you." Shavon looked away. "I remember someone telling me once that you and Tracy were dating. Is that true?"

She answered slowly. "Yes, we were but that didn't upset me. I did have a --"

"Shavon, was your son Tracy's child?"

Shavon's heart pounded as her palms began to sweat. She looked at him sadly because she knew she had lied.

"Shavon, you said your son's father had died. Why did you feel you had to lie to me?" There was a long moment of silence.

"Jerome, I'm sorry. I didn't want to lie but I had been through so much because of him and I guess I just wished he was dead. He wasn't there for his son before or when he did die. He might not know even now that his son is dead. It still hurts."

"Do you still care for him?" Jerome quickly regretted his question. She looked at him as if she had been slapped.

"No! Are you crazy? How could I care for someone like that?" Jerome gave her a shameful expression.

"Jerome, I love you. I wouldn't even think about another man. You must know how happy I am with you."

Jerome smiled. "I know, Shavon, that was a silly question. Shavon, don't ever think something is too bad or unimportant to tell me."

She grabbed his hand. "I won't, I promise."

Myah listened as Tracy poured out his heart.

"Myah, I have tried to stop thinking about her only because I know she doesn't want to see me anymore but I can't. I have to talk to her. How is she?"

"She's fine."

"She's still in the hospital, right?"

"No."

"What do you mean, no? I thought you were going to call me when she was released. Myah, you promised. I contacted you every few months to find out how she was doing. How could you lie to me like that? The last time I talked to you, she was supposed to be getting worse."

"I thought it was best that I didn't' tell you the truth."

"Did she ask you not to?"

"No. I probably won't see her for a couple of months."

"Why so long?"

"She's not in Detroit anymore. She lives in Los Angeles."

"What's she doing there?"

"She got a job as a fashion designer."

"Wow! That's great! Does she like it?"

"Yep, she's been at Executive Styles for about two years now and she absolutely loves it. She is really happy, Tracy."

"Myah, I have to see her."

"First you wanted to talk to her, now you have to see her."

"I know but I just can't stay away from her any longer. I have fought with myself so many times but I still love her. Can I have her address?"

"Tracy—"

"I know what you're going to say, Myah, but you have to give it to me. I can't give up without a fight."

"Tracy." He dropped his shoulders.

"Myah."

"Tracy, she's married." His eyes widened.

"Married? Married?" His heart sank as he fell back into his seat.

"I'm sorry, Tracy, but she married Jerome Ware a little while back."

Tracy was silent.

"Are you okay?"

"Yes," he answered despondently. He felt like crying and Myah could tell.

"Tracy, are you all right?"

"Damnit, Myah. How could you do this to me? Why didn't you call me?"

"Don't start that, Tracy! You know how she feels about you!"

"I'm just shocked. I guess she really meant it when she said she never wanted to see me again. What should I do, Myah? You're her best friend, you know her."

"Nothing. What can you do?"

"How long has she been married?"

"It was a year last month."

"A year!" Myah knew it was coming.

"Myah, if you had called me, maybe things—"

"Tracy you know that seeing her before she had gotten married wouldn't have made a difference."

"I disagree, Myah!" he yelled. He quickly calmed his tone. "Look, Myah, if I had reached her before she got married, I could have at least let her know how I still feel for her!"

"But, Tracy, she despises you."

He sighed. "Okay, Myah, I'll tell you what. Since you obviously don't want to give me her address, send her a letter for me. Deal?"

Myah hesitated before she responded. "Deal."

A week later, Shavon dialed Myah's number with anger.

"Myah, don't ever send anything here for him!"

"Okay. Calm down! He wanted to send it himself but he knew I wasn't going to give him your address. What did the letter say?"

"I wouldn't know. I didn't open it. I burned it."

"You really hate him, don't you?"

"Yes, I do. I don't feel anything but hatred for him."

"Shavon, he told me he never got your letter about Terrell."

"I don't care. He was still wrong no matter how you look at it. He is so selfish. Oooh, I just hate talking about him. He really irks me."

Myah could see that Shavon remained bitter and from that moment on, she would never mention him again.

Three weeks passed and Tracy had not heard from Shavon. He called Myah to find out if Shavon had received his letter. Myah only told him that she was sorry and that she couldn't do anything to help him. Tracy went through the Yellow Pages trying to jog his memory for the name of the shop Myah had told him Shavon was working for. Finally, it hit him. "*Executive Styles.*" That's it!" he yelled with relief. He made a call to the Los Angeles operator. His heart pounded to the thought of talking with Shavon. He imagined talking with her but it was nothing like the actual conversation.

"Where did you get this number? Did Myah give it to you?"

"No. Shavon, I need to meet with you. We need to talk."

"I don't even know why you're calling here. We don't have anything to talk about."

"Shavon, don't say that. I know you're hurt, I am too but…"

Shavon felt a wave of heat pass through her. "Don't you talk to me about how hurt you are, you don't know how it feels to be hurt! You only know how to hurt people."

"Shavon, I loved Terrell too, you know that. It hurts that I wasn't there for the both of you."

"I'm just sorry that it didn't hurt you enough, Tracy. How can you live with yourself? I can understand your neglecting me but not your flesh and blood son, not Terrell."

Shavon, don't do this."

You've already done it, Tracy!"

He wiped tears from his eyes.

"Shavon, if I could change things, I would. Just give me a chance to straighten things out with us, let's talk about it."

"You lost your chance when Terrell died. And if I were you, I'd stop calling me. You're wasting your time. As far as I'm concerned, you don't exist!"

Tracy didn't sleep that night. He was inclined now to believe that she really hated him but deep inside he refused to believe it. She had to be made to realize that she still loved him. For a week, Tracy thought of nothing but the things Shavon had said. He finally decided he had hurt her enough and that he wouldn't take things any further.

CHAPTER 27

Shavon smiled happily as she looked at her husband. "I'm so happy, Jerome."

"I see. You're glowing."

"Jerome, I have wanted this just about all of my life and now I've got it."

"I know that when you have your grand opening, you're gonna get a good crowd."

"I sure hope so, Honey." She spun herself around. "Oh, I'm so excited."

Jerome picked her up holding her lovingly in his arms. "I love you so much."

Shavon looked at him as if he had said something wrong. Hearing him say it that way reminded her of Tracy. She quickly brushed the thought away. "I love you too," she said with a hug.

Later that night after they had fallen asleep, Jerome was awaken by Shavon's tossing and turning.

"Shavon."

He called to her but she kept moving back and forth. He reached to touch her arm.

"Tracy," she whispered.

Jerome stared at her for a moment then moved back to his side of the bed.

When Shavon awoke the next morning, she found a note on the table.

Sweetheart,
Had to work early. Didn't want to wake you. See you tonight.
Love, Jerome

When Jerome came home, Shavon was finishing dinner.

"Hi," she said with gaiety. She reached for a hug and kiss as he yielded. He was hurt but he could never turn her away. She noticed he was dragging when he came in. "What's wrong? Are you too tired for me today?"

Jerome studied her face. "You are so beautiful."

Shavon wondered why he had such a serious expression on his face.

"Why did you marry me?"

"Don't be silly, Jerome. I married you because I love you. Why did you ask me that?"

"I don't know. I guess a man needs a little reassurance once in a while."

"Well, you can rest assure that you're the only man for me."

Jerome excused himself to get ready for dinner. He felt a little better because of the reception and answer she had given him.

***

Tracy went through a photo album as he sat at the kitchen table. Maria watched him as he became more despondent.

"Tracy, you ain't doin' yourself one bit of good. Why don't you forget about Shavon. She's married now and you just gotta accept it. I'm pretty sure they plan on startin' a family soon. You just wastin' away for a woman you never gon' have."

Tracy took a swig of beer. "Mom, it hurts so deeply."

"I know, Tracy, but--"

"You couldn't know how I feel. I love her more than my own life."

Maria's eyes grew wide. "It's over, boy! You need to accept it! She belong to somebody else now."

"No. She'll never really belong to anybody but me. I've tried to forget her but I can't. I know she still loves me, I know it!"

"Tracy! Don't be no fool! She already done made it clear that she don't want no parts of you." Tracy leaped up from the table.

"Where you goin?" Maria watched him as he packed his clothes. "No woman is worth all that!" she yelled as he walked out of the door.

As soon as Tracy arrived in Los Angeles, he went to *Executive Styles* to see Shavon. He was disappointed to find that she no longer worked there. He convinced the secretary that he was a relative and she told him about Shavon's fashion shop. For the rest of the week, he watched her as she closed the shop. He knew it was crazy to watch her but in his mind, he had no other alternative. She would never see him willingly.

His heart was filled with joy knowing she had put her dream in motion. The neon sign in the window read "*Shavon's Fashions*." He was so proud of her. He only hoped she would see that they could share the happiness of fulfilling both their dreams. He began to ponder the thought of following her home but quickly dismissed it.

Shavon was aware that Jerome had become somewhat distant. He seemed to stay more to himself. Most of the time he seemed happy but other times it seemed as if something was bothering him. She tried her best to reassure him that she truly loved him but it seemed he had become insecure about their marriage.

Shavon put her hands to her hips as she looked around the shop.

"I think I want something really exotic in this window. You know-- something that will reach out and grab people. I think I might use this royal blue sequin dress. What do you think, Delsey?"

"I agree. I bet that dress will be one of your best selling items. I think you should also feature that dress in your fashion show next month."

Shavon smiled as she glanced at Delsey. "How would you like to model it?"

"Shavon, be serious! I'm too big to model."

"If you haven't noticed, Delsey, we also have sizes 12 through 22."

"You really want me to be one of your models?"

Shavon put her arm on Delsey's shoulder. "I asked you, didn't I? Delsey, don't feel so negative about who you are."

"I don't, she said with laughter. "I really don't." Delsey looked out of the window. "He's nice looking."

Shavon looked up. "Who is?"

"That man who just passed the store. But you're' not interested, you're married."

Shavon laughed. "Yep and very satisfied with my husband. But, you Delsey, that's another story. You're what, about 18 now? And the last I heard, you weren't seeing anyone steadily. You can take your break now if you like. You might be able to get a better view."

Delsey laughed. "No, that's okay. He probably wouldn't like me anyway."

"Why do you say that?"

"He's kinda tall."

"So, what does that mean?"

"Shavon, you're not that old. Don't you know that tall men don't like short, not so small women?"

"Don't be ridiculous, Delsey; sure they do. And you're right, I'm not that old. I'm pushing 26 but I haven't quite reached it."

Shavon began setting up the display.

"Delsey, get that blue dress for me, please." Shavon ran her hand through a box of jewelry as she waited for Delsey. Yeah, I think this pearl necklace would be perfect with this dress." She held the pearls up to the mannequin. "Perfect," she whispered.

"They would look better on you." She jumped to the familiarity of the voice that had just spoken. She took one look at Tracy and began to sweat. She hadn't seen him in nearly five years and he was still as breathtaking as she remembered.

"Shavon, I had to see you."

Shavon stared in silence for a moment. "Tracy! I told you to leave me alone!" She tried to keep her voice down. "Please, go!"

"Not until we talk, Shavon."

"I told you we didn't--"

"Shavon, I know I was wrong for turning away from you and Terrell and everybody else, I know that now. I had a goal set and I was fool enough to let it take over. I've missed Terrell terribly but I don't know how to make up for that. Shavon, I have really suffered being without him and I still love you. I have tried to forget you but I can't. You're a part of me. I need you, please forgive me."

"You want me to forgive you? You've got a lot of nerve, you know that. You come in here like I should hear you out, as if I owe you something. Well, you owe me a debt you could never pay. Don't you dare come in here telling me how you love me! You're incapable of that and you've proven it! Where were you when Terrell was on his death bed asking for you? You didn't even care enough to call once in a while to make sure we were okay. I kept telling him you would be there soon. You only cared about yourself."

Tracy watched her as she became more and more emotional. All he could do was listen. He felt a thickness in his throat and he couldn't talk or swallow. She was yelling at him now. Delsey stood on the side watching as the customers were doing. She couldn't believe what she was hearing from Shavon. She had never seen her in such a fit of rage.

"My son needed a man and a father. Obviously you couldn't be either! I expect what you've done only from a teenager. I have learned, Tracy, and I have learned a hell of a lot from you. I'm not that young inexperienced girl who lacked fortitude that you used to know. I have gone through hell because of you and I'll hate you forever!" Shavon stared at him with eyes full of pain and anger. He reached for her arm. "Don't you dare touch me!"

"Shavon, I'm sorry I hurt you this way."

She quickly pulled away turning to Delsey who stared at the scene with her mouth hanging open. "Delsey, call the police, now!"

"That's not necessary; I'm leaving," Tracy said sadly.

***

Shavon explained to Jerome what had happened at the store. She was shaking when she told him.

"Okay, Shavon, I'm here. It's okay." Jerome held her until she calmed down. He couldn't help but wonder why she allowed Tracy to get to her that way when she didn't love him anymore. For the rest of the evening, Shavon lay on the couch staring numbly at the TV set.

"Shavon, let's go to bed." She stood up and held her hand out for Jerome's.

"I'm sorry, Jerome. I guess I've been a little out of it."

He took her hand leading her to the bedroom. After she undressed, she climbed into bed and turned her back to Jerome. He put his arms around her and began to kiss her. She slowly turned to him and responded to his passionate kiss. Suddenly, she broke their embrace.

"What's wrong, Shavon?"

"Jerome, I'm not in the mood."

Jerome turned over pulling the sheets over his shoulder. She touched him sympathetically.

"Jerome, I'm just upset about that incident with Tracy today, that's all. It's not you, Sweetheart."

Jerome held his breath before he spoke. "Don't you see it's hurting me too, Shavon?"

She sat up in the bed. "What's hurting you, Jerome?"

"If it were Tracy here tonight instead of me, would you make love to him?"

"Jerome! How could you say that?"

"Shavon, you have thought about him all day long. You say you don't love him but you bring him to bed with us."

"Jerome, you know how I feel about him. I've told you how I abhor his existence."

"Well, if you hate him so much, why does he get to you this way?"

"Jerome, another life was involved here. His son was asking for him on his death bed. You expect me not to feel pain from the memories he induced, the pain from losing my son!"

"Shavon, he would have died if Tracy had been there! It's not his fault Terrell died. Stop blaming him for that!"

"Don't you tell me not to blame him. You seem to be defending him."

"No, I'm not defending him but I think you're wrong for blaming him for that."

"But I'm not! It's just that Terrell was everything to me and he was hurt by his own father before he died. Jerome, I know he didn't kill Terrell himself but I still can't forgive him for not being there." Jerome got out of bed.

"Shavon, I know you still feel something for him. I have never seen you so shaken by anything, and I'm your husband."

"Jerome, are you implying that I still love him?"

"Shavon, you need to ask yourself one question. Are you angry with him for not being there for Terrell, or for you?"

Jerome stared at her for a moment then left the room.

That night Shavon slept alone. She was angry with Jerome for defending Tracy and walking out, but she wished they hadn't argued. The last thing she wanted to do was hurt him.

For the next three days, Shavon and Jerome hardly said anything to each other. They tried to make small talk but didn't get into any worthwhile conversations. By the end of the week, things were beginning to get back to normal. They had begun to have laughs and conversation again.

CHAPTER 28

Jerome and Shavon sat in the living room playing checkers. Jerome had five checkers remaining and Shavon had four.

"It's your turn, Shavon."

"I know that."

"Well, what's taking you so long? Should I get my pillow?"

"Let me do it my way, Jerome." Shavon made her move. Jerome moved taking one of her checkers. Shavon smiled and looked down at the board. "I don't know about the pillow but you might need a drink." Shavon moved across the board taking his remaining checkers.

"I don't believe it! No woman has ever beaten me. I don't believe I didn't see it coming."

"If you had kept your big mouth shut, you probably would have." Shavon laughed.

"I put my foot in it again, didn't I?"

"Pardon me?"

"Shavon, I said some things a few days ago that I never should have said. I wanted you to know that I was sorry about starting that argument. If you still loved Tracy, you wouldn't be here with me. I want you to know that I really believe that. I guess I was just a little jealous and I shouldn't have acted that way."

"I don't know that this argument was your fault, Jerome. You were right. I shouldn't have let him get to me the way I did."

"I don't know, Shavon. I guess I just found it really incredulous at the time."

"What?"

"I have never heard you say a mean thing about anyone but when it comes to him, it's just unbelievable. I have never seen anyone hate someone so much after loving them the way I know you two loved each other." He looked at her sympathetically. "I guess if I had been in your shoes, I would probably feel the same way." Jerome smiled as he thought of how silly he felt he had been. *You know she loves you and there is no reason whatsoever to question her love for you*, he thought.

"Hey, let's take the next week off and go to San Juan Island. I've never been there, have you?" he asked.

"No, can't say that I have."

"Well, let's go! You need a break. Let the girls run the shop for a while. It'll be good for them."

"Yeah, but will it be good for me to leave them alone?" she asked with laughter.

"You don't think they can handle it?"

"I don't know."

"Well, what about Debra? She's the eldest, right. She seems to be well organized and very capable of handling things for a week."

"I don't know, Jerome."

"Shavon don't worry, I've seen those girls working. Your shop will be in good hands. Do you think you can swing a week?"

"Do I have a choice," she responded.

"No."

"Then a week it is."

Jerome felt that getting Shavon away for a while would relax her mind and bring them closer together, which was something he felt a desperate need for. Once they were in Washington, Jerome felt closer to his wife. The Island of San Juan was spectacular. They enjoyed it immensely. They stayed at a romantic cottage and enjoyed the hot tub and massages to help them relax. They took the ferry to town to shop and enjoy a little sightseeing. They hated to leave but Saturday afternoon, they were home again.

Shavon stood in the mirror trying to decide which shade of blush she should wear. Jerome walked in with a towel around his waist. He leaned over her shoulder and kissed her on the neck.

"What shade would look best, Honey? Should I wear this plumb or the rose colored blush?"

"What are you wearing?"

"I'm wearing that two piece fuchsia pant suit."

Jerome frowned as he tried to remember.

"You know, the one you saw me making last week. The striped fuchsia and pink one you said you liked.

"Oh! Now I remember. I would definitely say the rose blush. It would go better with your complexion as well as your outfit."

"Hey, I didn't know you paid that much attention to things like that."

"Only when it concerns you, my dear."

"Jerome, I want everything to be perfect for my first fashion show."

"Don't worry. I have all the confidence in the world in you and your designs."

"Thanks, Sweetheart." She began to apply her blush. "I'm a little bit nervous about being the commentator but it would have been foolish to hire someone to do it. I think I would be the best commentator for my own designs."

"I agree." Jerome responded.

Shavon looked in her jewelry box. "Have you seen my pink beads, Jerome?"

"No, I haven't," he said as he laid out his suit. "I'll bet they're right in front of your face like those shoes you were looking for last week."

"You think so, huh," she said.

"Yep, and I'll bet I can find them."

"Help yourself," she responded.

Jerome tripped over the phone cord as he picked up the jewelry box. He tried to catch it but it fell to the floor. Shavon looked at him with a sarcastic expression.

"You klutz." He laughed.

"I'll bet if they were in there, they're probably in pieces now, she said."

Jerome spotted a diamond ring as he picked up the jewelry.

"Where did you get this? I've never seen it."

She turned around recognizing the ring immediately.

"Oh, I've had that ring for years."

"Oh, yeah. It's a nice ring. Why don't you ever wear it? Actually, it looks like an engagement ring."

Shavon turned back toward the mirror. "Tracy gave it to me."

Jerome continued picking up the jewelry. She could see that the mention of Tracy's name bothered him. She didn't want to say another word. She just wanted the moment to pass as quickly as possible.

The fashion show was successful. It proved that Shavon's shop would have a very lucrative future.

"You were really great as a commentator."

"Thanks. Having you in the audience for support did wonders for me." She sighed.

"Didn't Delsey look beautiful in that royal blue sequin dress?"

"Yes. She was absolutely stunning."

Shavon relaxed her head against Jerome's chest.

"Shavon."

"Yes, my love."

"Let's have a baby."

Shavon felt her heart drop. "Now?"

"Why not? We've been married over a year and I think it's time we had a family."

"Jerome, we don't have time right now. I'm just getting started with my career. Let's give it some time, at least two years."

"Two years!"

"Yes, why not?"

"Shavon, are you afraid to have children?"

"I must admit, it does make me a little nervous but that's not my reason for not wanting any now."

"Shavon, if we wait much longer our child is going to be born with dust on his head. We're not that young anymore."

"Listen, Honey, I really do want to establish my career first, yours is already established. I think I deserve the same."

He drew a deep breath. "You're right." He rubbed her shoulders. Jerome didn't want to admit it but the mention of Tracy's name surfaced his insecurity.

As they climbed in bed, Jerome pulled her next to him. He didn't want to start an argument but he had concealed his feelings all day and he was curious about something.

"Shavon."

"Yes."

"Why did you keep Tracy's ring?"

"I don't know. I guess I just forgot about it. If it bothers you, I'll get rid of it in the morning."

"No, don't do it on my account."

"No, really, Jerome, I will. I don't see why I should keep another man's ring."

'*Me either*,' he thought but dared not to say it out loud.

The following day, she went through her jewelry box for the engagement ring she had gotten from Tracy. She slowly slipped the ring on her finger momentarily and took it off. She was on her way out of the door when she had a memory of the day Tracy had given it to her. "I love you. Don't ever take it off," she heard him say. "What are you doing?" she whispered. She dropped the ring in her purse and went to work.

Shavon stood at the top of the stairs combing her hair.

"Come on, Shavon, move your car. I'm really in a rush. I don't want to be late for the meeting."

"Well, if you can't wait one more minute, you can move it for me. My keys are in my purse on the living room table." Jerome reached in her purse and found everything except the keys.

"I'm dumping your purse," he yelled.

As she ran down the stairs, he was dumping her purse. She quickly remembered the ring. She had not gotten rid of it as she said she would.

"Let me get them," she said trying to keep him from spotting the ring. It was too late. Jerome's eyes were fixed on the diamond ring she so willingly said she would get rid of the month before. She quickly grabbed the ring along with some Kleenex and threw it in her purse.

"Here we are," she said as she sprang from the couch. "Come on if you're still in a rush." Jerome followed her out of the door.

Shavon sat in the back office wondering if Jerome had seen the ring. She finally convinced herself that he hadn't.

A week passed before Jerome decided he couldn't take it anymore. He sat across the dinner table with a long face.

"And, Honey, things are really going well as far as my sales are concerned. I'm glad my husband is an accountant," she said with laughter.

"So, how have things been at your office? You haven't said anything lately."

"Well, something else has been on my mind."

"Oh, yeah. And what might that be?"

"I'm really trying to understand, Shavon, I really am."

"What's wrong?"

"Why did you try to hide the ring from me?"

She sighed. "I just didn't want you to be angry. I didn't want to argue."

"Well, did the thought ever occur to you that it would hurt me more if I found out you were hiding it?"

"No," she answered softly. "I really didn't think about that."

"Why do you still have it anyway?"

"Well, I intended to take it to the pawn shop but I guess it slipped my mind."

"You guess?"

"Jerome, I know how it might look but it's not what you're thinking."

"Well, what is it?" She didn't have an answer. "Is there some sentimental reason you can't get rid of it?"

"No, Jerome. There are no sentimental feelings about that ring. Come on, Sweetheart."

Jerome looked in her eyes then walked out of the house. She didn't try to stop him because she knew she couldn't convince him of anything different than what he already believed.

He needed to get out of the house and away from Shavon. He needed some time to think. He drove downtown to a small bar in Greektown where some of his buddies hung out after work.

Jerome sat at the bar with one of his closest friends and talked nonstop for hours about Shavon.

"Robert, I don't know what else to do. I love her so much and she loves me too but she is still in love with Tracy. I don't care how she tries to mask it the end result is the same. She is the most beautiful woman I've ever met, inside and out but I don't know if I should go on with a marriage I feel so insecure in. I keep having dreams that he walks into our bedroom, holds his hand out for her and she leaves with him. Man, you don't know how much it hurts to have a wife you don't really have. The worst part about it is that she doesn't even realize that she still loves him. She thinks she hates him. I only wish she did. She is really bitter now but sooner or later that bitterness will subside and I'm afraid that one day she'll realize that she really does love him. I've tried everything to make her fall deeper in love with me and every time I think she has, something happens. We can't relocate. He found her once and he'll do it again."

"Well, what about kids, Jerome? If you two have a child, she would probably feel obligated. You know, just like we do. I'll bet she wouldn't leave you then."

"I don't believe you just said that, Robert. That's the most ridiculous thing I've ever heard."

Robert threw his hands in the air.

"Besides, I already tried that," Jerome said sadly. "That's really not the way to go. If I can't have her willingly, I'll set her free."

"But look, Jerome, you're overlooking one important thing."

"What's that?"

"You can't hold what Cynthia did against Shavon. I believe you can trust Shavon."

"I know," he mumbled remembering Cynthia's brief period of infidelity. "I've thought about that over and over. I want to believe I can but that still doesn't explain why she would hold on to that ring. Obviously he made her a whole lot happier once."

"Well, you do what you like, Jerome, but I would never give up on a woman if I had feelings as strong as yours. I wouldn't give up unless she wanted me to."

As Jerome drove home, he thought a lot about Robert's last statement. The only bright side to the whole situation was he knew that Shavon really loved him. But lately he was unsure of just how much.

Shavon lay in bed wondering why she didn't have an answer to her husband's question. She wasn't sure of why she still had the ring. "You can't still love him," she whispered. She thought of Terrell. "No. I only have hatred for him," she told herself.

She jumped at the sound of his keys in the front door. She sat up as Jerome walked into the bedroom. She looked at him with a sad expression. She could only say what was on her mind.

"I love you so much, Jerome."

He went to her side and embraced her.

"I love you too, Shavon."

Shavon made love to him like never before.

"I totally forgot about the ring but I can't let it be the cause of problems for us, you mean too much to me for that. I promise I'll get rid of the ring first thing in the morning."

Jerome felt good lying in her arms, but didn't say very much for the rest of the night. Her promise did little if anything at all. He held his wife all night but he still believed there was more to it than she knew herself. He wondered what she would do when she came to terms with her true feelings.

For the next three weeks Jerome was thoroughly satisfied with the way things were going with him and Shavon.

Jerome came home for lunch on Friday. He was in a good mood. He took the paper and mail out of the mailbox and dropped it on the table. He began reading it as he waited for Shavon. He looked at his watch. It was 11:16 a.m. and Shavon wasn't there yet. Just as he was about to call her, the phone rang.

"Hi. You're supposed to be here."

"I know. I'm running a little late. I'll be there in ten minutes."

"Well, hurry up, I'm hungry."

"Well, read the paper to keep yourself occupied until I get there."

"I already did."

"Well, keep reading it, or read a magazine, the mail, I don't know. Find something to do until I get there."

"Okay, okay. Ten minutes, Shavon."

"Ten minutes."

Jerome had begun sorting the mail when he saw a handwritten envelope addressed to Shavon. He put it back on the table. *Maybe it's personal*, he thought. He picked it up again thinking it might be Myah's handwriting. The envelope didn't have a return address so he banished the thought of it being from Myah. Besides, Shavon had talked to her a couple of days ago. Jerome opened the letter.

Dear Shavon,
I'm truly sorry for what I did to you over the years and I wanted you to know exactly how I feel. I have written my deepest feelings, especially for you. And as I have said before, I still love you.

Tracy

I woke up in the night again with sweat upon my face
It seemed so real but as I reached, I found there was no trace.
I can't erase the wrong I've done or pain that I've bestowed.
Success had gotten hold of me. I let it take control.
I think of little Terrell and where I should have been.
I've prayed that God would bring him back to let me start again.
And, Shavon, I know the wound is deep. I share the hurt you feel.
I've often held him in my dreams but know I never will.
I think of you so often, Shavon, no matter what I do.
Sometimes I just break down and cry. I can't get over you.
I can't go on are remembering our love the way it was.
I'll die before my heart accepts your unrequited love.

Jerome slowly took his eyes off the letter as Shavon walked in. She immediately detected a disappointed expression on his face.

"What? I'm not that late!"

Jerome put his hand to his forehead as he often did when he was aggravated about something. Shavon could see that he was serious about whatever it was bothering him.

"Honey, what is it?"

"Have you ever denoted to Tracy that there might be a chance that you still have feelings for him?"

Shavon frowned, "Oh, Jerome, I thought we were through with that."

"I was but obviously somebody else isn't."

"What are you trying to say? I haven't seen him since that day at the shop. What brought this on?"

Jerome dropped the letter on the table. "Here. I believe this was meant for your eyes only."

Shavon looked at the letter then back at Jerome.

"Go on, read it," he demanded. Shavon read it half way then dropped in a chair. "Jerome, I don't know what to say."

"Don't say anything--Tracy already said it."

"Jerome, these are his feelings, not mine. You can't hold that against me."

"Tell me something, Shavon. Did you let your address slip when you were giving him a piece of your mind?"

"No! I don't believe you, Jerome. Why are you doing this? You know I love you. You're my husband and I would never do anything behind your back like that. I married you because I love you, not because I was on the rebound. My love for you hasn't changed! Jerome, I don't know how he got our address but I do know it's not hard to get. Don't you trust me?"

"Shavon, I have fought with this for a long time now. I think you are still in love with him. Every time I convince myself that you're not, something happens to convince me that you are."

"What! That's ludicrous!"

"No, Shavon, it's not. He gets to you more than anyone else can."

Shavon stood there shaking her head in disbelief.

"A few months ago I felt as if he were in bed with us." Her eyes widened with confusion. "Shavon, you even call his name in your sleep. Did you know that?"

Shavon stared at him in disbelief.

"Why would I do that?"

"Why would I lie?" She dropped her head.

"Shavon, I love you but I'm beginning to think I'm in love with another man's woman." Tears came to her eyes as she thought of all the tragedy she had encountered in her life, and now Jerome.

"I do love you. You have to believe that, Jerome."

"I do," he said softly.

"But I think you still love Tracy and I don't think I can continue to contend with that." He gave a short laugh. "Imagine my wife being pulled in two directions. Shavon, it might hurt me more to be with you than without."

"Jerome, that's not true. We can't let him come between us, we're happy together. We have too much to throw away just like that."

"Yes, we do. But I can't keep wondering when you're going to be honest with yourself and admit you love him. Where will I be then?"

"Jerome. I hate him, I swear I do. Why won't you believe me?"

"Shavon, I've seen this situation before and I know I'm right. I couldn't possibly win. I think Tracy has been your one true love and if you really love him, you'll eventually be with him."

"What are you telling me? I don't want to split up. I couldn't bear to be without you."

Jerome drew a deep breath, "I don't want to be without you either, but I think you need time to sort your feelings out and I'm willing to give you that time."

"You want to separate?"

"I think it's best for now, Shavon. I can't lie next to you anymore wondering if you want me or another man. I want you to work it out yourself. If you find that you are over Tracy, without a doubt, then we'll talk about my coming back home."

The next day Jerome packed some of his things and moved out.

"I'm taking what I know I'll be using right now. I hope you won't mind my leaving the gun. I know you probably won't be using it," he said trying to break the monotony. He knew she had always been uncomfortable with a gun in the house. Shavon turned away from him.

"Where will you be?"

"I'll get a room at a motel for now but next week, I'm going to look for something more livable."

She turned to him, "Jerome, don't do this. You're wrong about this!"

He dropped his head, "I'll call you, Shavon." Walking out on Shavon was the hardest thing Jerome ever had to do but in his heart he knew it was the right thing to do.

Shavon barely slept that night. All she could think of was how she lost the son that Tracy greatly disappointed and now there was a chance she might lose her husband; all due to Tracy.

Shavon concentrated on painful memories of Tracy to reinforce her hatred and anger toward him. She thought of how she and Jerome had been happily married for over a year and now Tracy had managed to split them up.

Chapter 29

Tracy sat in a motel room thinking about Shavon. He called his mother's house thinking Shavon might try and contact him but there was no message. Finally, he decided to go to her. He thought carefully about what he would say. He had planned to tell her he loved her dearly but if it meant hurting her anymore, he would stay out of her life permanently. That was the last thing he ever thought he would do but it was time to face the fact.

Shavon poured a glass of milk and opened a bottle of sleeping pills. She took an extra pill for quicker results. She was an emotional wreck, and she dreaded another night without Jerome. She moped around for twenty minutes before she dropped off to sleep. She began dreaming. She could see Terrell Ray in the hospital with tears in his eyes calling Tracy.

"Daddy-Daddy, I need you."

Shavon watched as Tracy turned his back. She could see him signing autographs as his secretary called to him.

"Shavon's on the phone. She says your son is sick and he needs you, Mr. Gaines."

She could see him brushing her off.

"Tell her I'll call her later."

She began crying in her sleep.

When Tracy arrived at Shavon's house, he could see that Jerome's car wasn't there. Perfect, he thought. He felt nervous as he walked toward the door. As he proceeded to knock, he heard a scream.

"No! No! Don't turn your back on us!"

Again, she had a flash of him turning his back.

"No!" Her scream echoed throughout the house.

"Shavon!" he yelled. Tracy broke a small window near the door but he still couldn't reach the knob. He quickly remembered the file on his key ring. He put the file in the door and was in the house in a matter of seconds.

"Shavon!"

Shavon awoke feeling half drugged from the sleeping pills she had taken. She heard a voice and she knew it wasn't Jerome's. *Who was it?* Still dazed, she fumbled to find the gun. She found the gun and held it tightly in one hand while reaching for the lamp with the other. Her eyes were unfocused.

"Shavon, it's me, Tracy. You screamed. Are you all right?"

Tracy couldn't see the gun in her hand.

"Please don't be angry. I just want to talk to you, that's all. You've got to hear me out."

She paid no attention to what the intruder was saying. She found the switch on the lamp and turned it on. The lamp tumbled to the floor. She could see the shadow of a man with the familiarity of Tracy. She didn't know if she was dreaming or if it was real.

"Shavon, it's me, Tracy." Tracy could see the gun clearly now. "Shavon, it's me. Put the gun down."

She felt the anger from her dream and screamed, "No! Get out of here! I hate you! I hate you! How could you hurt my baby like that? How could you?" She crawled to the left corner of the bed, "Somebody get him away from me!"

"Shavon put the gun down. It's Tracy, Shavon." Tracy took two steps forward. She cocked the gun. "Don't Shavon!"

She could feel her finger slipping on the trigger. It was all happening so quickly. She could see the intruder raising his hands as she saw his lips move. She could only hear the sound of the monitor the day Terrell died. She lost control and pulled the trigger. She watched as he fell to the floor while she screamed repeatedly. There was no movement as she stared at the seemingly lifeless body which lay before her. She dropped the gun and moved closer. Suddenly, it all seemed so real.

"Oh, my God! Oh my God! Tracy? Tracy? This is not real," she reiterated. She looked at the gun and began to shake. She stumbled to his side. "Tracy, I'm sorry. I'm so sorry. I didn't mean to. I've got to get help!"

She called for help and rushed back to his side where she cried as she held him in her arms. Her gown was covered with blood as she held him.

CHAPTER 30

Shavon sat in the waiting room in a panic as she prayed over and over for Tracy's life. She cried herself to sleep as she waited for the doctor. She jumped when the doctor touched her. Her eyes grew with fright and she couldn't speak.

"Hello, Mrs. Gaines, I'm Dr. Green. Your husband made it through the surgery but his condition is critical. We were able to remove the bullet from his abdomen. Tears ran down her face. "You can rest assure, Mrs. Gaines, that we are doing everything we can. Your husband is in very good hands."

"Can I see him doctor."

"Yes, you can look in on him but the anesthesia hasn't worn off yet. He'll be asleep for several more hours.

Shavon dreaded calling Maria but it had to be done. She only told her that Tracy was shot accidentally and his condition was critical. She gave Maria the information she needed. Maria couldn't get a flight until that afternoon. Shavon was exhausted. She slept sound the rest of the morning, and once again cried herself to sleep.

Shavon was at the hospital by noon. Tracy remained in the ICU in stable but critical condition. She said a silent prayer of thanks for his life. Shavon knew she shouldn't see Tracy while he was awake. So she looked in on him as he slept. "What have I done," she whispered. She couldn't help but wonder what if anything he was dreaming about. She thought back to their first date.

She stared at the screen while Tracy watched her profile. Oh, God, he's staring at me. I wish he would just watch the movie, she thought. She remembered he had slowly slid his arm over her shoulder and she became more nervous. She smiled at her thoughts and once again focused on Tracy as he lay there. She drifted again. "So, how did you like the movie?" he asked. She remembered his smile as he pulled his arm back. He knew he had made her uncomfortable. "Do you feel better now?" he had asked. "I won't hurt you. When you're with me, you're in good hands." "That's not what I heard, she remembered saying with laughter.

It hurt to see him lying there by her hand. "I'm sorry," she whispered as tears dropped from her eyes. *Look what I've done to you,* she thought. *No matter what you did, I never wanted this to happen*. She turned to leave. When she got to the door, she took one last look before leaving.

"Myah, what flight did you say you were taking?"

"I'm coming on the eight p.m. flight. That's the earliest one I can take. How is he?"

"He seems to be hanging in there. I saw him this afternoon."

"What did he say?"

"He was asleep."

"Shavon, Tracy knows how you feel about him and it's no secret to the rest of us either. I'm only going to ask you once. Was it really an accident?"

"I don't need to hear this from you, Myah. What I need right now is consolation from a friend. I mean, what if he--"

"Shavon, stop it. Don't ask for trouble. He's still breathing isn't he?"

"Myah, please."

"Well."

"Myah, I'm not sure what happened last night. Maybe by the time you and mama get here, my head will be clear."

Shavon returned to her empty house. She walked into her bedroom and saw Tracy's blood on the floor. She leaned against the wall. "God, help us," she pleaded. She mopped the floor then took a long hot bath to soothe her nerves. The phone rang many times but she didn't feel up to talking to anyone. The girls at the shop had been calling all day so she checked in with them. After bathing, Shavon unplugged her bedroom phone and fell into a deep sleep.

At 4:30 p.m., she awoke to noises outside. "Tracy." She remembered what had happened. It still seemed like a bad dream. She rose quickly, got dressed and headed to the hospital. She was afraid of him seeing her, but she had to know if he was all right.

When Shavon approached the ICU, she saw Maria crying in the corridor. She stopped in her tracks. She feared Tracy had taken a turn for the worst. Tears filled her eyes as she watched. Neicy came out of the room shaking her head. Shavon couldn't move any closer. Maria spotted her as she looked up the hall.

"What you doin' here?"

"Is he all right?"

"What do you care? Why did you come here, to finish the job?" Neicy yelled. Neicy had never been so angry in all her life. "How could you do this? You knew how much he loved you." Neicy ran toward her and knocked her against the wall and began hitting her. Shavon felt the punches but didn't bother to defend herself. She understood Neicy's feeling of hatred toward her.

"Mama was right about you all along. How could I have been so stupid? Look at him. Look at him! He's suffering now because he loved you. You are the most unworthy person of his love in this world. He regrets ever meeting you!"

Neicy reached for Shavon's arm and pushed her toward the door.

Tracy stared at the ceiling never acknowledging her presence.

"What's wrong with him?"

Neicy closed her eyes tightly as she balled her fists. "Mama, get her out of here before I kill her."

Maria stared at Shavon with hatred in her eyes. "I hope you're happy now," she whispered.

Shavon went to the desk and asked for Tracy's doctor. After a briefing of his condition Shavon sat in the visitor's lounge thinking about what the doctor had said.

"After he heals, it's highly possible that he won't ever walk again. That's not to say for sure, but things don't look good for him." The doctor paused a moment before he continued. "I really shouldn't share this information with you. I understand you're not his wife and in fact, you're the person who shot him." Shavon dropped her head in her hands. "I only shared that with you because I also heard he broke in your house. Unfortunately, I am unable to talk with you any further."

Shavon nodded with understanding. She was experiencing more emotions at one time than she ever thought possible.

When she got home, Dana was waiting at the door. She looked at her mother for a moment then embraced her. Once inside, Dana sat nervously on the sofa. She had no idea where she should begin. She didn't know what state of mind her daughter was in. Shavon caught her mother's eye. She knew she should explain but before she got a chance Dana began.

"Honey, it was an accident. I would shoot to kill if someone broke in my house too. Anybody in their right mind would. There was no way you could have known it was him. You said it was dark in the room, right?"

Shavon put her hand over her eyes. Dana went to her side and hugged her. "Let's just hope the worst is over."

Shavon expressed no relief from her mother's comment. "How did he say he was feeling?"

"I didn't talk to him. I saw him twice when he was unconscious and again when his mother was there. I only peeked in his room then."

"She gave you a hard time, didn't she?"

"Not really. It was Neicy who couldn't control herself, but I fully understand. I would have done the same to her if things had been reversed." Shavon explained in detail what happened.

"Where was Jerome when all this happened? Is he out of town?

"No, Mama, he's in town. He left me."

Dana fell back against the couch. "Oh, Honey, why didn't you tell me?"

"That's not the sort of thing you brag about."

"I know, Honey, but I wasn't aware that you two were having problems. I'm sorry."

"Me too. I just hope it's temporary."

"Shavon, do you mind if I ask why?"

"Mama, he's insecure."

"Insecure about what? You and other men?"

Shavon nodded in agreement.

"Why? Have you given him any reason?"

"Believe it or not, Mama, he feels threatened by Tracy."

"Tracy? Jerome has left you because he's insecure about a man that I didn't know you still see. What was Tracy doing here anyway? Were you and Tracy having an affair?"

"Talk about ludicrous. Mama, Tracy hurt me too much for me to even want to see him, let alone have an affair. Tracy had to go and send a letter here. Mama, I was so happy with Jerome. I don't know why Tracy would do a thing like that. He ruined my marriage."

"Shavon, did the letter indicate that you two had been seeing each other?"

"No. He just explained how he felt about everything that happened years ago."

"Did you sit down and talk to Jerome about how you felt about things?"

"Yes, I did." Dana still looked puzzled. "Mama, he said I called Tracy's name in my sleep one night. I must have been having a nightmare about him. There is no other reason I would call his name. I tried my best to convince him that I don't love Tracy but he insisted that I wanted to hate him for losing my son, and that one day I would realize my hatred was really love. He felt like I needed time to think. He says he wants to be sure it's him I want. Mama, how could he leave like that? He gave up so easily."

"I don't know, Sweetheart. You can live with a man a life time and never know him. Shavon, does Jerome know what's happened."

"I don't know where he is yet, but I sure do need him. He left Monday and he's going to call when he gets settled."

Dana hated to ask the next question but she was curious. "Shavon, how *do* you feel about Tracy now?"

"I don't know how I feel about him. I know one thing, once again I'm hurting for something he did. I feel a huge emptiness being without my husband, but I feel damned sorry for what I did to Tracy."

Later, Dana went to see Tracy. Tracy was extremely bitter. "Don't give me that bull about Shavon being sorry. I don't buy that. She knew what she was doing all along. Oh, God, why didn't I leave her alone when she asked me to? I didn't believe her when she said she hated me but I sure as hell believe it now. How could she do this to me? If she wanted revenge, revenge is what she got." Dana walked toward the door. "And will you do me one last favor, Dana? Tell your daughter, I will never cross her path again!"

On the way back to Shavon's house, Dana thought about all of the problems her daughter had encountered. Shavon didn't deserve it, but her life had been such a mess. Dana couldn't help but to take notice and be proud of the way Shavon was handling yet another bout of adversity. She had a strength Dana hadn't seen before, and greatly admired.

"How is he?" Myah asked as Dana walked in. She dropped onto the couch as if she was drained of all her energy.

"Well, did he talk to you?" Shavon asked.

"Well, you could say that."

"I can image what he had to say," Shavon commented.

"We really can't blame him Shavon. He's hurt and he's got to have an outlet."

***

Tracy held his breath as the doctor pricked his toes. Dr. Garrett was disappointed to see his lack of reaction. "Hmmm... Still nothing, huh?"

Tracy shook his head no.

"Tracy, there's a very slim chance that you will walk again." He could see the disappointment in Tracy's eyes. "I wish I could guarantee that you could walk out of here by the end of the week but I can't. I'm here to tell you the facts. So far, it doesn't look promising. Outside of immobility and the psychological aspect of it all, you're looking pretty good."

"Doctor, how long will it be before I can have another pain pill?"

"Tracy, we don't want to overdo it. Are you in great pain? We may be able to increase the dosage on the drip."

"That's fine. I think mentally, I'm in more pain than I can deal with."

"Would you like to see one of our staff psychiatrists?"

"Right now, I don't want to see anybody."

The doctor left with direct orders that Tracy didn't want to be disturbed by anyone outside of the staff for the rest of the evening. But the most important order came last. Tracy informed him that he didn't want Shavon anywhere near him.

Maria paced with anger in her motel room.

"Neicy, this don't make sense. I'm his mother. Don't he know we here 'cause we love him? I didn't come all this way to be barred from seeing my son. Oooh, he makes me so angry! I wish his father could see what his son was doin' now. Your daddy would whoop him good ole' fashion style."

"Mama, you sound like me now. I think Tracy just needs some time by himself. Can you imagine being deeply in love with someone and they try to kill you? He'll probably be all right in the morning. Give him some time."

"Neicy, I just don't know what happened to Shavon. I never thought she would do anything to hurt Tracy."

"Mama, she should be in jail. Did Tracy say he broke in her house?"

"He didn't say nothing except she knew what she was doin.' That's what the paper said Shavon told the police."

"She probably set the whole thing up, and let him in and shot him."

"I don't know, Neicy. He been such a fool for her already, I wouldn't put it pass him to break in. The policeman said there was a window near the door that he musta broke to get in."

"Why would he go to her house anyway she's married, Mama?"

"I know child. I don't know what your brother's problem is. He certainly ain't the man I thought he was. Maybe now he'll come to his senses about her."

"I think he will, Mama. He's got to."

Maria nodded in agreement but didn't believe it for a second.

***

Myah, Dana, and Shavon sat in the living room making small talk.

"Is anybody hungry?" Shavon asked.

"I am, Sweetheart." Shavon pulled out a half thawed chicken.

"How long will it be, Shavon?"

"If I put it in warm water, it'll be ready in no time."

"I don't think I can wait, Shavon? Why don't we go out and get something to eat, my treat."

"Mama, it really won't take that long."

Dana turned to Myah. "Are you hungry?"

"I really am, Mrs. Thompson."

"Why don't we just let Shavon eat the chicken and we'll go out to dinner?"

"That's all right with me," Myah agreed. They headed for the door as Shavon watched.

"Oh, no you don't." Shavon threw the chicken in the freezer. "Sorry, Mr. Chicken, we'll have to deal with you later."

They laughed as Shavon opened the door. Jerome stood before them. The laughter ceased. Neither Shavon nor Jerome knew what to say.

"Are you all right?"

"Yes, I'm fine." She turned to Dana and Myah.

"Why don't you two just go on ahead? I'll grab something later."

Jerome hugged Dana then Myah.

"Did I come at a bad time?"

She assured him he hadn't. After they had gone, Jerome reached for Shavon holding her tightly. He held her until the mist in her eyes subsided. She could feel his unspoken love. She wasn't sure if he knew about what happened or not. She explained everything to him. He consoled her then he was gone.

The following morning, Myah went to see Tracy. He was civil but he kept making snide remarks regarding Shavon and his condition. Myah described her visit to Dana.

"Mrs. Thompson, he is really bitter. He kept saying things like, 'I wish I could walk out of here right now.' Then he would laugh and say, 'But I can't. Your best friend shot me.' Mrs. Thompson, I felt like slapping him."

"I know, Myah, but like you said, he's bitter. I try to imagine how I would feel if I couldn't walk after all these years of being independent."

"I see what you mean but he induced his own suffering. He may not have deserved it but he sure earned it."

"You are absolutely right, Myah. If he had not been at the house, this would have never happened."

Jerome stood in the doorway of Tracy's hospital room. Tracy laid down his pad and pen when he saw Jerome.

"Jerome."

"How are you, Tracy?" Tracy expelled bitter laughter. "Shavon tells me you've been here nearly a week."

"You haven't changed much," Tracy said ignoring his comment. Jerome looked him in the eye.

"Neither have you."

"Yeah, well look, man, if you came here to fight, as you can see, I'm—"

"I came here to talk to you man-to-man, Tracy. I love my wife and I was extremely happy with her before you interfered. I don't blame you for still loving her, but it's over. I advise you to stop chasing my wife. What she felt for you is dead and gone and I can promise you that."

Tracy glared at Jerome with anger. "Why don't I save you some time and breath, Jerome. I wouldn't take your wife if you threw her at me. And as far as chasing goes, I won't be chasing anybody ever again. I wish the both of you a very happily married life."

Jerome's eyes focused on Tracy's legs. "Yeah, whatever you say."

Tracy picked up his writing pad. Jerome turned to leave but stopped in his tracks. "Before I leave let me say this, if you hadn't been after my wife, you wouldn't be here now."

Jerome turned and walked out before Tracy could say anything else. What he didn't see is the realization on Tracy's face that Jerome was right.

***

Shavon waved to Dana and Myah as they boarded the plane. When Shavon got home, she relaxed with a glass of wine. All she could think of was Jerome.

"Call me if you need to talk," he had said. She didn't dare ask him to come back home. She needed him more now than ever and she felt that as her husband, he should have known being there was the right thing to do. But she could see no indication of willingness to do so.

CHAPTER 31

Ronny shook his head. He found it hard to believe that Shavon had encountered so much tragedy. He never imagined that such a benevolent person would suffer as she had done. Myah curled her hair as she explained in detail what had happened. Ronny looked at Myah who was almost in tears. He had some idea of what she felt. Shavon was the sister she never had. Myah had been depressed many nights when Shavon was in the institution and Ronny would always try and comfort her.

Terrell's death had made Ronny think about the now forgotten child he and Myah had conceived. With regret, he recalled telling her to get an abortion. He laughed as he remembered her saying, "No problem, it's not your baby anyway." *The life of a child is the quintessential treasure,* he thought.

Myah screeched from the hot curlers as she burned her ear. Ronny jumped from his seat.

"Are you all right?"

Myah looked at him suspiciously. "What's the problem? All I did was burn myself."

He smiled and walked back to his seat. Myah laughed out loud. "What's on your mind," she asked.

"Nothing," he lied.

Myah laughed again. "You'd better stop acting so concerned. I might get the erroneous impression that you're a man in love."

Ronny laughed. "Who, me? Never," he said as they laughed.

Ronny didn't come in when he dropped Myah off from the hair show they had just attended. Myah fell in a chair as she reviewed what she had seen at the show. She planned on how she would go about learning more about cutting hair. She did extremely well with chemicals and styling hair but she could use some improvement on hair cutting. The phone interrupted her thoughts.

"Hello?"

"How's my favorite girl?"

"Hi, Kenny."

Myah had met Kenny three months back when she was out one night with some of her girl friends. Kenny impressed Myah to the utmost. He was a computer whiz for a major computer company. When Myah first laid eyes on Kenny, he was handsomely dressed in a double-breasted, Armani suit which flattered his slender body. Kenny was an average looking guy but his maturity and intelligence made him much more attractive. Myah admired him for his articulation. Most guys she knew didn't care how their words came out as long as they got the point across.

"What are you doing?"

Myah smiled as she looked at her watch. "Waiting for you."

"That's just what I wanted to hear."

"Have you eaten?" she asked.

"No. I was trying to wait for you."

"Are you cooking or are we going out for dinner, Kenny?"

He laughed, "I've prepared some baby back ribs, corn on the cob, bake beans and apple-cinnamon muffins, my dear. Is there anything else the lady would like to know?"

"No. That sounds perfect. I'm going to pick up something to drink. I'll be there in a half an hour"

After dinner, Myah and Kenny sat on the couch too full to move.

"Myah, I've cooked for you about four times. When are you going to cook for me?"

"Patience, patience," she said with laughter. "It's just that once I cook, you'll want me to cook all the time."

"Are you that good at it?" he asked.

"Of course I am. I'm good at just about anything I put my mind to."

Kenny admired Myah's assertiveness. She reminded him of himself, except he didn't brag like she did. He walked Myah to the door and kissed her passionately.

"Myah, why won't you stay the night?"

Myah leaned forward and kissed him softly. "Do you really want me, Kenny?"

"You know I do, Myah."

She pulled her keys out of her pocket. "Stand in line," she whispered.

She left Kenny standing in the doorway wondering why she thought she was so special. The part that bothered him the most was that he did too.

***

Time went slowly for Shavon. The more she thought of the situation with Tracy, the more guilt ridden she became. She called him a few times but she always managed to call him when he was out of his room for testing. She left messages but he never returned her calls.

She tried to busy herself in her work to keep her mind off her problems. Her sales had increased but she wasn't sure if it was because people had heard about her designs or if they had heard about the shooting and wanted to see her out of curiosity and ended up liking her designs. She had heard whispers. "Is she the one? She doesn't even look like the type."

Later she would laugh to keep from crying. She prayed over and over that Jerome would come back to her but he still wasn't ready.

Jerome often thought of his confrontation with Tracy. He particularly remembered one of his statements to him. "What she felt for you is dead and gone and I promise you that." Jerome couldn't make that promise even to himself. He wished many times that he could go home and be with his wife and have a normal life but he still had doubts that she loved only him.

Sometimes when she and Jerome met for lunch she would bring up Tracy. She explained the best way she could that the guilt was overwhelming and she couldn't help being concerned. Jerome would always interpret it as love behind her concern but he continued to comfort her.

He often wondered why she couldn't see that it was painful for him to talk about Tracy. He kept in mind that what she did to Tracy was just as painful for her. Jerome sat thinking about how much he wanted to be back with his wife again. He packed his things in a hurry one day after remembering what he shared with his wife.

When he arrived, he got out happily leaving his bags in the car. He wanted to ask her if he could come home. Shavon was on the phone. "I don't know if he has shown any signs of improvement. All I know is that he's out of the hospital. Would you do that for me? Oh, thank you, Myah." Jerome stayed for an hour and left. He decided not to tell her the reason for his visit.

Three weeks later, Shavon got a call from Myah.

"He wants to see you, Shavon."

Shavon felt nervous. "See me? I just wanted to know how he was doing. I can't see him."

"Okay, I'll let him know. What is it going to hurt, Shavon?"

"All right, Myah, maybe I will go see him. Where is he staying?"

"He's in his own apartment down town. Brace yourself, Shavon. He's still in a wheelchair."

The following week Shavon got up the courage to visit Tracy in Detroit. Her first stop was to see her mother. She wanted her mother's opinion about her going to see him. It was obvious to Dana that Shavon's hatred had subsided. She encouraged her to mend fences with Tracy if at all possible. Her second stop was Jerome's parents' home. Jerome's mother was very fond of Shavon. She knew they were separated but avoided any questions regarding their marriage.

Shavon smiled at his mom's last statement. "He loves you, Shavon. You may never understand a man's pride but give it time."

Shavon felt nervous about seeing Tracy but she wanted to tell him how sorry she was and how much she wanted to be of help to him if he needed her. A lady dressed in a nurse's uniform opened the door. Shavon felt a stab of pain as she looked at Tracy in the wheelchair. His expression was bland.

"Shavon, this is my physical therapist, Brenda." They shook hands and Brenda excused herself. Shavon tried to read his emotions but couldn't.

"How are you, Tracy?"

"Fine, considering."

She didn't respond. He motioned for her to have a seat. She moved toward the chair across the room.

"I'm sorry, Shavon. I would get up but--"

She turned in the other direction speaking quickly.

"That's a nice picture of you on the mantel."

He eyed her but didn't speak.

"I hear you're a pretty popular guy now." She smiled.

He laughed. "Somewhat."

"I heard you met R& B mogul Jimmy Knight."

"Yeah, we collaborated on a tune."

"How did it feel to work with him?"

"Quit the small talk, Shavon, and tell me what you came here for." Her eyes widened with surprise.

"Wait a minute. You asked me to come. Why did you ask me?" There was a long moment of silence before she spoke again.

"I came to see how you were doing. When you were in the hospital, I called a few times. I understand why but you didn't return my calls."

"I'm glad you understand."

"Tracy, come on. If I can let go of some of my bitterness, you should at least give it an honest try."

"I'll keep that in mind."

"Tracy, I came here to tell you how sorry I am for doing this awful thing to you. It hurts me to see someone who was so active, immobile now. I wish I could do something to change things. I know it's probably the worst pain you've ever dealt with but--"

"No, it's not." She looked in his eyes.

"The death of my son was the worst. I consider it an honor being shot by you."

She stared at him momentarily then rose from her seat. She grabbed her purse and pulled out a pencil and piece of paper and scribbled a number on it.

"Here, I'll be staying at Mama's when you decide to be civil."

Shavon was angered by his reception. She decided to leave Saturday afternoon. There was no sense in trying to reach him.

As the months passed, Shavon's sales continued to climb. She was very pleased with her professional life. She gave more fashion shows and came up with more ways to augment her popularity. She and Jerome had been separated four months now and she barely heard from him anymore because of their busy schedules. She missed him terribly but more and more, she believed he wasn't coming back. It was hard on her some nights being without him but she always found the strength to make it through another day.

As fall progressed, when time allowed, she would take long walks to clear her mind. There always seemed to be so many thoughts. Shavon finally realized that if she had been stronger, her life would have been totally different. In spite of all her problems, she was proud of who she had become. She had accomplished so much in a few short years.

Shavon had one big project after another. She wore herself ragged preparing for her old friend Kim's October wedding. She was ecstatic when Kim asked her to design her gowns. She explained that she didn't have time to be in the wedding but she would try her best to be there.

Shavon was very pleased to see Kim walk down the aisle in a wedding gown she designed. Everyone agreed that Kim was a radiant bride. Shavon had worked very hard and seeing the bridal party was well worth it. Everyone loved the gowns and subsequently, that put more gowns on the cutting board for *Shavon's Fashions*. As Shavon laughed and talked with some of her old friends, she spotted Tracy in the back of the church. She could see him looking in her direction. She wanted to say hello but someone walked up and began talking to him so she opted not to interrupt.

She didn't attend the reception. She flew home immediately after the wedding.

The following week, Shavon spoke with her mother.

"Hello."

"Shavon, where have you been? I've been calling you for the last few days."

"Mama, I've been so busy."

"Honey, you really need to slow down a bit."

"I know, Mama. I'm taking some time off in a week or so."

"Good. Shavon, listen. What I wanted to tell you was that Tracy called here for you last Sunday. He said he had seen you at a wedding."

"Yeah, but he was talking with someone, and I never got a chance to say hello. How did he sound?"

"Like his old self."

"You mean he wasn't grouchy or sarcastic."

"No. He was very pleasant. As a matter of fact, it sort of reminded me of when you two were friends."

Shavon laughed, "Friends, huh?"

"Before the wedding, how long had it been since you two last saw each other?"

"About six months ago. Mama, he was so bitter that I didn't care if I didn't see him for six years."

"Well, he didn't sound like that when he called. And come to think of it, you don't sound angry with him anymore either."

"No. I guess I'm not. I think I've done some growing up. I took a long look at myself and realized that if I hadn't been so weak--"

"Shavon, don't be so hard on yourself."

"It's true, Mama. I should have been stronger. Maybe I should have leaned on you and Myah more. I just couldn't stop thinking about Tracy. I knew Terrell had those problems when he was born but I couldn't handle it, and I needed to blame it on Tracy for not being there. After I saw his anger, I understood my own. I was wrong, but Mama, I really believed what I had felt at that time was right."

"You are really something, Shavon. I'm so proud of you. You have really come a long way." Shavon smiled.

"Let's just hope Tracy has."

Shavon dreaded calling Tracy. As she dialed, she had memories of their last meeting. She hoped he wouldn't answer."

"Hello."

"Hi, Tracy. How are you?"

"I'm fine, how are you?"

"Fine," she answered. "Tracy, this is—"

"I know, Shavon."

"How did you know it was me?"

"Your voice hasn't changed." He paused. "Shavon, are you busy this weekend?"

"Probably so. Why?"

"I thought we could talk."

"Tracy, I really am busy. I don't think I can get away."

"Shavon, I promise I won't treat you like I did the last time we met."

She didn't know what to think.

"Tracy, I really can't get away until maybe next weekend."

"Well, next weekend will have to do."

"Are you okay, Tracy?"

He sighed, "I just need to talk to you."

They agreed to meet the following weekend.

Shavon stood at Tracy's door wondering what he might have to say. *I hope this isn't another bitter meeting*, she thought. When he opened the door, they both displayed bland expressions.

"Hello, Shavon. How are you?"

"Fine." She tried to read his facial expression.

"I'm glad you could make it," he said as he led her to the living room. "Would you like a drink?"

"Do you have some… Canei?"

They said it simultaneously and laughed.

"You didn't think I'd remember that did you?"

She smiled. She was afraid to get too familiar with him.

"Well, I never really drank much outside of wine anyway. Would you like for me to get the glasses?" She briefly thought about what she had always heard about handicapped people not wanting special treatment. She wished she hadn't asked. To her surprise, he welcomed her assistance.

"Sure. They're in the kitchen cabinet near the end on the top shelf."

Shavon was surprised the glasses were stored in such a high place. She had to ask, "Why aren't your glasses stored in a lower cabinet?"

"My regular housekeeper has been off for a couple of weeks and my new housekeeper is in a world of her own. She makes everything convenient for herself."

"Why don't you just ask her to move them?"

"I didn't want to offend her but I guess I'll have to do just that." Tracy poured the wine. "So, how's business?"

"Business is great. I think the word spread quickly about my shop."

"For one, I think you picked a pretty good location."

"Me too. And people seem to like my designs. My staff is getting larger. I have really been working hard and it seems to have paid off."

Tracy nodded with pleasure. "I knew you would be successful given the chance." There was a long pause. "Shavon, I really didn't know what to say to you today. There's so much on my mind." He sighed. "For so long, I've wanted to tell you how sorry I am about everything. I wanted you to know that I understand the hurt and hatred you have felt. I lay awake at night and wonder what was wrong with me. Why couldn't I understand when it counted? I have missed my son terribly. I know staying away made it seem as if I didn't care, but I cared more than you will ever know. Shavon, I loved him more than I loved you." Tears were in his eyes. "I guess I was just blinded by my own needs. I won't even attempt to excuse myself but after Terrell died—" He dropped his head. "I still wish it had been me. It's so hard for me to go on with a normal life knowing what I did to you and my son. You two meant so much to me. I can't explain, nor will I ever understand my actions. I know it won't help any now but I see everything clearly. You and Terrell paid dearly because of my foolishness. I wish I could make up for it. I think I've finally grown up. It's a shame it took the loss of God's most precious gift to me and your sanity to make a man out of me. After I found out Terrell had died and you were in that hospital, I nearly went berserk. I had to seek counseling to go on. I know I was bitter and angry when I found out I may never walk again but since the last time I saw you, I've done a lot of thinking. If I never walk again, it won't be enough punishment for deserting you and Terrell."

"Tracy, I have a confession to make. I have never hated anyone the way I hated you. I really wanted you to suffer for what happened to me and Terrell. But when I found out you were paralyzed, my hatred was dispelled. I still had a strong dislike for you." She looked into his eyes. "I felt I had lost my husband because of your interference and my sanity because of your neglect. You are guilty of both, interference and neglect but I grew up some too. I lost my husband because he was insecure and my sanity because I couldn't handle the grief or neglect. I blamed you for so long and I was wrong for that." There was a long pause. She signed as she looked at her watch. "I'd better be going. I have an appointment I have to keep." Tracy shook his head in agreement. She saw herself out.

***

Shavon and Myah ate lunch at Gregg's Cafe.

"So, what we did was air our feelings. He told me how sorry and wrong he was and I admitted I blamed him for other people's insecurities and weaknesses."

"So, are you two friends again?"

"Myah, I really don't know how I feel about things. He said his piece and I said mine. I guess our admissions brought closure. I don't really expect to hear from him again."

"Well, I'm just glad you two can be civil toward one another." Shavon quickly changed the subject.

"So, how are you, Ronny and Kenny getting along?"

Myah giggled, "Couldn't be better."

Shavon laughed, "Myah, when are you going to learn?"

"I have learned! When I was so deep in love that I only cared about what Ronny wanted, I was hurting myself. I had to face reality. If a man says he loves you, then he should be with you and only you."

"He always loved you, Myah."

"Yeah, but he had other women on the side. I'm just another player in the game of life, Shavon."

"Myah, you need to quit. You know that only works for men. It doesn't turn out the same for us."

"I don't know about that. He had his fun and now it's my turn."

"Two wrongs don't make a right," Shavon commented.

Myah frowned, "Aw, loosen up, you stiff. You only live once."

***

Shavon stayed in Detroit for a few days then returned to California. Things were going fine at the shop, so she relaxed and went on with her vacation to the Bahamas. She thought a lot about her meeting with Tracy. She still didn't know what to think of it but she was glad he admitted how wrong he was for neglecting Terrell.

Friday morning some problems came up at the shop and Shavon decided to return to work early.

"Shavon."

"Hi, Mama. I was just packing to surprise you with a visit. I'm coming to take measurements for some prom gowns."

"Oh, Honey, that's great. When are you leaving?"

"In the morning."

Dana looked forward to Shavon's visit. "Oh , Shavon, I almost forgot. Tracy wants you to call him. He said something about some friends needing a good designer. He recommended you and he wanted to know if it was all right."

Shavon agreed telling her mother she would contact Tracy later.

During her visit, Shavon enjoyed a cruise and a Brian McKnight concert with some of her old friends. She admitted she hadn't had that much fun in months. Shavon's friends were the kind of girls who loved to party.

She felt awkward at the nightclub but her friends helped her to relax and enjoy the party. She danced very little but she enjoyed watching her friends. She felt lonely as she watched everyone slow dance. She found herself thinking about Jerome. She excused herself to go to the rest room. She heard a familiar voice.

"I think you've had too much to drink," the male voice had said.

The female responded, “Why don’t we just dance it off.” Shavon turned to see Jerome and Cynthia.

The following Monday Shavon was back to work with more energy than she had for some time.

“That time off did wonders for you. You seem to be even more rested than you did after your Bohemian trip,” Delsey told her.

She promised herself she would take more days off and not wear herself down so. She appointed Debra as her assistant manager, which assured her that the shop would be in capable hands. As the months passed, she made arrangements to accommodate the growth of her warehouse. Business was booming and she needed to keep up with the demand. Tracy had referred some of his friends in the entertainment business, which she was very grateful for. She had begun to see artists making television appearances in her designs, which gave her a great pleasure.

Shavon found herself lying around watching soap operas. She hadn’t seen one in about two years. She became bored and turned on the radio. As she did her housework, she was interrupted by the phone.

“Hello.”

”Hi, Shavon, how are you?” There was silence.

“I’m fine.”

“This is Jerome, Shavon. Did I catch you at a bad time?” She dropped the broom.

“No, Jerome. Is everything all right?”

“Shavon, I need to talk to you.” There was another pause. “Shavon, did you hear--”

“Yes, Jerome. I heard you.”

Jerome sensed a different attitude in her. "Are you okay, Shavon?"

"Yes, I'm just fine. Uh, how about lunch tomorrow at the delicatessen on the corner?"

"See you at 12."

CHAPTER 32

Myah crawled out of the bed and went into the bathroom as quietly as possible. A few minutes later, she dressed quickly and headed for the door.

"Myah! Where are you going?"

"It's 2:30 a.m. and I think it's time I get out of here," she said never missing a step.

Kenny reached for the light switch. "Myah, hold on." He grabbed his robe off the chair beside his bed and went into the living room where she stood waiting. "Myah, I want you to stay. I want to hold you for a little while longer." He began to unbutton her coat.

"I really do have to go. Ronny might be wondering where I am."

Kenny took off her coat as he kissed her.

"Kenny," she murmured. She began to return his kisses.

"He'll never know," he whispered. Myah made love with him again. She thought about Ronny for all of two seconds and dropped off to sleep.

The following day Myah left her hair salon at 4:30 p.m. When she pulled in the driveway, Ronny was sitting on the porch.

"I called you 12 times last night, where were you?"

"I was with some girl friends."

"What girl friends?"

"What is this? Don't you trust me?"

"Myah, lately you've been spending a lot of time with girl friends."

"So damned what! I do as I please, Ronny."

"If you're going to yell, Myah, let's go inside," Ronny said calmly.

As she turned the key, she felt nervous. '*What have you gotten yourself into*?' she thought. They were barely in before Ronny began.

"What friends, Myah?"

"Look, either you believe me or you don't! I don't have to tell you who I hang out with."

"About two weeks ago I called you at one in the morning and you told me the same story you're telling me now."

"Ronny, 1 a.m. is not late for somebody who goes out to party. You know everything closes at two a.m."

"Funny you should mention that. Last night I called you at 2, 3 and 4 a.m."

She sighed, "My phone was unplugged."

"Sure it was, Myah. You and I both know you never unplug your phone."

"Well, I did last night!"

"Well, I don't want to argue any further about this. If you have something to tell me, I wish you would do it right now."

"I don't have anything to tell you except that I was with Sherry and Drena. We went to that little bar on Outer Drive. Somebody broke into Sherry's house and took her stereo and VCR and all of her savings. She felt pretty bad so we took her out to help her forget." Myah's face expressed a pitiful look. She was so convincing. Ronny felt bad for pressing her the way he did.

"Come here." He hugged her tightly. "I'm sorry. I guess I got a little carried away."

"You guess?" she said with laughter. He returned her laughter.

"I love you," he whispered.

***

Three weeks passed before Shavon's warehouse was renovated. She spent many hours of hard work to get things in order. She often thought about her lunch with Jerome. He wanted to come home. She couldn't take him back. She was afraid of his insecurity. She reminded him that he left her because he was unsure about her feelings, feelings she had expressed and explained numerous times to keep him. She asked what made him so certain now. Jerome didn't have an answer. He only told her he loved her and he couldn't stay away any longer. She told him as gently as she could that he had walked out of her life, and it wouldn't be so easy to come back.

She loved Jerome and wanted him back but she believed in her heart that he would be insecure about any man who showed interest in her. Shavon found it very odd of how adamant Jerome was when he accused her of being with Tracy. Now she wondered if he had just needed a way back to Cynthia and suddenly changed his mind again.

When Shavon called Tracy to thank him for referring his friends to her he was out, but he returned her call as soon as he came in.

"Shavon, it's got to feel great to see your designs on big name entertainers. It gives you a rush, huh?"

She laughed, "Yeah, I guess you could call it that."

"Shavon, I need to ask a favor of you."

"Go on, what is it?"

"There's going to be a party in California next week and I would like for you to go with me. I could use your help in getting around. It's a publicity party."

"A publicity party? I don't think that's a good idea."

"Why not, Shavon? You would love it."

"I doubt it. Where is it, in Beverly Hills?"

"Well, as a matter of fact--"

"No. I think I'll pass."

"Shavon, you could meet some very important people at this party. This could benefit your business."

"Sorry, Tracy. I can't mix with your crowd."

"Shavon, I need your assistance."

"What about your housekeeper?"

"She's not back yet."

"Well, I'm really sorry, Tracy, but I'm sure you'll get along fine without me."

"Okay, Shavon, but if you change your mind..."

"Sure. I'll call you."

Shavon knew going to the party would link her to Tracy as a love interest. And worse than that, everyone knew who put him in the wheelchair. She didn't want or need that kind of publicity.

***

"Ahhh!" Shavon pulled the phone from her ear as Delsey screamed into the phone.

"Shavon, are you there?"

"Delsey, is that you?"

"Yes and Shavon, the commercial was fantastic! Me and Debra looked like glamour girls.

"You saw it?"

"Yes! A few minutes ago. My friends have been calling me left and right to find out how I got on TV. I'm so glad you let me be a part of it."

"Of course I would, Delsey. You and Debra have been with me from the very beginning and if you two didn't know before how much I appreciate you, I want you to know now.

"Thank you, Shavon. Well, let me go. I'm sure my fans are trying to get through," Delsey said with laughter.

Shavon smiled as she hung up the phone.

"What would I do without Delsey?" she said with a smile.

Shavon jumped as she felt herself dozing. She found the marketing seminar very interesting but she had stayed up late last night. She looked at her watch wondering if she could endure 30 more minutes. Immediately after the seminar, she headed for the water fountain.

Shavon looked twice when she saw a familiar face. She could only see him from a profile and he looked a lot like Tracy. A woman pushed his wheelchair to the door then leaned forward and kissed him. He then cupped her hand and revealed a wide grin. Shavon could see a better view now. Tracy looked very happy.

Shavon lived five miles from the auditorium. On the way home, she wondered about the woman Tracy was with. Her last thought was of how she hoped he was as happy as he looked.

Shavon sat working on her plans for her upcoming fashion show when Delsey came into her office. "Excuse me, Shavon, but someone is here to see you." Delsey immediately sighed when Shavon asked who it was. "It's Tracy Gains," she said reluctantly. Shavon smiled.

"It's okay. Show him in."

Tracy looked around the office, "Very nice, very nice."

She smiled at him, "So what brings you here?"

"I was here on business and I thought I'd stop and say hello before I leave."

Tracy informed her that he would be leaving in a few days. They talked further and decided they would get together for a drink. Shavon proceeded to see him out but someone called her to the front desk. While she stood at the desk, she turned and saw the same woman that was at the seminar helping him to the car.

The next day Shavon combed her hair into a bang and ponytail. She chose a light colored rose lipstick and slipped into her gray corduroy pants and her favorite gray angora sweater. She was supposed to meet Tracy in an hour.

Shavon nervously knocked at the door of his hotel room. As she knocked, she had an awkward feeling meeting him at the hotel. Tracy opened the door slightly surprised to see her. He never thought she would meet him there.

She was there for 40 minutes before the woman from the seminar came by. Dale's face revealed a negative reception as Tracy introduced them. Shavon gave a short smile. The three of them sat uncomfortably for 15 minutes before Shavon excused herself. Dale stared at Tracy as Shavon closed the door. Her anger was obvious towards Shavon.

The following day, Tracy called Shavon to explain how sorry he was for Dale's interruption. He asked Shavon to meet him for dinner at the Chef's Inn.

Shavon and Tracy enjoyed a hearty bowl of Mexican Chili with toasted garlic bread and a tossed salad. Tracy talked Shavon into drinking a Long Island Ice Tea instead of white wine. She drank one glass and giggled the rest of the evening. Tracy called a cab to make sure she got home safely because she was a little too high to drive. Shavon was getting out of the cab when he called to her. She turned to him and saw a serious expression, which caused her to drop her smile.

"I really enjoyed tonight."

She smiled, "So did I."

"We'll go back and get your car in the morning," he told her.

Shavon dropped off to sleep before she could get her clothes off. She had no thoughts or dreams that she was aware of, only peaceful sleep.

Tracy lay awake in his bed thinking of Shavon. She looked beautiful tonight. Could she read his mind when he called to her as she got out of the cab? Of course not. She didn't notice anything after drinking that Long Island Ice Tea. Tracy hoped things would be different. He had hoped it would at least end with a kiss on the cheek. *I guess she really is over me*, he thought. He set his clock for 7 a.m. and fell asleep.

Tracy hung up the phone and laughed. *She must still be asleep*, he thought as he reached in his coat pocket for the keys he had taken from her the night before to keep her from driving. *I'll bet she had a hangover.* He called his friends Patrick and John to help him get Shavon's car to her house. John rang her bell several times but there was no answer. He tried knocking but there was still no answer. Tracy assumed she was still asleep.

When they arrived in front of the Chef's Inn, Shavon's sparkling burgundy Grand AM was gone. His first thought was that someone had stolen it. Patrick talked him into going to Shavon's shop before he assumed the worst. Patrick looked at John and scratched his head.

"Hey, man, isn't that a burgundy Grand AM over there?"

"I don't know," John responded. "It looks like it could be a Grand AM or a Cadillac." They laughed.

"Tee he," Tracy mocked. "I guess she didn't need my help after all. Would you guys like to meet her?" Patrick smiled.

"Man, I was on my way to the gym when you called."

"And I was on my way to the laundry mat," John added.

"Come on guys. This is the one I told you about. The one I was with in high school. John and Patrick bucked their eyes and burst into laughter.

"Uh, sorry man, I didn't wear my bulletproof vest," Patrick said with laughter. John began walking away.

"Where are you going, man?" Tracy asked.

"Look, man, I never even got the chance to make out my will."

Tracy rolled himself in as they laughed following close behind him.

"Shavon these are my old buddies, Pat and John. They're writers also."

"Pleased to meet you," Shavon responded.

"I didn't mean to interrupt you. I just wanted to make sure you had your car. After last night, I didn't know if you were up to picking it up.

"I managed," she said.

"I also wanted to know if you would like to come to dinner tonight?"

"No. I can't."

"Come on, Shavon. I'll do the cooking."

"I've got other plans, Tracy."

John and Patrick glared at each other.

"I can't accept that," he said trying to hide his embarrassment.

"I really must get back to work, Tracy."

He handed her the keys and she was gone.

"No wonder you wanted us to meet her. She is gorgeous, Tracy."

"Yeah, I know."

"Look, man, we may as well tell you, we felt the tension. What did you do to upset her?" Pat asked.

"I wish I knew, man."

"Don't feel bad. We're all rejected once in a while," Pat said.

Tracy laughed as he and John spoke simultaneously, "Hey, speak for yourself, man."

***

Tracy stared at the clock as he tried to concentrate on his writing. He couldn't understand Shavon's sudden change of attitude. What's with her, he wondered. Last night she said she enjoyed herself.

Shavon swung her hair back and picked up the phone.

"Shavon's Fashions."

"Shavon, this is Tracy. What did I do to you to make you so angry? Last night you said you had fun and today you did an about face. What's the problem?"

"Look, Tracy. Don't you ever give anybody the impression something is going on between us. I didn't like that one bit. You had to bring not one but two of your friends up here. Oh, and what was that you said, 'after last night'."

"Shavon, I didn't mean it that way. I'm sorry if I offended you. I'll tell you what, Shavon. Since I see we really can't be friends, I'll leave you alone. I'll be leaving in a couple of days and I won't contact you again. Tracy sat by the phone telling himself to forget her. "You are so unforgettable, Shavon," he whispered.

CHAPTER 33

Kenny walked Myah to the door. “Myah, I really wish you would reconsider.”

“Don’t even try it, Kenny. Listening to you almost got me in trouble last month.”

“You’re not married, he doesn’t own you! Myah, what are you afraid of? I know you want to be with me. I feel it every time we’re together.”

She couldn’t’ believe her ears. This was the man who said he didn’t want to get serious with anybody and here he was acting as if he were head over heels for her.

“You’re unbelievable, you know that! You knew from the beginning that I would never leave Ronny alone. I’ve been with him, it seems like forever. There’s a lot between us.”

“Myah, just give us a chance. This is the first time I’ve ever had a woman who satisfies me in every way.”

“Stop it Kenny! I’m in love with him!”

Kenny stared at her for a moment then slowly walked to the couch where he fell into a slouched position. She tried her best to explain that she enjoyed and cared a great deal for him but her and Ronny had been through so much together. Myah wrapped her scarf snugly around her neck before putting on her coat. Kenny grabbed her hat from the shelf.

“Myah, do what’s best for you.” He kissed her softly. “But if things don’t work out, give me a call.”

Myah gave a positive nod. She waved good-bye to Kenny when she reached her car. She really liked Kenny but she never intended to get too close to him or anybody else. It was all for the sake of fun and excitement. She glanced in her rear view mirror and pulled off with caution to avoid a collision with the car behind her which seemed to be leaving.

She felt bad about the way things had turned out. Kenny was a wonderful person and she didn't want to hurt him. She had no idea he would be so serious about things after telling her he only wanted to be friends. Myah thought about Shavon's comment when they last met. "Maybe the stiff was right," she mumbled with laughter.

She went two blocks and turned right. She looked in her rear view mirror and saw a car close behind her. It appeared to have the same type of headlights as the car that was behind her on Outer Drive. She was almost sure it was the same car but the glare from the headlights prevented her from seeing the make of the car. She decided to turn off at the next light. The car followed close behind her. She made a left turn down Wyoming to be sure that she wasn't just paranoid and that she was in fact being followed. When she saw the car coming down Wyoming, she began to panic. She sped up the street through stop signs until she got back to Six Mile Road. She looked in her mirror again. She had lost him.

Myah nearly broke the door down trying to get in the house. She called to her mother but no one was home. She rushed to the phone to call Ronny. There was no answer. Someone knocked at the door. She stood quietly afraid the stranger had followed her to the house. She heard a second knock. She grabbed the phone.

"I've got a gun and I've called the police!" she yelled.

"Myah, let me in."

"Ronny?" She looked out of the peephole. Show your face!" she yelled.

Ronny moved over just enough to let her see it was him. She quickly pulled the door open and hugged him once he was inside.

"Ronny, look outside and see if you see a strange car." Ronny only stared at her. "Did you hear what I just said? Somebody was following me tonight! Would you please look outside?" His expression was stoic. "What's wrong with you?"

"Myah, why would someone follow you?"

"How the hell am I supposed to know?"

"Maybe because you were somewhere you weren't supposed to be."

She looked at him with surprise. "What does where I was coming from have to do with anything?"

"Where were you coming from?" His voice was calm.

"Terry Smith's house, where are you coming from?" she asked cynically.

"What did you and Terry do?"

"We played cards. What's with all the questions? You just won't get off of this accusation will you?"

He continued to stare at her. She leaned to pull off her boot. "How insensitive can you be? Somebody could have killed me tonight and you're still on that cheating kick."

He walked toward her. "So, you still say you're not cheating on me?"

"Get outta my face with that garbage, Ronny." She went to the window.

"Who do you know on Outer Drive, Myah?"

"Outer Drive?"

"Yeah, you know that street your so called lounge is on."

"Nobody. Why?"

"I saw you come out of a house on Outer Drive."

Myah dropped on the couch. "That was you following me?"

He didn't respond. She sighed. She knew there was nothing she could say to get her out of this one.

Shavon thought about Tracy for most of the morning. *I was hard on him*, she thought. *What's wrong with me? I have really become an ogre. I can't call and apologize to him. Maybe I should. Why did I let this get to me?*

Shavon finally dialed his number. A woman answered the phone. After she asked for him the woman immediately dropped the phone.

"Hello."

"Hi, Tracy, please don't be angry. I just called to apologize for the way I acted. I was really cruel and you didn't deserve that." She heard laughter.

"You have got to be kidding. Is this Shavon saying these words or is it an impostor?"

"Come on, Tracy. I'm trying to make amends."

"Thank you, Shavon. I knew you weren't that cold hearted person you were trying to be."

"Hold your compliments. I didn't mean to give you the impression I thought I was wrong about what I said. I just think I should have found a better way to say it." They laughed.

"Well, I know you have company so I'll—"

"Can we get together for lunch soon, your treat?" he asked. She snickered.

"Sure." To his surprise, she agreed. She gave him her home number.

Tracy approached the door with a bottle of wine in his hand. He was glad she had changed it from lunch to dinner. That would give him more time with her.

She let him in with a smile on her face.

"What are you smiling about?"

"Oh nothing. Come on in?" she said. She prepared pepper steak with potatoes, gravy, black-eyed peas and a crumb cake.

After dinner, they sat in the living room and slowly sipped on the wine. They felt more comfortable with each other tonight. They talked about old times and the new. They even talked about Terrell.

As they sat on the couch, Shavon began to pour out her feelings about Terrell. Tracy reached for her and she fell willingly into his arms where they cried together. The tears began to subside but he continued to hold her tightly as she returned his firm hug. Tracy knew what he was feeling but he wasn't sure about her. He broke the embrace and looked into her eyes and wiped her tears. He wanted so much to kiss her. He placed his hand upon the side of her chin and leaned forward. To his surprise, she didn't hinder his affection. He felt a familiar warmth and excitement when their lips met. He was overjoyed when she welcomed his kiss. He felt her embrace him. He didn't want the kiss to end because he was afraid he wouldn't get another one. Before the night was over, he kissed her three more times without rejection. He knew now that he had been right all along about their connection. Shavon still cared for him.

Shavon remembered last night clearly. She thought of every detail from the night before. She was surprised by her onslaught of tears but she knew part of her grief was seeing how painful it had been for him over the years. She lay in bed wondering what Tracy might be doing. "I do still care for him," she whispered.

Tracy sat talking to his agent, Matt.

"Tracy, I'm glad you decided to come out here. Quincy says he's happy about the way things are going on the set. They should be through in three months. As a matter of fact, he invited us to the studio today if you feel up to it."

"You bet I do," Tracy conceded.

Off and on all day Tracy thought about last night. He had lost his concentration several times that afternoon but he was very pleased and interested in the way things were going on the set. He was known for writing adventure novels but didn't want to be stereotyped so he decided he would give romance a shot. He never dreamed the producers would want U*nrequited Love* for a TV movie.

Tracy left the studio at one 1 p.m. He picked up the phone and quickly put it back down. He wanted so much to hear Shavon's voice but he had second thoughts about his certainty of her feelings. He remembered not long ago when they had gone to dinner. He knew she had enjoyed herself but the next day, she found a reason to reject him. He was afraid that overnight she may have had a change of heart.

Shavon smiled as he told her about the movie. Tracy was hesitant but he had to tell Shavon that the movie was based on the love they had shared. She was a little disappointed at first because she knew it would hurt Jerome. Tracy told her he changed major details and all the characters names. She empathized with his need to tell their story. He reminded her of how she had always been a sucker for love stories.

Shavon told him how lucky she thought he was to get this opportunity. She quickly retracted her statement.

"It's not luck," she told him. "It's pure talent."

"You always did believe in me, didn't you?" She nodded positively. She wanted to kiss him but she couldn't. She knew how she felt, but being with Tracy again was a pleasurable but strange aura.

As Shavon put away the dishes, she thought about the way things were going with her and Tracy. The time they spent together was wonderful. She wanted to help him as much as she could. She began giving him massages in between his physical therapy.

Tracy's improvement was rapid. He felt positive about everything he had once considered a problem. He was slightly disappointed when he had heard that the leading actress in the movie needed time off for illness but even that couldn't dampen his spirits. Being with Shavon again meant the world to him.

As Tracy worked out, he thought of the intimate night he and Shavon had shared. He knew his lovemaking wasn't the same but he knew his handicap was an obstacle he would soon overcome. He had been to his doctor and his improvement was miraculous. He kept it to himself out of fear of hindering his good fortune. His doctor told him that his new attitude seemed to have done wonders for him. Tracy could stand up now but only momentarily.

Tracy remembered the softness of Shavon's body. She had trembled as she yielded. Hearing her whisper his name made him feel as he did years ago when they were in high school. Though he always wanted things to be this way, he never thought they would be. Over the last few weeks, he had told her time and time again how much he loved her and he was pleased that she returned his confession.

Shavon smiled at Tracy as he slept on her sofa.

"Well, it's you and me again," she said referring to the television. She began switching channels when she spotted a Jimmy Knight clip on Entertainment Tonight. "Tracy, look! Jimmy Knight is working on a new album. Do you believe that?

He could have consulted with you first. I thought you two were close." She concluded with loud laughter. He was too far gone. He hadn't heard a word she said. She turned to see his expression but there was none. She took a blanket from the linen closet and covered him with it. With a solemn expression, she grazed her fingers through his wavy hair. She felt good being close to him. She briefly thought of the past problems between them but quickly brushed her negative thoughts away. The memories were still too painful. She dropped her head for a moment then began to get up.

"Hey!" Where are you going? You're not leaving me, are you? She smiled.

"Of course not. I'm going to get some water. My throat feels kind of parched."

"Maybe this will help." He kissed her as if it were his last time.

"Okay, okay." She laughed

"Can a girl have a break?"

"Sure." He gave her one last peck then backed up. She looked at him with a half smile.

"What?" he asked.

"You give up too easily!" She began kissing him with little pecks which slowly climaxed into a passionate kiss. He could feel the warmth of her body as she aroused him. He knew she wanted him and he wanted her but not now. He wanted to talk. She began undressing him. He made an attempt to resist but instead he returned her passionate kisses as he touched her. He began to fight his inclination by pulling away. She slowly opened her eyes.

"What's wrong?"

"Nothing. I love making love to you but I just want to hold you and talk with you for a while."

Shavon stood up.

"I think I'd better get two glasses of water." She placed her hand on his head. Are you all right? Should I call a doctor?"

He laughed, "Come on, give me some credit here. I didn't stop because I don't desire you. I want it just as much as you do. I stopped because I'm in love with you and sex is just a small part of my love. I just happen to believe in the art of communication."

"Well isn't sex an act of communication?"

He touched her face as he held his solemn expression. "Yes, but a wink of passion will never transcend what I feel for you." Her smile vanished. "Shavon, if I never make love to you again, I can assure you that my love will never fade."

She leaned her head against his chest. They held each other for the rest of the night.

Tracy went home to Detroit for the weekend to see his family and to take care of business matters. Business delayed him a few more days than he had hoped. Not only was he anxious to get back to Shavon but he was also excited about what was going on at the studio. He was careful not to tell anyone about it. Shavon was the only one who knew. He knew that in the entertainment field, nothing was definite.

Shavon smiled as she talked with her mother.

"Mama, he is wonderful. For the last few months, we've gotten to know each other better and he seems to be a very mature person. He really has changed. I never wanted to admit it," she sighed. "Or maybe I just didn't realize it but I still love Tracy. I don't think I ever stopped." Dana was silent. "Why are you so quiet, Mama?"

"Sweetheart, I'm sorry. "I'm just wondering if you have really gotten over all of the pain."

Shavon stuttered. "Well. Well, yeah. Sort of."

"Shavon, how can you be sort of over the pain?"

"Well, actually sometimes it still hurts. I sometimes wonder if I can really trust him to be there for me no matter what, and then there are times I study him as he talks and he is so sincere. I'm not saying that because I love him. He really does seem to be more mature." There was a long pause. "Mama, I know what you're thinking. Jerome chose his life, he left me. I don't know why I hung on for so long anyway. I still love him but it's over. I realized it when I saw him out that night. I don't know why I ever thought there was a slight chance he was miserable without me. I guess because I was miserable without him." She drew a deep breath. "Jerome is never going to trust me the way I need him to. Mama, I'm going to go on and file for a divorce."

Dana held her breath. She knew going through a divorce would mean a lot of pain. "Shavon, I only have one thing to say. Whatever you do, make sure it's what Shavon wants. Don't try to please anybody else. You know how I feel about Tracy and you know how I feel about Jerome. I love them both. They are really good men and it won't matter who you choose as long as you choose the one you love and trust the most. I hope you don't make your choice for the wrong reason."

"Mama, Jerome hasn't really given me a choice. He made what he wanted very clear to me. He hasn't asked me for a divorce but he hasn't been breaking down the door to get back in either."

Dana had nothing else to say. The choice was Shavon's and Dana was confident she would do the right thing.

Shavon turned each page of the photo album remembering everything that happened on every occasion. She and Jerome were so happy. She spotted a picture where they stared intently into each other's eyes. She quickly remembered her thoughts. She still loved him. She always hoped things would work out between them but seeing Jerome with Cynthia was painful. How could she ever forget that he rushed to her so quickly after their separation? After all, she never dated Tracy until after she believed she had lost Jerome. She felt now that it couldn't have been as strong a marriage as she initially thought. She shook herself from her thoughts and left for the shop.

The day seemed incredibly long. Shavon tried to keep herself busy but thoughts of her husband crept into her mind for most of the day. She reminisced on wonderful times they had shared. She remembered when Jerome asked her to have a child. After their separation, there were many times when she thought she wanted one too. I wish I had given him a child, she would say. Even though she had a slight regret, she would always remind herself that a child would be the worst thing she could have done at that time in her life. She knew she wasn't ready to be the mother she wanted to be. She didn't have time.

Tracy greeted Shavon with a smile.

"I have really missed you."

She leaned to hug him. "And I, you." Instantly her spirit was lifted again.

"Did you drop in to see Mama before you left?"

"No."

He eyed her. "Shavon, your mother has always been a fair person but I have hurt you so much in the past that I don't really know how she feels about me now. She's still cordial over the phone but I don't know how she would feel with me sitting in her living room telling her how much I love her daughter."

"Tracy, just as you said, Mama is an unbiased person and she still loves you. She would never hold your past against you."

"I love her too and when I go home again, I will visit her." Shavon assured him Dana would be happy to see him.

She offered him a drink and excused herself for a phone call. Tracy wheeled himself into the dining room for a magazine. He pulled out a few copies of *Readers Digest* and set them on the table. He finally decided he would watch TV instead. He began putting the books away when he noticed another book setting on the table. He didn't recall taking that one out.

He opened the cover of the photo album and found himself glaring at Mr. and Mrs. Jerome Ware. He wondered why he felt jealous. *She's with me now*, he thought. The second page was of Shavon and Jerome kissing in front of the minister. Shavon looked beautiful. He then looked at her husband. In his eyes, it was him instead of Jerome. He was deep in thought and hadn't heard Shavon walk up behind him. She cleared her throat.

"These are wonderful pictures. Who took them?"

"Steve," she answered as she took the book. "We don't want to put a damper on this evening. You just got back."

He smiled politely.

"Are you still in love with him?"

"Tracy, I don't want to talk about Jerome." Her statement ended the conversation.

As Shavon and Tracy listened to soft music, he had an inspiration. "Shavon, get a piece of paper and pen."

"What?"

"Hurry or I may lose it." She was up and back in about 12 seconds. She stood by watching as he scribbled. Minutes later he handed her the sheet of paper.

"What do you think?" Shavon read the poem.

She was so confused she took a walk along the shore
There she was alone to contemplate what life had stored
That's when she heard the music as it was getting loud
She looked into the sky and saw a figure through a cloud

She ran to hide for fear of him or what this thing could be
His eyes were warm which gave her hope that he might set her free
She tried to make a sound but she couldn't even scream
She kept repeating to herself, "It's got to be a dream"
She was so afraid that she began to cry
He stared and took control as he looked into her eyes
"I'm from another world," he said "Land of Eternity"
She looked at him with pleading eyes "Why have you come for me?"
This land is not for you," he said "Won't you come with me?
We could reign together in my land Eternity"
He spoke with such conviction of such a land of love
He told her everything except, who or what he was
She thought of what he said and she decided not to go
She couldn't adapt into a world of those she didn't know
He softly touched her hand upon her cheek he put a kiss
She slowly turned to see him disappearing in a mist
She thought of what he told her not knowing where it was
She wondered was it really real, a land so full of love

This is really good, Tracy. You are so talented!"

"And so are you. That's why we're so good together. Hey! We could start our own greeting card company!"

"Oh, yeah?" She laughed. "Who's going to do the art work?"

"With that artful eye you have?"

"I'm into fashion and that's all I can draw. Let me know when you want me to design a gown."

"Come on, Shavon!"

"Nope. That sounds like a job for Mama," she laughed.

"It was worth a try," he told her.

***

Over the next few weeks, Shavon and Tracy were getting closer to having the relationship they had once shared. She listened to him when he had things on his mind and he in turn was there for her with support. In the following month, the movie was finished. It was time for Tracy to go home. He invited Shavon to his hotel to tell her.

They sat on the bed eating pizza. Shavon was in a very good mood but she noticed Tracy wasn't. She rubbed his side burns.

"What's wrong?"

"Shavon, since the cast is finished filming the movie, I think it's time I head home."

Her face expressed disappointment. She wondered what he expected her to say. She knew she wanted more than just a fling of a relationship. He waited patiently for her response. She cleared her throat.

"When are you leaving?"

"In three days." She tried to camouflage her obvious disappointment.

"When will I see you again?"

He frowned. "I don't know but I don't want to lose what we have. If I could stay, I would. You have made me feel so good these past few months. I can honestly say I haven't felt this way since we parted. You mean the world to me and I don't want you to think I'll forget about you. I'm not going to make that mistake twice."

She smiled. "Yes, you do have a history of giving people the wrong impression," she teased. He returned her smile.

"I'm going to San Antonio for a few weeks on business. When I get back, we need to talk about our relationship. I don't want to talk about it now but I really need to know how you feel and what you want for us."

She hugged him. As she held him, she thought of how she would miss him.

Tracy spent most of his ride thinking about Shavon. He was sure she loved him but she also loved Jerome. Knowing Shavon as he did, her love for Jerome was probably deep. She would never have married him if she weren't deeply in love with him. He only hoped the love she smothered for him all these years would be uncovered and surpass what she felt for her husband. He wondered how he and Shavon would work things out. There was only one answer if they chose to be together he would have to move to California. California wasn't a bad place to live but he longed to be back in Detroit. Shavon couldn't leave. She no doubt wanted to manage her own day-to-day operations. It was more feasible for him to relocate since he traveled so often anyway.

He wondered how she would feel when he had to go away on business. She was fair. He knew she would understand as long as he didn't lose touch for long periods of time. He reached for his notebook. He began thinking about his project with Carla Trenton.

Carla was a beautiful, Caucasian actress he had met at a Hollywood party. Her husband, Don, had introduced them. He had explained to his wife that Tracy was the writer she was looking for to write her biography. Carla inquired about his experience. She was hesitant when she ascertained he had never done a biography. After reading some of Tracy's novels, her doubt was dispelled. She called him the following day. Tracy was a writer with an exceptional ability to grab his reader's attention from beginning to end. Carla had a great story to tell and with Tracy's help, she would have a phenomenal book.

Tracy had a strong feeling the finished product would be a winner. Anybody who was somebody knew Carla. Many rumors followed her career and that was an asset in itself to Tracy. He had heard many times that Don's best friend was Carla's lover and the father of their 10-year-old daughter. Carla had promised to be candid with Tracy and discuss all of the rumors she was associated with, even if it hurt. He was excited about working with her. If the book was a hit, it would open more doors than he ever imagined.

Carla had a car waiting at the airport for Tracy when he arrived. As he admired the mansions, the limousine drove down Willow Lane. The driver pulled into a long driveway and stopped at the gate and dialed a code. Once inside, Tracy was flabbergasted. Her house was nothing short of what he had seen on the *Life Styles of the Rich and Famous*. She took his jacket then offered him her finest champagne.

"Would you like some Krug Champagne? It's simply marvelous. I order it from France." Tracy decided not to pretend to be rich. Besides he had never heard of Krug champagne.

"No, I'll have a beer."

She turned to her butler.

"Get the gentleman a beer."

Tracy's bags were taken upstairs to a room he would be staying in. He was amused when Carla asked him what kind of furniture he liked. "Contemporary, why?" he asked.

"There's a different style of decor in every room. I want you to be comfortable while you're here."

He laughed. "You've got to be kidding."

She looked at him and said nothing. He eyed her as she turned her back to him and walked to the nearest chair.

"Before we get started, I want you to know that you shouldn't be surprised by anything I say."

From that moment on, Tracy was sure this trip was well worth it.

Shavon went through the jewelry box in the back of her closet. She pulled a diamond ring from the box. She clasped the ring in her hand. She closed her eyes and a drifted for a few moments. She made her way to the phone as it rang.

"Hello, Shavon."

"Tracy!" How are you?"

"Missing you but everything is going fine."

"When are you coming back?"

"Shavon I'm going to be here for another week."

"Oh, Tracy, I was looking forward to seeing you tonight. I hoped you would be calling to tell me you were on your way back."

"I'm sorry, Shavon. I looked forward to seeing you too but I think I need to stay for one more week."

"Well, just keep in touch, Tracy."

"I will," he assured her.

Shavon reviewed her day. She dialed her lawyer's number twice today but she couldn't go through with it. *I'm not ready*, she thought. She remembered the woman he was with when she was out that night. If it had been any other woman, she wouldn't have taken it so hard but it was Cynthia, his ex-wife. Cynthia was beautiful. Her figure was exactly as it was in high school and her face was prettier than ever. Seeing him with her shattered Shavon's inclination of hope for their marriage. She remembered how insecure she felt after seeing Cynthia. She had gone home that night and done sit-ups.

She knew how Jerome had once felt about Cynthia. He loved Cynthia even after she left him. She believed seeing them as she had meant they were probably renewing their relationship. She wondered if Jerome was secure in his relationship with Cynthia. Then she asked herself the same question about her relationship with Tracy. She was still uncertain but she knew time would help her find a definite answer to all of her questions.

When Tracy arrived at Shavon's house, he stood at the door waiting. Shavon screamed.

"Oh! Tracy. This is the most wonderful present I've ever had." She hugged him numerous times. His legs were stronger now and seeing him standing there was like a dream come true. Shavon and Tracy had a wonderful night together. The following day, neither of them wanted to be the first to initiate the conversation regarding their future.

Tracy's throat was dry. "Well, what's on your mind, Shavon."

She bit her lip. He braced himself.

"I don't know yet, Tracy. It's too soon. I'm sure I love you and I enjoy you thoroughly but I can't make a decision right now. I need more time."

He nodded in agreement. They had missed each other terribly and it was clear that he would stay the night.

Shavon awoke at 2:30 in the morning and it appeared Tracy was gone. She got out of bed and peeked into the living room where he sat in a chair. She tip toed her way to the chair and hugged him from behind.

"I love you," she whispered. Without turning around, he reached over his right shoulder for her hand.

"Come back to bed," she whispered.

"I'll be in there in a minute or two. I was just thinking about how to end that manuscript I've been working on."

Shavon returned to her bedroom. She didn't know what else to say to him. She knew very well what was on his mind. After going to bed, Tracy lay awake for a half an hour thinking about what he knew could end all of his happiness with Shavon. She was no doubt very much in love with her husband.

Tracy was packing his clothes for another trip to San Antonio as the phone rang. It was Shavon.

"Shavon, I'm going to miss you."

"I miss you already," she told him.

"I'll be gone again for about three weeks."

"Three weeks seems like so long but I won't ever try to interfere with your career. I just hope you'll be here for me."

"Shavon--"

"I know, I know. Believe in you," she quoted.

Shavon got off the scale.

"Oh no! 139 pounds. Something is wrong here. She reset the scale to zero. Again it read 139 pounds. Her first thought was of the monthly water weight gain. That must be it she assured herself. She checked her calendar. She was a week late. She panicked. She slowly raised her shirt then dropped on the bed.

"Oh, no. It can't be true!" Her breaths were short and rapid. "God, please don't let me be pregnant."

She became more anxious as the conversation with the receptionist went on.

"Well, can't I get an earlier appointment?"

The receptionist explained to her that she couldn't.

"Well, what about cancellations!"

The receptionist asked her when she wanted to come in.

"This afternoon." Shavon waited on hold while the receptionist checked the doctor's schedule. She returned in a matter of seconds and explained to Shavon that she couldn't possibly squeeze her in. Shavon made an appointment for Friday morning. She was exasperated.

"Friday!" she said in anger as she hung up the phone.

For the rest of the day, Shavon was in a daze. She never once thought about her career. Her thoughts were fear of producing another child that might only see kindergarten. Tears poured from her eyes as she remembered her pain. After her tears subsided she found herself going through a photo album. Her fingers glided across a picture of Terrell when he was two years old. She began talking to the picture.

"Baby, I know it would make you happy to see me and your daddy together and I wish you could. I think if you were here, you would have wanted me to forgive him for leaving us and I have." She sniffled. He loved you so much, Baby," (she put her hands to her cheeks) and so do I. You don't know what I went through when I lost you. But when I look at your father, I see you again. I feel like I still have a part of you."

She closed the photo album. It was 11:30 a.m. but she was suddenly exhausted. She lay down and slept for the rest of the day.

When Tracy called, Shavon tried to appear normal but he knew something was wrong. He never let on that he was aware of her sadness but he said everything comforting he could think of to let her know that no matter what, she had his support.

Shavon lay on the bed and thought about her conversation with Tracy. He was really wonderful but talking to him didn't help matters. She wondered how he would react if she told him she might be pregnant but that didn't matter either. She only prayed she wasn't.

Mrs. Ware studied her son's face.

"Jerome, why don't you call her?" He shrugged his shoulders.

"Mom, it's been so long. I love her just like before but I know I can't get her back now.

"How do you know for sure, Jerome?"

"Mom, she saw me with Cynthia, remember."

"Well, there was nothing going on between you two."

"Well, Shavon didn't see it that way. She believes something was going on because of the way Cynthia was acting. I don't know what kind of game Cynthia was playing that night but I haven't heard from her since. Actually, I think she was using me to make some guy jealous."

"Did you tell Shavon that?" He sighed and shook his head no.

"Maybe I should have but when she told me nothing was going on with Tracy, I kind of turned my back on her." He went to the window, "I was a fool. I thought I would be unhappy if I had stayed with her." Jerome's mother listened as she shook her head. "I haven't been the same since I left. At first, I thought I would get over it but I have really missed her. Months back I started to file for a divorce but I couldn't. I still love her and I don't know where to begin to get her back."

He walked across the room and fell into the leather recliner in the east corner of the living room. "I thought that after Shavon saw me with Cynthia, she would never take me back. I asked her if I could come home once, and she said no. I wanted to go home so many times before that incident, but I guess my pride was in the way. I understood her not believing me about Cynthia. It's the same exact thing that happened to her regarding Tracy. I was too stupid to believe her. I know now that she really didn't want him."

He admitted that she had every reason to mistrust him and think he would be jealous of every man she came in contact with. "It's just that I know how she once felt for him. He was her first love and the father of her child. I had heard from so many people that once they truly loved each other and I believed there was an unbreakable bond. I just didn't want to get caught up in a tangled web." He scratched his forehead. "Of all the bad decisions I have made in my life, that one was the most asinine. I walked out on a perfect relationship over pride."

"Jerome sometimes you have to accept that other men may want your wife. That doesn't mean she'll want him." Jerome's mom walked toward him taking both his hands in hers. "Honey, you can't expect her to keep hating him."

"I know, Mom, but I sure wanted her to." He grabbed his jacket.

"Are you going to talk to her?"

"I don't know but if I could have her back I wouldn't be so foolish the second time around."

After Jerome left, his mom expelled a sigh of relief that there might be a chance they would reconcile. She never understood why they had broken up in the first place. She only hoped it wasn't too late.

***

Shavon waited nervously on hold to ascertain her test results. So many thoughts entered her mind. She felt the tension of a soon to be headache. She was on the edge of her seat when the receptionist returned to the phone.

"I'm sorry Mrs. Ware but the test was negative."

She was momentarily impassive.

"Negative. Are you absolutely sure?"

"Yes. I'm sorry."

"Don't be sorry. That was just what I wanted to hear."

Shavon's mood changed instantly. She went to the mirror. "Boy! You look a mess!" She bathed and put on her favorite wrap-around lime green skirt with a matching sexy tulip print, green and white t-shirt. She had designed it herself and it was a perfect fit. She took a look at her legs. She loved wearing dresses but her legs were far from the most beautiful. She had just escaped the category of the woman with the skinny legs. She curled her hair and put on some makeup. She felt like a million bucks. And now that her pregnancy scare was over, things could get back to normal.

Shavon sat at her desk singing and going over the inventory report she always hated doing. Today even doing inventory was a pleasure. It was much better than designing a line of maternity clothes, she thought. Delsey peeped in the door and informed her she had visitor. Shavon smiled thinking Tracy had returned early. Delsey's face evinced a perplexing expression. Shavon tried to read it but before she knew it, Jerome was standing before her. She was astonished. She never expected it would be Jerome. Jerome acted as if he didn't know what to say. Shavon noticed Delsey was still there and staring at the both of them.

"Thank you, Delsey, she said. Delsey knew Shavon and Jerome had been separated for some time. She also knew Shavon had been seeing Tracy. She couldn't wait to see what was going on.

Jerome suddenly looked nervous.

"Have a seat." She directed her hand to the seat next to her desk.

"No, I only came by for a minute."

She was slightly disappointed. “Did you come for a match?”

“Sort of,” he said with laughter. She looked puzzled. “Would you like to have dinner with me tonight?”

She hesitated before she answered, “Sure.” She squinted her eyes. “Is everything all right?”

“Yes, things are fine. I’ll pick you up at seven thirty.”

Shavon was glad to see him but she hid her excitement. She had no idea why he came to see her. She thought there could be only one reason, he wanted a divorce. She dreaded hearing that but if he was ready, she wouldn’t contest it. She reminisced again on all the happy times she and Jerome had shared. She remembered a time when they were dating and he had taken her to the skating rink. What fun they had. She thought about the trip to Washington. There will never be another time like that, she thought. She remembered playing checkers, going to basketball games and many other things that made them close. But now, it was all gone. Sadness swept over her. Accepting the end of her marriage was worse than she ever thought it would be.

At 7:00 p.m., Shavon dialed Jerome’s number. She couldn’t face him tonight. She had to get used to hearing herself say the word divorce for a couple of days first to prepare herself when he said it. She knew that tonight it would be impossible to hide her pain. The phone rang seven times. Jerome wasn’t there. She hoped he would call before he came so she could give him an excuse for tonight.

Shavon sat across the table from Jerome feeling as if her world was about to crumble. She tried telling him she was tired but he wouldn’t accept that. She was half way through a meal she didn’t want to eat when she spoke up.

"Jerome, I can't wait any longer. Will you just say what you have to say so that we can just get it over with?" He was surprised by her apprehension but yielded to her request.

"It's really hard for me to ask you this, Shavon, but are you involved with anyone?"

She looked away puzzled for a few seconds then turned back to him and sighed, "Maybe. Why is that important to you, Jerome?" Without letting him respond, she retorted. "Are you seeing anyone?"

"No." Her harsh expression softened. He spoke before she could say another word.

"I'm still in love with you. I know I don't have a right to try to come back into your life after all of this time and expect the same. I don't know any other way to say it but I want you back."

She couldn't believe what she had heard. She was so sure he wanted to end it all. She didn't know what to say. She felt silly. All the time she had spent preparing to end things and he wanted to start over. She was happy to hear it but she remained calm.

"Jerome--"

"Shavon, I want to come back home and be with you as a family. I was a fool to leave you. I know you didn't want Tracy. I don't know where my mind was at that time but if you give me another chance I'll never let you down again." She tried to speak. "Wait. I want you to think about this. I don't want you to make a quick decision. If you still love me, just give it some consideration."

She took a deep breath. He would die when he found out she was seeing Tracy but she had to tell him. It would be worst if he heard it from someone else. She was surprised he hadn't already known considering Tracy's notoriety.

"I am involved with someone." He dropped his head.

"I expected that."

"I want you to know who he is."

"Shavon, please. I would rather not know. It is only natural that you get on with your life. I messed up. I just need to know if there's still a chance for us." He paused. "Shavon, do you still love me?"

"Yes," she heard herself say. She immediately retracted. "No. I don't know, Jerome." She had been so sure she wanted Tracy but as Jerome sat before her she realized their love was stronger than either of them had known. She felt confused. He could see from her reaction that she was serious about the other guy.

"Do you love him, Shavon?"

"Jerome, I need to think. I can't answer anything right now."

She could feel the pain in her husband's eyes but it couldn't be avoided. She didn't want to confirm or deny her love for Tracy.

Jerome walked Shavon to the door.

"I'll wait for your call." He hugged her with tears in his eyes. "I love you," he whispered.

Shavon closed the door and leaned against it. She knew she wouldn't sleep tonight. She had a choice to make. Her decision would determine her happiness for the rest of her life.

Shavon tossed and turned for the next few days. She couldn't believe it was possible to love two men the way she did. She had missed Jerome terribly when he left and she remembered believing she would never get over him. Seeing him again made her realize just how much she missed him. Feeling his hand against hers reminded her of the affection they once felt for each other. It was still there. But Tracy had been the perfect mate since they had reunited. She was absolutely sure now that he would be there for her. He had really matured. She thought of how she always looked forward to his visits. She remembered how she felt in his arms the night before he left. It was a tough choice but it had to be made.

She thought about Myah. When Myah was torn between two men, it was funny. But she had almost lost Ronny in the process. But her situation was different. It was hardly a game loving two men. She was still deeply in love with a man she had vowed to be with for the rest of her life but on the other hand, she had spent years with Tracy, her high school sweetheart whom she loved for so many years. They had shared so much, even a child. Her last thought was of Terrell.

That night, Shavon prayed for wisdom. She knew who she wanted and she hoped she had made the right choice. She gathered her thoughts for preparation of what she might say to them. No matter who she chose, she would always love them both.

Wednesday afternoon when Shavon returned from lunch, she found a message on her desk from Tracy stating that he would be home Thursday. She stared at the message for a moment and drifted into thought. Each time she thought of him, she thought of Jerome and vice-versa.

As Shavon opened the door she smiled.

"Hi." Tracy handed her a dozen roses. He leaned to kiss her. She held him slightly tighter than usual. It didn't take long for him to realize something wasn't right. He kissed her passionately and she yielded. He knew whatever it was, it certainly wasn't her passion for him. Though her kiss was genuine, he felt awkward. He took her hand and led her to the couch.

"Okay, let's talk about it," he said. She hugged him again.

"I love you, Tracy," she whispered. He pulled away.

"Then why are you ending it?" Tears came to her eyes.

"I never thought I would ever feel this way about you again but God knows I do. You mean so much to me. You always will." He sat silently as she continued. "While you were away, I did a lot of thinking. I was almost ready to file for a divorce but something happened to make me realize I can't be the wife you need."

"What do you mean?" he asked. "I don't want to change you?"

She stared at him a moment then went into the den and came back with pictures little Terrell had drawn when he was four years old.

"What does Terrell have to do with this?"

"Everything, Tracy. Don't you understand! When you were away, I thought I was pregnant. I almost went crazy. I went through hell when I lost him. I love you but I wouldn't go through that again for anybody! Remember that night we cried together?" He didn't respond.

"Do you?"

"Yes, Shavon, I do."

"Well, I strongly believe that if our second child was born with the same problems and died, our relationship would end immediately after."

"Shavon, they don't know why Terrell was born the way he was. There's a chance it may not happen to our second child!"

"Tracy, that's just it. There's a chance it will and there's a chance it won't."

"Shavon, chance pertains to everything in life!"

"I know!" She realized she was getting loud and calmed herself. "I know it, Tracy, but my fear of us having a child together is stronger than my love for you!"

She could see that her last statement nearly crushed him. She went to his side. "Tracy, I don't mean to hurt you but I have never stopped hurting for Terrell. I wish I had the courage to take that chance but I don't. I just hope you'll forgive me."

There was a long pause of silence. Tracy stood and reached for her hand. He pulled her close.

"Always remember that I love you," he said. She tried to speak.

"Shhh," he urged. "I understand more than you will ever know. He led her to the door. He saw no reason for prolonging their departure.

She reached into her pocket and pulled out a ring. Tracy instantly remembered the ring he had given her before he went to New York. He knew getting the ring back meant things were finally over. Knowing she had kept it all those years meant more than she could ever say.

***

"Mom, I really feel good about this. I want to thank you."

"Thank me?" she said putting her hand to her chest.

"Yes, you." He hugged her.

"If it weren't for you, I may have lost Shavon forever. I thought it was too late but you had faith in us and that had an impact on my decision to make an effort to get her back."

Jerome said good-bye to his father as he and his mother headed toward the door. He leaned to kiss her on the cheek.

"I wish you would stay a little longer. What's the rush?" Jerome smiled slowly.

"I've got some packing to do."

Mrs. Ware closed the door behind her son and smiled. Her prayers had been answered.

Jerome was going home.

ORDER FORM

To place mail orders, please send money orders payable to Yvonne Weems to:

Second Time Media & Communications
P.O. Box 401367
Redford, MI 48240

16.95 + tax (MI sales tax 6%) = 17.96

Turnaround time is 5-7 business days.

Number of Books _____ x $16.95 _______________
Tax _______________
Subtotal: _______________
Shipping & Handling $2.95 _______________

Total: _______________

Shipping Information (REQUIRED)

Name:____
Address:____
City:________________ State:__________ Zip:___________
Contact Number (optional):____________________________
Email :____

Your support is appreciated!

Yvonne A. Weems

Breinigsville, PA USA
05 March 2010

233672BV00002B/1/P

9 780984 066070